SIDE EFFECTS

What Reviewers Say About VK Powell's Work

To Protect and Serve

"If you like cop novels, or even television cop shows with women as full partners with male officers…this is the book for you. It's got drama, excitement, conflict, and even some fairly hot lesbian sex. The writer is a retired cop, so she really writes from a place of authenticity. As a result, you have a realistic quality to the writing that puts me in mind of early Joseph Wambaugh."—Teresa DeCrescenzo, *Lesbian News*

"*To Protect and Serve* drew me in from the very first page with characters that captivated in their complexity. Powell writes with authority using the lingo and capturing the thoughts of the law enforcers who make the ultimate sacrifice in the fight against crime. What's more impressive is the command this debut author has of portraying a full gamut of emotion, from angst to elation, through dialogue and narrative. The images are vivid, the action is believable, and the police procedurals are authentic…VK Powell had me invested in the story of these women, heart, mind, body and soul. Along with danger and tension, Powell's well-developed erotic scenes sizzle and sate."—*Story Circle Book Reviews*

Suspect Passions

"From the first chapter of *Suspect Passions* Powell builds erotic scenes which sear the page. She definitely takes her readers for a walk on the wild side! Her characters, however, are also women we care about. They are bright, witty, and strong. The combination of great sex and great characters make *Suspect Passions* a must read."—*Just About Write*

Fever

"VK Powell has given her fans an exciting read. The plot of *Fever* is filled with twists, turns, and 'seat of your pants' danger...*Fever* gives readers both great characters and erotic scenes along with insight into life in the African bush."—*Just About Write*

Justifiable Risk

"This story takes some unusual twists and at one point, I was convinced that I knew 'who did it' only to find out that I was wrong. VK Powell knows crime drama, she kept me guessing until the end, and I was not disappointed at the outcome. And that's not to slight VK Powell's knack for romance. ...Readers who appreciate mysteries with a touch of drama and intense erotic moments will enjoy *Justifiable Risk*." —*Queer Magazine*

Exit Wounds

"Powell's prose is no-nonsense and all business. It gets in and gets the job done, a few well-placed phrases sparkling in your memory and some trenchant observations about life in general and a cop's life in particular sticking to your psyche long after they've gone. After five books, Powell knows what her audience wants, and she delivers those goods with solid assurance. But be careful you don't get hooked. You only get six hits, then the supply's gone, and you'll be jonesin' for the next installment. It never pays to be at the mercy of a cop."—*Out in Print*

"Fascinating and complicated characters materialize, morph, and sometimes disappear testing the passionate yet nascent love of the book's focal pair. I was so totally glued to and amazed by the intricate layers that continued to materialize like an active volcano...dangerous and deadly until the last mystery is revealed. This book goes into my super special category. Please don't miss it."—*Rainbow Book Reviews*

About Face

"Powell excels at depicting complex, emotionally vulnerable characters who connect in a believable fashion and enjoy some genuinely hot erotic moments."—*Publishers Weekly*

Visit us at www.boldstrokesbooks.com

By the Author

To Protect and Serve

Suspect Passions

Fever

Justifiable Risk

Haunting Whispers

Exit Wounds

About Face

Side Effects

SIDE EFFECTS

by
VK Powell

2015

ISBN 13: 978-1-62639-364-6

This Trade Paperback Original Is Published By
Bold Strokes Books, Inc.
P.O. Box 249
Valley Falls, NY 12185

First Edition: August 2015

Credits
Editor: Shelley Thrasher
Production Design: Susan Ramundo
Cover Design By Sheri (graphicartist2020@hotmail.com)

Acknowledgments

To Len Barot and all the other wonderful folks at Bold Strokes Books—thank you for making this process so amazingly enjoyable and painless and for turning out a quality product every time.

My deepest gratitude to Dr. Shelley Thrasher, editor and sister author, for your guidance, suggestions, and kindness. Working with you is a learning experience and a pleasure. Our stolen minutes of conversation at conferences and writer events keep me on track and always reaching for unattainable perfection in my work.

For BSB sister author, D. Jackson Leigh, and friend, Jenny Harmon—thank you for taking time out of your busy lives to provide priceless feedback. This book is so much better for your efforts. I am truly grateful.

To all the readers who support and encourage my writing, thank you for buying my work, visiting my website (www.vkpowellauthor.com), sending e-mails, and showing up for signings. You make my job so much fun!

Dedication

To Trish and Jacqui for providing a soft place
to land when I needed it in London and for
the perfect setting in which to write this book.

CHAPTER ONE

Sergeant Milton's jowls drooped like melted rubber into a permanent scowl as he shoved the morning paper across his desk toward Jordan Bishop and her partner Rebecca Ward. "I don't need another shit storm on my desk at the moment. Have you seen this?" She leaned away from his hacking smoker's cough and offending news.

Jordan glanced at Bex and let her do the talking. She was senior detective, and Jordan hadn't exactly been on the sergeant's good list lately.

"No, Sarge. What's up?"

"What's up? Goddamned protestors are creating a ruckus in Raleigh and the stench is spreading our way. Ed Branson, an abortion doctor based in Greensboro and a consultant to the governor's office, was assaulted last night in the parking lot of his clinic. Serious injuries, but he'll make it. The attacker tagged his car with graffiti. *Stop or next time will be worse.* Something like that. Definitely abortion related."

"Did the tag actually mention abortion?" Bex asked.

"No, but what else could it be? Abortion doctor plus assault equals *right-to-lifer.*" Milton emphasized the phrase like they were kindergarteners.

"But we're Special Investigations, not Crimes Against Persons." Sometimes Bex had a gift for stating the obvious.

Milton rolled his eyes, and Jordan remained silent. They weren't here to talk about an assault case, and a prickly feeling up the back of her neck signaled she wouldn't like the real reason.

"Another doctor has received threats—*you'll be next* or some such crap. The chief wants us to provide protection for her until this blows over."

"But, Sarge—"

"I don't want to hear your objections, Jordan. It's not your call. Hell, it's not even my call. The chief wants this done, so it gets done. Am I clear?" Clearer than his bloodshot eyes trained on her. He pushed a file toward them. "Whatever it takes. We have a mutual-aid agreement with Raleigh PD and the North Carolina State Highway Patrol. Shouldn't be a problem for us to be on their turf. They don't want this hot potato any more than we do."

Bex looked as confused as Jordan felt. Special Investigations handled gang-related crimes, terrorist activity, and subversive groups, anything out of the ordinary not covered by the other departmental divisions, but they'd never pulled a babysitting job.

"Just read the damn file and make a plan." He flipped his hand at them like they were a couple of annoying insects. "I'll expect it on my desk by the end of the day."

"What the hell just happened?" Jordan asked as they made their way back to their desks in the bullpen. The other detectives discussing cases, talking on the phone, and telling one-up stories faded into the background as she focused on her partner. She didn't have the patience for this kind of assignment right now. She needed to be active, not playing nursemaid to some doctor.

"We got shafted with a job nobody else wants. Must carry some clout if the order came from the chief's office. Let's find out." Bex pulled her wobbly roller chair alongside Jordan, propped her feet on the battered desk, and opened the file. She flipped through the first few pages before placing a picture on the desk in front of Jordan. "That explains a lot."

"What?"

"Doctor Neela Sahjani."

"Who's that?" Jordan glanced at the photograph, and dark, soulful eyes rimmed in deep amber pulled her in. Long black, silky hair and flawless olive skin completed the image of a woman who could've graced the cover of a magazine.

"Jesus, Jordan, do you ever watch the news? Read the paper?"

"Don't own a television. Don't read the rags because it's always bad news, and I get enough of that at work. Just tell me what you're on about."

"Neela Sahjani."

"And why should we protect someone who could be the proprietor of an Indian restaurant?"

Bex shook her head with a disbelieving expression Jordan had seen far too frequently the past several months. "Prejudiced much?"

"I'm not prejudiced. Just confused." She leaned back in her chair, propped her feet on the roller spokes, and tapped her foot. Sitting still wasn't a strong point.

"Doctor Neela Sahjani is the North Carolina State Health Director."

"We have to protect a politician? The sergeant just said she was a doctor."

"And apparently a pretty liberal one, based on her work in the previous administration. Not bad duty though. She's quite a looker, don't you think?"

"She's pretty. So what?"

Bex slapped her on the back as though she'd won a prize. "Hallelujah, she lives. Do you have any idea how long it's been since you've noticed a woman you weren't planning to bed, much less admitted she was attractive?"

"Don't start with that again."

"I'm just saying you need to get out, see people."

"I see people—and not dead ones either. I look in on my elderly neighbor, Mrs. Cherry, every week and take her dog for a walk when it's raining."

"But do you actually talk to her?" Bex was trying to make a point, but Jordan wasn't interested in her armchair therapy. She got enough shrink-wrapping from her real therapist, when she bothered to keep an appointment.

"Neither one of us is much for conversation. It works."

"How about an occasional date?"

"She's too old for me. Besides, I'm pretty sure she's straight," Jordan said.

"Smart-ass. I mean a real date. It doesn't have to be for life."

"Seldom is." She hadn't found anyone who could or would put up with her long enough to try forever. "Let it go, Bex."

"You've been distracted lately. I just want to see a spark in your eyes again."

"I'll buy fireworks for the Fourth of July. Now about this freaking detail. Isn't it the highway patrol's responsibility to protect the governor's staff?"

"Usually just the governor and any dignitaries he deems worthy. They obviously don't care enough about Doctor Sahjani to be bothered. Maybe they're trying to get rid of her."

.   "Why would anyone want to get rid of her?" Jordan asked.

"Maybe her pro-choice stance, or some conservative asshole doesn't like a woman of foreign descent or a woman of color in a high-level position. Somebody might object to her stem-cell research. That's a pretty contentious subject at the moment. If they're trying to force her out, this whole threat scenario could be internally motivated."

"Even more reason for us not to get involved. Plus, she works in Raleigh."

"Yeah, but she lives in Greensboro, Hamilton Lakes. Face it, Jordan. We're involved whether you like it or not. Read the file and let's talk strategy." She rolled back to her desk and pulled a yellow notepad from the drawer. "We've got until the close of business."

Bex left Neela Sahjani's photo on her desk, and Jordan glanced at it periodically as she skimmed the file. Sahjani was definitely attractive, one of those women who captured admirers with her looks and slowly drained them of life with her clingy neediness. Fortunately, Jordan didn't have much life left—no passion, no hope, and no belief in the fictional happily-ever-after. The only emotion she could identify recently was the anger that sustained her.

"What do you think?" Bex asked.

"I don't want any part of this. I've got problems with everything she represents. Politicians aren't my thing, especially ones who are supposed to advocate for the poor or underprivileged but turn a blind eye to what's happening right under their noses."

"What are you talking about? You don't know what she's like. Besides, we help people we disagree with philosophically every day. Comes with the badge. What's so different about this one?"

"Just trust me, Bex. Doctor Neela Sahjani and I are not a good fit. Get one of the guys to help you."

"You're my partner. Besides, we'll need more guys to run a twenty-four-hour operation. I was thinking Phil and Harry. Okay with you?"

Jordan pushed her chair back from the desk, suddenly needing more space. The room felt close and stuffy, and the scorched-coffee smell from the leaky drip machine irritated her nose. She stood and started down the hall. "I'm getting out of this."

"I wouldn't advise it." But Jordan was already halfway to the sergeant's office.

She knocked and waited for Milton's grunt of permission before entering the office that reeked of cigarettes and apathy. "Sarge, I'd like to be reassigned from this protection detail."

"No." He didn't even look up.

"You didn't hear my reasons."

"Don't care." Still no eye contact.

"I can't do this." Her insides tightened as she recalled an edict from her Catholic upbringing: *Most politicians are corrupt, and nobody but God should make decisions about life and death.* Though she'd formed her own beliefs, she still occasionally struggled with premature judgments of people based on ingrained intolerance. She hated her inability to completely shake the small-mindedness of her past and the people it tethered her to.

Milton placed his pen on the desk and slowly raised his head. "Do you think the police department is a fucking democracy?" His face flushed and he erupted into a sputtering cough that sounded like he was bringing up a lung. She stepped back. "You don't get to pick and choose assignments. What's up with you anyway? You used to be a good, focused detective, but lately you've been going through the motions, barely talking, doing only what you have to, and zoning out during operations. If this case has gotten a rise out of you, I think that's great."

"I've got a conflict of interest."

"I don't give a happy horse shit. And while we're on the topic of conflicts, maybe I had to manage a few to get you in this division. You'd only been on the force four years and were the youngest detective in the department, but you'd made a name for yourself with informants and good solid police work. Don't make me regret my decision, Bishop. Get your head back in the game before you get somebody hurt and while you still have a job."

She flinched. She'd hoped her recent distraction had gone unnoticed. The only thing she had left was her job and her motorcycle rides. She couldn't afford to lose either. She tried a different tack. "We don't have the budget to pull the trigger on this operation. We need more manpower."

"I don't give a damn. The chief has green-lighted the funds for overtime. Now finish the op plan and get to work. If one hair on this woman's head is disturbed, it better not be on our watch."

As Jordan walked back to her desk, she tried to analyze her objection to protecting Neela Sahjani. She'd never met the woman so her reluctance couldn't be personal—but it felt very personal. Her reasoning just wasn't logical or professional. She dropped onto the corner of her desk and crossed her arms. Bex didn't speak. She'd become much more economical with her words recently. She was probably afraid she'd set Jordan off. "He wouldn't even listen."

"What's your problem with this case?"

"Just forget about it, Bex. Really."

"Guess I don't have a choice. You're not talking to anybody about anything these days." When Jordan glared at her, Bex shrugged. "Well, you're not."

Jordan slid off the desk and headed toward the exit. She needed some air.

"Hey, some of us are going for a drink after work. Come with us."

"Can't. Sorry."

As the door slowly closed behind her, she heard one of the other detectives say, "Told you. She never hangs out with us any more."

Was that true? So what? They'd only want to rehash why she was still single, live vicariously through her latest sexual escapades, and offer well-meaning but useless advice. She didn't need to rake through the shallows of her unfulfilling life to know she was unhappy. And she certainly didn't need more opinions about it. Her therapist had hit some hot spots recently and dredged up things she'd rather not think about. What she did need was a long, fast ride on her Ducati, but she wasn't likely to get that today, thanks to Neela Sahjani. This woman was already disrupting her life.

❖

Neela twirled her reading glasses and tried to conceal her disappointment as she looked around the conference table at her small group of subordinates in the North Carolina State Health Department. For the first time in more than a hundred years, Republicans controlled the governor's office and the legislature. Matt Lloyd, who had taken office only six months earlier, was the first Republican governor in the state in twenty-eight years. Everybody in the room knew what that meant. The state now had its most conservative government ever, and their jobs as part of the previous Democratic administration were on the line. "What do we know?"

The other three in the group looked at Rosemary, Neela's administrative assistant and trusted friend, to deliver the bad news. "Before his election, the governor said he wouldn't make any changes to the current abortion law."

"That's good news, so why do all of you look like someone stole your smart phones?"

"He lied," Rosemary said.

"Rose, please." She didn't allow outright insubordination in her department, even if she totally agreed. She was never entirely sure who was listening or through what means.

Rosemary dipped her head in a quasi-apology everyone knew she didn't mean. She called it as she saw it, one of the things Neela admired and respected about her. "We're hearing he's given a completely different directive behind the scenes. His strategist and moneyman, Elliot Ramsey, is supposedly running objective," she finger-quoted the air, "surveys across the state to garner support for his agenda. They're planning to bury the abortion language in a bill on motorcycle safety."

Neela looked up from her iPad. "Motorcycle safety, really?" *Nothing subversive going on here then.* She admonished herself and tried to stay on track. "Do we know how bad it is?"

Her liaison on the Hill spoke up. "Not exactly, but I'm hearing it could be the most restrictive legislation we've had in decades, could set us back fifty years."

Everybody around the table groaned and talked at once, voicing their concerns. Neela reflected on the past four years of her career under a reformist female Democratic governor, who'd championed significant advancements for the state. Under her leadership North Carolina was becoming more progressive, and people were relocating here as a result. In a matter of months the new regime could obliterate everything she'd accomplished and make it more difficult to reverse their antiquated rulings for years to come. The legislature didn't have enough votes to defeat any bill the Republican stronghold put forward. What could she possibly say to comfort her coworkers and friends? She shared their discomfiture and the growing sense of doom that had hung over their heads since the election.

"Let's not get ahead of ourselves. We don't have definitive information yet. Everybody keep your ears to the ground and let me know the minute you hear anything new. In the meantime, stay focused on your jobs. Free up as many funds as you can for community projects, and let's do some good with the time we have left." She looked around the room, meeting each gaze with as much encouragement and compassion as she could muster. "Anything else?" When no one spoke up, she said, "That's it then. Have a good evening, everyone."

Rosemary stayed behind as the room cleared, checking her iPhone before handing Neela a list of messages.

"Anything I need to handle right away? I wouldn't mind a cup of coffee and a chat with my best friend." She smiled and placed her hand on Rosemary's arm. "You're my rock. You know that, don't you?"

"Likewise, but a couple of detectives are here to see you."

"Have our law-enforcement liaison assist them."

"They're not state highway patrol or Raleigh police. They're Greensboro police, and they asked for you specifically. Wouldn't say what it's about. Fancy a drink after work? Looks like you could use one."

"Can't. Have some research to do and then hopefully home before midnight."

"And that's exactly why you need a drink. You've got to slow down, Neela, or you'll crash."

"I will." She stopped short of promising, because she couldn't see any break in sight. Neela tucked her iPad under her arm and walked toward the exit. "Tell the detectives I slipped out before you could catch me. They'll just have to come back tomorrow." She blew Rosemary a kiss. "Once more into the breach."

CHAPTER TWO

The next morning Neela stepped into her office and came to an abrupt halt. The two women standing in front of her desk couldn't have been more opposite. One wore bright clothing, appeared to be in her thirties, with short, dark hair, deep-brown eyes, and a sporty build. Her companion, maybe mid-twenties, looked like she'd stepped out of a vampire movie, chiseled from alabaster with a snowcap of white hair and dressed entirely in black, down to heavy biker-type boots. Neela's breath caught in her throat. Both of these women were attractive, but she'd remember the taller androgynous one if she passed her on the street years from now.

"I'm Detective Rebecca Ward with the Greensboro Police Department's Special Investigations Division." Ward, the sporty one, greeted her with a warm smile and cordial handshake. The other woman with thick white hair barely touching her collar and cobalt eyes didn't speak. Ward jerked her thumb in her direction and said, "This is Detective Bishop."

As Neela dropped her briefcase beside her desk, she fixed her gaze on the woman who couldn't be bothered to introduce herself. The energy around her vibrated with recklessness and impatience. Neela pictured her on a Harley-Davidson zooming down the road while doing a handstand on the handlebars. She had a tiny scar on the right side of her lip, and Neela wondered if she'd been injured in the line of duty or taken a tumble while performing some daredevil stunt.

"How can I help you, detectives?" She addressed her question to Bishop, determined to make her speak. Instead, Jordan Bishop simply stared at her until the room became uncomfortably quiet.

"So much for public relations. Have I done something to offend you, Detective Bishop?" Neela never backed down from conflict. She wouldn't have survived long in politics if she had.

"Being here offends me, *Doctor.*"

Bishop's voice, deep and sultry, would've been more fitting in a bedroom than an office. Her tone rumbled through Neela, stirring up heat, while her words were a cold blast of liquid nitrogen. Neela started to speak but words failed. How could she respond to someone she didn't know, had nothing in common with, and had somehow offended by her very presence? Jordan Bishop turned and walked to the bank of windows overlooking the athletic field in front of their repurposed school building. Neela stared at her back for several seconds before raising her hands in resignation.

Ward stepped closer and whispered conspiratorially. "You don't want to know."

"Would either of you care for coffee? I think we might even have some croissants." Ward shook her head and Bishop didn't respond. "What can I do for you, detective?" She waved for Ward to have a seat and tried to ignore Jordan Bishop, which proved harder than it should've been for someone so rude. Bishop's taut frame and dark clothing seemed to block the light trying to seep in around her. Neela decided to give this woman a wide berth.

"Actually, we're here to do something for you," Ward said as she handed her an official-looking document.

"How so?" Neela put on her glasses and skimmed the assault report on Ed Branson.

"You've received some threats recently, and in light of the assault on one of your associates, we've been assigned as your protection detail until the case is solved."

Neela's heartbeat increased as she imagined spending time around the woman standing across the room. Was she afraid of Jordan Bishop, or had her strong reaction been something entirely different? Either way she didn't need more complications. "Why would they target me?"

"You're pro-choice, a liberal in a conservative administration, and a stem-cell researcher. Some people take offense to all those things. And let's not forget you're a *politician,*" Jordan said from the window. The way she emphasized the word sent a chill through Neela.

Her normally even-keeled temperament rankled at having to address Bishop's back when she spoke. Her rudeness was the epitome of disrespect. "Well, I—"

"Branson was probably attacked because he's an abortion doctor," Jordan said.

"I appreciate your concern, but I don't perform abortions and I don't need protection."

"Great." Jordan finally turned from the window and started toward the door. "And we don't need to waste our time."

"Might I suggest an attitude adjustment before you cross my threshold again? At the least a little common courtesy, or don't they teach that in the academy?"

"Sorry if I offended you, Doctor Sahjani. You won't see me again." The words were appropriate but Jordan's tone dripped contempt. With such an attitude, how had she survived in law enforcement long enough to become a detective?

"Perfect." Neela couldn't stop her childish response. Detective Ward stared back and forth between them like she'd been dropped into a sibling dispute.

"Jordan, sit your ass down. Sorry, Doctor Sahjani."

Jordan stared ice bullets at Rebecca and her nostrils flared. "I don't need to be here."

"Yes, you do. Sit. This is the job, whether you like it or not."

Neela watched their interaction over the rim of her glasses while trying to appear nonchalant. Rebecca seemed to penetrate Jordan's haze just enough to make a difference. Jordan's icy gaze melted to a light frost, and she raked her fingers through her white hair.

She sat down in front of Neela's desk but didn't make eye contact. Her right leg bounced constantly. Nervous tic or restlessness? "Sorry if I was…abrasive."

Abrasive didn't begin to cover it and Neela was about to tell her so, but Rebecca shook her head. "Where were we?"

"As I said, detective, I don't need protection. I've received these so-called threats for the past several years. They're always fairly generic and nothing has come of them. I'm sorry Doctor Branson has been hurt, but it has nothing to do with me."

"That's not the way our boss sees it. You live in our jurisdiction, and you're a high-profile state employee who's been repeatedly threatened. We can't have anything happen to you. Wouldn't look good, especially after what happened to your associate."

"How did you find out about these threats? I certainly haven't reported anything."

Rebecca referred to her notes. "Doesn't list a complainant, but it's obviously someone who's concerned about your welfare."

"What if I refuse protection?" How could she possibly do everything in her busy schedule with cops following her around, not to mention her after-hours activities? She didn't have the time or inclination to put up with the intrusions of a detective with a chip on her shoulder.

"Still have to do our job, but without your help, it would be more difficult," Rebecca said.

Neela didn't know how to ask her next question. While she was used to tiptoeing around delicate egos in the political arena, Jordan Bishop seemed more volatile. "Would the two of you be my detail?"

"Unfortunately," Jordan said. Her eyes stared at her through dark lashes that contrasted with her stark-white hair, and Neela's nerves pulsed. She pushed her glasses up to divert her attention from the woman in front of her.

"Yes, that part is non-negotiable, but we'll also have another team covering our off time. Twenty-four-seven coverage," Rebecca said.

"Great." It was anything but; however, Neela was stuck with the situation whether she wanted it or not. "What do I have to do to facilitate this surveillance?"

"We'd like to install a camera in your office and two more outside your residence, front and back. Nothing inside the house at this time."

"Absolutely not. I won't allow cameras in or around my home. What you do here is up to you, with the governor's approval of course. But my home is off-limits. Is that understood?"

Rebecca scratched her head. "We'll just work around it."

"What does that mean exactly?"

Jordan stood, placed her hands on Neela's desk, and leaned toward her. "What that means exactly is you've just made our job harder than it needs to be. We'll have to sit outside day and night in rain, sleet, or snow to make sure nothing happens to you when we could've been dry and warm in a van with a camera setup. But hey, we're here to serve."

Jordan was so close Neela watched the irises of her eyes turn dark like an animal on the prowl. Her voice rippled over Neela's skin like thunder, and when her breath brushed Neela's face, it was like a blast of summer heat. Something dangerous lurked beneath Jordan Bishop's beautifully packaged exterior. Neela's survival instinct screamed for her to flee, but she inched forward instead and removed her glasses. When she violated Jordan's personal space, the undeniable scent of arousal mingled with a fragrance that reminded her of innocence. There was nothing innocent about this woman. Neela modified her caustic response only slightly. "Just remember, detective, that I didn't ask for this any more than you did."

Jordan started to say something else but slowly straightened and walked out of the room.

"What's her problem?"

"You really don't want to know," Rebecca said.

"If she's part of my protection detail, I certainly deserve an explanation. I don't need more pressure and stress in my life right now."

"She'll calm down. Besides, you might be exactly what she needs—somebody to stand up to her. Too many people have been handling her with kid gloves lately."

"I'm not a babysitter, detective."

"Rebecca, but everybody calls me Bex."

"I have enough problems without adding an unpredictable cop to the mix. I don't want to complicate her issues, but sort her out or I'll ask for a replacement."

"Understood. I'll have a talk with her. Now, if I could ask for a few more details, we can get the ball rolling on this assignment. Is there anywhere else you frequent that we need to be aware of? It's better if we have an idea of your relationships and routines."

Neela didn't think this whole exercise was necessary and was certain it wouldn't last long, so she chose to keep some aspects of her life private. "No."

"Sure? You hesitated."

"Sure." If Bex examined her too closely, she'd discover Neela wasn't a very good liar. "If there's nothing else, I have a busy day."

"Of course. Thank you for your cooperation, doctor."

"If you're hanging around, you might as well call me Neela. When does this protection begin?"

"We'll have a detail at your home this evening. If you need to contact us, here's my card." Bex wrote her cell number on the back and handed it to her. "I'm sorry. I know it's inconvenient to have the police shadowing your life. Hopefully we'll clear everything up soon."

When Bex left, Neela collapsed in her chair, vibrating with energy from the interaction with Jordan Bishop. She finally drew an unrestricted breath. Was she angry, frustrated, or aroused? Whatever she was feeling, these particular emotions hadn't been churned up in a very long time. She was a consistently stable and even-tempered woman who got along with everybody—everybody, it seemed, except Jordan Bishop.

"That went well, don't you think?" Bex stared at Jordan, forcing her to respond before she cranked the car and started back down I-40.

"Like a turd in a punch bowl."

"This woman probably has enough clout to get us both fired. And before you say it, I know you don't care, but I do. I happen to like my job and being able to pay the mortgage. If you're determined to crash and burn, don't take me down too. You've never been so rude or hostile before on the job. I've tried to get through to you, Jordan, but I'm reaching my limit."

"Whatever."

"That's the best you can do? I'm really worried about you, and I need to know what's going on."

Jordan shook her head. "No, you don't."

"It might help to talk, not keep it bottled up."

"Now you sound like my therapist. Talking won't change anything. I know you're just trying to be a friend, and I'm sorry for being such a shit lately."

"Is your shrink picking at old scabs?"

"I'm fine," Jordan said.

"Fucked up, insecure, neurotic, and emotional. Roger that. Whatever you say." Bex drove in silence for a few minutes. "I could go for a woman like Neela Sahjani. Love her hot-for-teacher glasses, and she's got balls of steel to stand up to you. Admit it. You liked her, especially when she didn't back down."

"So what? She's attractive. We've already covered that ground."

"Would you at least try to be a little less glacial? It might help if my best friend isn't glaring at her in the background when I make my move."

"She's probably not even a lesbian, and if she is, she's got a waiting list as long as the Great Wall of China." The idea of Bex hitting on Neela Sahjani felt wrong, but Jordan brushed it aside. They could do whatever they wanted. It had nothing to do with her.

As Bex drove back toward Greensboro, Jordan stared out the window thinking about Neela. She would certainly appeal to the masses, far more attractive in person than in her picture. Her curvy figure had been swathed in a pale-yellow suit that few women could wear without appearing like a tacky centerpiece. A white scarf highlighted the ensemble, a touch that was neither too flirty nor too professional. Jordan had skimmed the clothes before being sucked into the penetrating gaze that hadn't shied away from her. And when Neela licked her full lips and stood her ground, Jordan felt her words like a challenge to her soul. She'd wanted to grab Neela's long silky hair and yank her into a frenzied fuck right there on her perfectly organized desk.

Why had she been so affected by Neela, so irritated and rude? Was she trying to get a rise out of Neela, to piss her off so they'd get thrown off the case? Maybe she just wanted to feel something besides the numbness that had become her life. She hadn't felt anything real in months...until a few minutes ago in Neela Sahjani's office. When she'd leaned over Neela's desk and she hadn't backed down, Jordan had wanted to vault to the other side and claim her just to prove she was still capable of emotion. Neela's obsidian eyes had shown a flash of fear, but she'd remained controlled and confident. Her defiance registered in a part of Jordan that was still barely alive. But she didn't want to feel again, and she didn't want to protect this politician. She wanted to hold on to her illogical dislike of her and carry on with life as usual. The known was safe.

Maybe her early Catholic indoctrination about absolute right and wrong was getting in the way. Perhaps she distrusted politicians and public entities that were supposed to advocate for the less fortunate. But she couldn't let her past interfere with her job. She was a professional who dealt with adversity every day, but no one had affected her like Neela. If she had to accept this assignment, she'd just stay as far away from Doctor Sahjani as possible. Protection details were all about surveillance and apprehension. She could do that—no personal contact required.

After Bex dropped her off, Jordan rolled her Ducati out of the underground parking garage and headed for the back roads north of town. They twisted and curved through wooded areas and around the lakes, just enough to keep her mind off the new assignment and the old feelings she didn't want to remember.

She opened the throttle and killed the headlights, savoring the challenge of navigating by moonlight. The damp air off the lake tingled, and an occasional bug stung her face. As she increased speed, the adrenaline she thrived on flooded her system. Her skin dimpled and tingled. Her heart raced and she panted to catch a breath. The need in her pulsed and throbbed, feeling more powerful than the machine roaring between her thighs. She pumped her fists in the air, let go of the handlebars, and screamed at the sky. "Yes!"

When she looked back down, a white dog stood in the middle of the road. She grabbed the brake and squeezed steadily. If she jerked, she'd go over the handlebars or throw the bike into a skid. No matter how much pressure she applied, she would hit him if she didn't ditch.

"Love you too." She mumbled, wiping at wet kisses. Jordan opened her eyes and met a pair of bright-blue ones staring back at her and a huge tongue ready for another swipe across her face. "Stop." The dog she'd almost hit stood beside her. She did a physical survey of her body before moving to make sure nothing was broken. Urging the dog aside, she gently rose. "Who are you?" The dog wagged his tail for the first time, as though relieved she wasn't badly injured. "Do you live around here?" *I must have a head injury. I'm talking to a dog and expecting him to answer.*

The dog's fur was as white as her hair and clean except for some leaves across his back. She reached to brush them off, but the animal twisted his hindquarters away as though her touch was painful. "You're hurt. Come here, fella." She urged him closer and checked for obvious injuries and a collar. She didn't feel comfortable leaving him alone on the side of the road with no idea who he belonged to or if he had internal injuries. "We probably need to have you checked out."

Jordan pulled her bike out of the ditch, grateful it didn't appear to be damaged. She got on and motioned for the dog to join her. He placed his paws on the side of the gas tank and waited for help. When she reached down and grabbed hold, he leapt up and stretched himself across the tank and her legs. "Good boy. You've been riding before." With her new charge in tow, Jordan drove much more carefully to the nearest emergency vet, wondering how the night had turned from one of carefree riding to concerned parenting.

After work Neela drove to the North Carolina State University campus where she conducted her stem-cell research, parked outside the College of Veterinary Medicine, and dialed her home number before going inside. "Bina, how are you?"

"Fine, honey. How are you?"

"Good. Listen, I'm—"

"Working late."

"Can you manage? I've left some dinner for you in the fridge. I shouldn't be too long."

"You work too much. Come home. We can have a nice hot meal and talk."

"I wish I could, but not tonight. I'll see you before bedtime. Love you."

"Love you too."

A wave of guilt blanketed her as she walked to the back door of the college. She should be home, not just tonight but every night, but she had to make sacrifices for the greater good. God, she sounded like a recruiting slogan. She swiped her access card and wound her way through the corridors to the stem-cell lab. Her research partner, Liz Blackmon, was already hunkered over a tray of specimens, tendrils of her red hair escaping the mesh net.

She pulled on a pair of scrubs, snapped a net over her hair, washed her hands, shoved them into latex gloves, and entered the sealed room. "Sorry I'm late."

Liz continued working. "You're never late, honey. I'm actually early. Look at this." She shoved a microscope toward Neela and kissed her lightly on the neck. "I missed you last week. When will you be free again?"

"Soon, I hope. I could use some stress relief."

"Ouch. After a year, I'd hoped to be more than just stress relief."

"Sorry. You know what my life is like. Besides, I don't want the university to pull our funding if they get wind of our...special friendship."

"Relationship, Neela. It's called a relationship. You can't even say the word. Besides, we're three years into this project and making great strides. They wouldn't cut us off if we screwed on the lawn naked in broad daylight."

"We're in the conservative South, Liz. I'm pretty sure that would get us fired and maybe banned from working again." Their friends-with-benefits arrangement worked well for Neela because she didn't have time to date and Liz was a satisfactory lover. But was satisfactory enough? She hadn't considered anything personal in so long the thought seemed foreign. She looked through the viewer. "What have you got here?"

"You tell me. I know what I think, but I need another opinion."

"It looks like some of the stem cells we injected into the spinal-cord specimen have made their way to the injury site. Is that what you're seeing?"

"Yep. The question now is, will they simply create a healing environment for repair or become part of the repair itself?"

"This is fantastic. Finally some progress." She hugged Liz and felt her arms tighten around her waist.

"You feel so good. Let's wrap up and celebrate. I'd really like to be with you tonight."

"I...shouldn't," Neela said.

"We can't do anything with this at the moment. It takes time. Bina thinks you're working anyway. We might as well make the best of it."

"But it's not right."

"What difference will another hour make? My place is only five minutes away. You deserve a bit of happiness. Please."

Liz ran her hands over Neela's backside and wedged her knee between her legs. She weakened as Liz rocked back and forth. "All right, but I can't stay long."

"It won't take long."

As she put the specimens away and made the short trip to Liz's apartment, Neela battled with guilt. She should be at home with Bina, not having sex under the guise of working late. She wasn't being honest, but she needed this so badly. Sex with Liz was the only physical release she had. She just didn't have enough time for anything that didn't come neatly sandwiched between work and home. She was already partially undressed as she walked into Liz's bedroom.

"Come here and stop worrying." Liz pulled her onto the bed, rolled on top, and kissed her. "Let me help you forget."

She tried to release the unpleasant thoughts and immerse herself in the physical. Liz sucked her breasts and Neela felt a tendril of arousal. Next Liz would slide her hand between Neela's legs and circle her clit in a slow clockwise motion just before slipping her fingers inside. Liz wouldn't go down on her yet. She always needed a quick release first to dull the urgency. Her technique never varied. It was efficient but hardly inspiring.

Liz's moans filled the air, and Neela tried to tap into her enthusiasm. She looked at Liz's face, hoping her arousal would stimulate her as well. But instead of Liz's green eyes blazing with passion, she saw the startling blue gaze of Jordan Bishop. The slight stirring pounded to life. Fire sparked through her, and she was instantly wet and aching. She closed her eyes and held onto Jordan's vision as Liz's fingers entered her. The stress and worries of her life vanished, and she came over and over. "Oh my God."

Liz pulled her close as her breathing slowly leveled. "Gorgeous. You needed that."

"You have no idea."

CHAPTER THREE

Jordan and Bex pulled in front of the ranch-style house in Hamilton Lakes just before six the next morning. The sprawling *House Beautiful* property had a manicured lawn with a border of azaleas, small carriage house, and a double garage at the end of the driveway.

"Working for the state obviously pays better than city government," Bex said.

"And who said politicians weren't corrupt?" Jordan sipped from her travel mug and looked away from the house toward the lake in front. Neela's home made her long for things she'd never had. The redbrick structure with a tidy yard and shuttered windows symbolized home. "Nice view. Beats the hell out of my empty rented studio flat overlooking the parking garage."

"I'm sure Neela isn't on the take. She seems too principled."

"Oh, it's *Neela* now, is it? And how would you know?"

"Shut up. I'm practicing. Told you I could go for that."

"Shut up." Jordan repeated their bantering phrase even though she meant it a little more than usual this time. Bex's reputation with the ladies was nearly as notorious as hers. Between the two of them, they'd bedded almost every eligible woman on the market and some who weren't.

Harry Styles and Phil Morris, the night-shift officers, pulled up to the driver's side where Jordan had slumped down sipping her coffee.

"What's up, guys?" Bex asked.

Phil held the surveillance sheet in front of him and read in an exaggerated show of giving a full report. "Boring as hell. Four coffee runs, three piss breaks, and a doughnut-retrieval operation. Whoever got us assigned to this shit detail owes us big-time. Doctor Sahjani got home shortly before midnight, but somebody else either lives here or stayed overnight."

"She didn't mention that." Bex made a note on their surveillance sheet.

"Surprise, surprise," Jordan mumbled. Why wouldn't she live with somebody? She was attractive, accomplished, and gutsy. Women like her didn't usually sleep alone or remain single for extended periods of time.

"We saw movement inside, and the lights went on and off throughout the house until Sahjani came home. Then everything went dark. How will we coordinate relief? This woman apparently doesn't keep a regular schedule, and we need to know if we're driving to Raleigh to relieve you or meeting in Greensboro."

"I don't know yet," Bex said. "We'll get a better handle on her activities and give you a call later. If we have to, we'll debrief by cell."

The guys pulled away and Bex asked, "What do you make of that?"

"Why are you constantly amazed when people aren't forthcoming about their lives? You're a police officer, for God's sake."

"And why are you always looking for the worst? Guess I prefer to be an optimist."

The front door of Doctor Sahjani's house opened, and Jordan nearly spilled her coffee when she jerked upright. She rifled through the glove compartment and looked toward the backseat. "Where are the binoculars?"

"Haven't gotten them out of the trunk yet. I didn't think we'd need them so soon."

Neela, curvy and long-haired, appeared in the doorway wearing slacks and a multi-colored blouse that complemented her mocha complexion. She hefted her suit jacket onto her shoulder and kissed a slightly shorter woman before walking toward her car. Something inside Jordan tightened like an over-wrought spring. She strained for a closer look at the woman left behind, but the door closed too quickly.

"What do you know, the doctor has a girlfriend. No mention of that either," Jordan said. But they hadn't specifically asked her that question. And Jordan's behavior when she met Neela hadn't exactly promoted trust and sharing. Why would she confide anything about her personal life? But everybody lied, evaded, covered up, or glossed over something. Why should Neela Sahjani be different? A small part of her was glad she wasn't.

"I knew there was something I liked about her, besides her feisty attitude," Bex said. "My chances just got better."

"Not if that's her partner and she's actually faithful." Her voice sounded smug, but Jordan couldn't help it. She cranked the car and fell in behind Neela as she weaved along the tree-lined streets of the Hamilton Lakes neighborhood.

The hour-and-a-half drive to Neela's office in Raleigh was like following a race driver around the track, and it reminded Jordan of her years on the motocross circuit. Every time she got close, Neela glanced in her rearview mirror and sped up. Where had she learned to drive like that? Jordan loved the exhilaration of the chase, and the attractive woman behind the wheel didn't hurt either.

"She has no idea this is like foreplay for you."

Jordan let off the gas and Neela's vehicle pulled away. Bex knew her too well. "You know how much I love games." The pulsing adrenaline was her drug of choice, and her body thrummed. She tried to stop the arousing thoughts and breathe through the building tension like her therapist, Molly, had suggested, but the exercise did little to blunt the pull.

She'd struggled with her sexual urges for years, trying to reconcile puberty with what felt like a curse to her. She'd had no role model for love or healthy boundaries, so she'd gone from the harsh strictures of her Catholic keepers to promiscuity. A never-ending string of sexual partners seemed perfectly normal. But she had no idea what to do if she met someone who mattered.

"I know you love speed. Combine that with a gorgeous woman, and even I'm getting a little worked up." Bex slid her hand between her legs. "Oh, yeah, baby. I'm horny."

"Shut up." Jordan felt moisture gather uncomfortably in her crotch and grimaced at her failure once again to control her body.

"Can you imagine that woman on the back of your Ducati, legs wrapped around your waist, hand in your jeans? Jesus, I could come just thinking about it."

"Seriously, shut up." She squeezed her thighs together and tried to erase the image Bex had planted in her mind.

"Yeah, you're right. You couldn't handle a woman like that on the bike. A dog in the road distracts you. I'm glad you didn't hit him, but you look like a poster child for road rash."

"Your constant prattle and this rush-hour traffic are making me feel like throwing this thing in the ditch." She gunned the accelerator, cut a figure S between three cars, and caught up to Neela again. "How much farther?"

"The next exit. We need to find out more about her routines when we get there."

"You talk to her."

"Fine by me. The tech guys should've installed the cameras last night. Makes our job a lot easier. We can monitor on the tablet from the car. Where will you be?"

"Out front." She needed to stay away from Neela Sahjani. Maybe the spring air would erode the layer of discomfort that thinking about her had created.

❖

"Good morning, det—Bex. Riding solo today?" Neela was relieved not to see Jordan. After her liaison with Liz the night before and the images of Jordan that had brought her most satisfying orgasm in memory, she didn't need to come face to face with the object of her fantasy quite so soon.

"She's outside cooling off. I think you got her worked up."

Neela dropped her briefcase and nearly toppled her coffee over on the day's schedule. "Sorry?"

"I think your little race down I-40 got her adrenaline pumping. She's a speed freak, especially on her motorcycle, but in the absence of that, any careening projectile will do."

"I see." Neela tried to erase a picture of Jordan Bishop aroused and astride a motorcycle pulsing between her thighs. *Too late.* She sat down before her legs failed. "How can I help you this morning, Bex?"

"I don't mean to be indelicate."

"But you're going to anyway."

"Occupational hazard. The surveillance team from last night noted you didn't get home until almost midnight...and someone else was in your house during that time. I really hate to pry, but if we don't know your normal routines—people, places, and so on—we can't properly protect you."

Neela rose and walked to the window overlooking the athletic field. How much of her life should she share? Was anything sacred? When she glanced toward the track, she saw a lone figure sprinting along the outside lane—Jordan. She'd recognize her lean, androgynous frame and striking white hair in a mob, but alone in a field she was an arresting sight. A short-sleeved blue T-shirt stretched tightly over back and shoulder muscles shaped by hours of physical effort. As Jordan's powerful legs and arms propelled her faster, Neela's breath hung in her throat like the first time she'd seen her.

"That's her way of letting off steam," Bex said.

Neela started. She'd been too engrossed to notice Bex walking up behind her. "Is it a frequent thing?"

"Not for some time, so I'm actually glad to see her worked up about something, even if I don't know what it is."

Neela watched Jordan more closely as she made another turn around the track. A red rash ran down her left arm, and her gait slightly favored that side. "What happened to her arm?"

"She was riding last night and ditched her bike to avoid a dog."

"Really?" The Jordan Bishop she'd seen so far gave the impression she wouldn't brake for a person, much less a dog. Her curiosity was piqued. But why would a woman who was rude, volatile, and so seemingly opposite her on every spectrum interest her?

"Why's she so intense?" Neela had no right to pry, but if her life was being splayed open to these people, a little reciprocity didn't seem out of line.

"Can't really say. I mean I could, but she's my best friend as well as my work partner, so it doesn't seem right."

"I understand. I'm having trouble coming to terms with the violation of my own privacy. Guess I should know better. Forgive me." Neela forced herself away from the window and returned to her desk. "You asked about my home situation. I live with another woman. She's there most of the time. As far as my other activities, I do research at NC State's College of Veterinary Medicine several nights a week."

"Any particular type of research? Just curious."

"Stem cells and their potential on various diseases and types of injuries. Right now we're working on spinal-cord injuries in dogs and cats."

"Impressive." Bex shifted uncomfortably in her seat and flipped a couple of pages in her notebook.

"Ask your questions, detective."

"What about your personal life—husband, boyfriend, girlfriend, exes? Anywhere you might be spending the night? We'd need to provide coverage."

"No." Bex looked surprised, and Neela smiled. "I told you I live with another woman. I spend my nights at home." She didn't mention Liz because she seldom spent the night at her place. She might have to suspend their liaisons entirely until this unpleasantness blew over.

"Right. Can you think of anyone who might have a grudge against you, personal or professional?"

"I've been in administration for several years, pretty low-key. Life consists of my work here, research, and family, quite stable but not exactly exhilarating. No disgruntled employees or jilted lovers. I'm not aware of anyone who would want to threaten or harm me."

Bex started to respond, but the door of Neela's office burst open and Jordan strode in.

"Are you about finished?" She looked at her watch, and Neela noted the huge Tag Heuer that dwarfed her small wrist. Sweat beaded Jordan's forehead, and her T-shirt clung to her compact breasts like plastic wrap. "I wanted to test the cameras."

Neela's mouth dried and she licked her lips. "G—good morning, detective."

"Morning." She didn't look at Neela but watched as Bex repositioned the cameras.

"I see your manners haven't improved since yesterday." What was there about this woman that rubbed her the wrong way? *Rubbing. Oh, God.* The image from last night flashed through her mind again. Her fantasy stood in front of her—hot, sweaty, and looking so edible that Neela ached. She'd never responded to a woman this viscerally.

Jordan swirled her leather jacket off her shoulder and pulled it on. "Sorry?" The word sounded like a question instead of an apology. She zipped the jacket and then tapped her fingers against the side of her thigh as her eyes roamed from Neela's three-inch heels to the top of her head and back down before finally meeting her gaze. Neela warmed as though a hot sun had broken through the window, but Jordan seemed unfazed.

"Yeah, well, let's test those cameras," Bex said.

Before Neela composed herself enough to speak, they were gone and she clung to her desk for support. "Wait." She ran down the hall after them. "Wait." She was within arm's reach of Jordan when a heel snagged on the carpet and she stumbled forward. Jordan turned just in time to stop her from taking a nosedive into the worn, stained carpet.

When Jordan's arms encircled her, the liquefaction she'd felt between her legs seconds ago spread throughout her body. *I can't breathe.* She'd expected this woman's touch to be cold and stiff, but as she stood supported against her, Neela felt only warmth and strength. Jordan held her as if she were weightless, and the muscles beneath Neela's fingers rippled with energy. "I'm so sorry. Low-bid government carpet."

"Or three-inch heels." For a second Neela caught a glimpse of humor in Jordan's eyes before the frosty barrier slid back into place. "Something you needed?"

You. She shook her head and formed her words before daring to speak. "I wanted to ask if these cameras are audio as well as video. Certain things need to remain private."

"I certainly hope so." Jordan released her and slowly pulled away. Neela was tempted to stumble again just to feel Jordan's arms around her once more.

"Are you okay?" She nodded, and Bex cupped her elbow and walked her back to the office. "They're just video."

"Great. Thanks." Why didn't Bex's soft touch have the same effect on her as Jordan's? If she was having some kind of hormonal spike, surely any woman would do. Her reasoning sounded weak, but after tangling with Jordan, she was too exhausted to examine her reaction further.

As she settled back in her chair, she sent up a silent prayer that she wouldn't see Jordan Bishop too often. She wasn't sure her heart or her body could stand the intensity. Why was she suddenly attracted—and she was definitely attracted—to a woman who conveyed more hostility than warmth and terrified her on so many levels? Even if her life wasn't a complicated mass of responsibilities and deadlines, Jordan would be the last woman she should be interested in.

Neela tried to ignore the blinking red camera light from the corner of her office and the gnawing feeling that her life was about to change. She pulled up the governor's latest internal email. Nothing new from on high, at least nothing His Holiness deemed worthy to share with the masses.

"Ready for the morning dish?" Rosemary popped her head into the office with two fresh cups of coffee. Her unruly mass of gray hair on top of her pencil-thin body made her resemble a very adorable scrub brush.

"More than. You always know exactly what I need."

"You're easy. You're a coffee slut."

"And you're a lifesaver, Rose."

"That's not what I hear. Rumor has it that particular job goes to a tall, gorgeous, slightly dangerous-looking cop roaming the building. There's a line of women, straight and lesbian, primping in the restroom as we speak. Care to comment?" Rosemary pulled her swivel chair up to the desk and caged Neela's legs between hers.

"Seriously, Rose, you're worse than my gay friends with your gossip. If I hadn't known you and Wayne for twenty years, I'd swear you batted for our team."

"If that yummy thing you fell all over is an option, I might be persuaded. But from where I'm standing it looked like you had her all wrapped up." She poked her in the side and did the hand fan like they were still in high school.

"Since we're on the subject of my protection detail, are you the one who notified the police about the threatening notes?" Rosemary fiddled with her smart phone and didn't answer immediately. "Rose?"

"I was worried about you, especially after what happened to Ed. I couldn't live with myself if someone hurt you and I hadn't done anything about it. Forgive me?"

"Don't I always, but it's really a waste of their time. And what's with this close-proximity briefing?" She indicated the scant distance between them.

"Just wanted to check your body temperature after your close encounter with Dracula's cousin. I've never seen you so flustered, not even for redheaded Doctor Blackmon. Do I need to alert the fire department or maybe the paramedics?"

"Shush." She pointed toward the camera but remembered Jordan and Bex couldn't hear them—thank God. "Very funny. Back off and give me the bad news for the day."

Rosemary cupped Neela's elbow and waited for her to look up from the computer. "You know I'm kidding, right? I just want you to be happy, really happy."

Neela hugged her and let the sincerity of Rose's words sink in. Would she even know what happiness felt like if it came along? She recognized passion from across the athletic field, but true happiness was another matter entirely. "I know."

"Okay, boss." Rosemary rolled her chair back and scrolled on her phone. "Nothing new regarding our staff conference the other day. Everything's quiet, which is always a worry. I'm not sure if that means nothing is happening or we're just not hearing about it."

"All we can do is wait and keep doing our jobs. Stay on top of our projects and make sure nothing falls through the cracks. I want our folks working like superstars. If the new man wants to get rid of us, he'll have to dig deeper than performance issues."

"Our folks are on board with that."

"But I still worry about them. Most of our employees have families to support. It's always bothered me how newly elected officials conduct a firing sweep like they're cleaning house, without regard for the people behind the jobs."

"You don't understand it because you're not morally bankrupt like some politicians."

"Thanks, honey, but that won't help much if the powers that be decide we have to go."

"Don't worry so much about what hasn't happened yet. You've got enough on your plate. Anything else for me?" Rose gathered her tablet and phone and had bent to give Neela a hug when the office door swung open.

"No, honey. What the—" Jordan Bishop stood framed in the doorway with a scowl across her beautiful face that looked almost painful. "Do you *ever* knock?"

Without answering, she glared at Rosemary and crossed to the camera. "Got a glitch. Picture's gone."

Rosemary smiled at Neela and started toward the door. "I'll leave you two alone."

"Rose, no." But Rosemary was already closing the door behind her. Great. She was in a confined space with a woman who exuded so much sexual energy she found it hard to breathe. "I'm trying to work here." Her voice sounded dry and scratchy.

"So am I. I have to see you."

In another context those words would've had her horizontal in seconds. She was practically there now. She straightened in her chair. "Would you please knock in the future before barging in? The governor could be in here...or anyone."

"So I noticed." Jordan pulled a chair from beside her desk and stepped up to reach the camera. "Pretty chummy with your *assistant*, aren't you?"

Neela was out of her chair before Jordan finished the sentence. "My relationship with my *assistant* or anyone else is none of your business." Hands planted firmly on her hips, she looked up to confront Jordan and was perfectly eye-to-crotch level. *Seriously? Give me a break with this woman.* Jordan's normal height was daunting enough, but this was like David and Goliath. "Come down here, this instant." She sounded like a scolding parent, but to her amazement Jordan complied. And she wished she hadn't. They were entirely too close.

"Yes?"

Even in heels Neela was still shorter than Jordan, but she refused to be intimidated. After the way Jordan had treated her, she should order her out of her office once and for all. She hadn't asked for this situation and certainly didn't believe she needed protection—and if she did, it was most likely from Jordan Bishop. The energy between them was almost tangible, and she couldn't walk away without understanding the dynamic. "You obviously have a problem with me. Are you able to put it aside until this unfortunate situation is resolved?"

"I don't know."

Neela had expected another smart-ass remark, not something that sounded like an honest, almost contrite answer. "Can you tell me what's going on?"

"I'm trying to fix the camera."

Neela tried again. "I mean with us."

"Stop talking."

She should stop. Whatever was going on with Jordan was none of her business, but she couldn't deny she wanted to know more about her. Was it her raw sex appeal, the pain she saw in her eyes, or just Neela's savior complex that made her keep pushing? "In case you haven't noticed, I don't take orders very well. When you held, or caught, me earlier, you seemed sad. Is it something I've done?"

"Please, stop."

"Why are you so rude and—"

"I just can't be around you…you remind me…I mean…forget it."

Pain shadowed Jordan's eyes and Neela was captivated. She slid her arm around Jordan's waist, pulled her firmly against her, and, without a word, kissed her. Jordan's lips were so soft and hot and wet that she melted into them and opened herself to Jordan's probing tongue. Her skin dampened with a sheen of pleasure sweat, and arousal trickled between her legs. While Neela's mind urged her to run, her hunger surged and swelled. As Jordan kissed her, the irrationality of her actions disappeared, and all she felt was this single perfect moment. She was plummeting out of control when Jordan pulled away and left her gasping for air.

"That was so wrong." Jordan stared at her for an instant, her eyes full of fire and regret, before she sprinted from the room.

Neela dropped into the chair Jordan had vacated and stared after her. "Oh, God. What have I done?"

Chapter Four

Bex met Jordan halfway back to the car. "You're really on the edge, aren't you? We're on the job. This is her place of business. Do I need to go on?"

"Hey, I didn't kiss her first."

"But you didn't back off."

"Would you?"

Bex grabbed her arms and made her look at her. "From where I'm standing, that was just reckless." Bex paused, trying to understand. "Why do you suppose she did that?"

"She wanted to?" Jordan was desperate to change the subject because she didn't understand why she'd responded so passionately to the kiss. Neela had been too close, asking too many questions, calm and relaxed, and acting like she cared. The energy inside Jordan spiraled and she had no time to count or breathe, no way to control it. And the look in Neela's eyes had been like an invitation, almost a plea—to reach out, to connect.

"My chances just went up in smoke. Why did you have to kiss her back?"

"She wouldn't stop asking questions I couldn't answer. It was the only way to shut her up." Jordan paced in front of the car, unable to settle. What she'd thought might be a stop button on a sound bite had turned into something entirely different.

"What kind of questions?" Bex asked.

"Why I dislike her, why I'm rude to her, why I'm sad, blah, blah, blah."

"Oh, you mean emotional questions? Questions normal people ask? Questions designed to help people get to know each other? Those kinds of questions?"

"Yeah."

"Well, I think you succeeded in shutting her up because she's been sitting in that chair since you left without saying a word. This is a dangerous game you're playing, Jordan, on more than one level." Bex counted on her fingers. "She's work, she's with someone, she's at least ten years older, and you're not really interested."

"It just happened, okay? It doesn't mean anything. I'm going to check out the protestors at the capitol. You can handle this, right?" Without waiting for a response, Jordan jogged away.

"You're running all the way to the capitol building?"

"It's only two miles, Bex. I've got my cell, and I'll be back before she leaves for the day." Jordan hoped running would clear her mind and help her figure out what had just happened. When Rosemary had come into Neela's office, she'd watched their interaction, and the more she watched, the more rattled she'd become.

She replayed the tape in her head. Rosemary had brought Neela coffee, a nice gesture for her boss. Rosemary had pulled her chair close to Neela's desk. Strike. Rosemary had opened her legs, straddled Neela's chair, and moved closer. Strike two. When Rosemary had leaned over to hug Neela, the reception froze. Strike three. Their interaction appeared more intimate than friendly, and Jordan didn't understand. For her, intimacy equaled sex. So why did Neela encourage such behavior in a professional setting? She'd sprinted across the parking lot and passed Rosemary on the way out of Neela's office. She wanted to tell her to stay away from Neela. Surely her assistant knew she lived with someone. Jordan was angry with herself for getting so worked up. It wasn't her job to protect Neela's relationship or her honor, just her personal safety.

As Jordan had adjusted the camera, Neela wouldn't stop talking, trying to connect with her, trying to understand her. She stood too close. Neela's brown eyes drilled into her until she couldn't think clearly. And when Neela had pulled her close and kissed her, something inside had snapped. At that moment, she'd wanted Neela's kiss more than her next breath. It was wrong but she couldn't stop. Neela had deepened their kiss, apparently unconcerned about her partner at home—the death knell. Was she simply an attractive woman who encouraged flirtations in the workplace and succumbed to the attraction of strangers? Was that why Jordan had returned her kiss? Had it turned out exactly as she'd hoped? Did she need to find a flaw in Neela?

She'd felt something the day they met and assumed it was a competitive spark, the result of Neela's defiance. But her behavior today, while it had inflamed Jordan's overactive libido, had doused any spark of real interest. She could never be serious about a woman who cheated on her partner. Bex would probably be next. The thought was like a roadblock and she stumbled, barely regaining her balance before lurching into an intersection.

She walked the last block to the capitol and joined the group of Guilford Citizens for Equality protestors gathered in front of the building. Several held signs objecting to Governor Lloyd's cutbacks to teachers' salaries and health care. Others chanted about proposed changes to voting guidelines. She hung out in the area between the more vocal group and the organizers toward the front, who talked about strategies and upcoming events. No one mentioned abortions or waved posters on the subject. She'd read all the literature on the Guilford Citizens for Equality group, and everything indicated they were peaceful, more liberal than their Republican counterparts, and supportive of a woman's right to choose. Her observations seemed to confirm those assumptions.

She made it back to the car just before five o'clock and settled in beside Bex. "Anything going on here?"

"Not since you left."

"Ha-ha."

"Nope, all quiet. You?"

"No sign of any radical right-to-lifers around the capitol. If all the protestors are as nonviolent as the ones I saw today, this case could be harder than we thought. They seem like an educated group who have genuine concerns and just want to be heard. Extremists aren't likely to mingle with the more docile crowd anyway, but it was worth a look."

"I'm still hoping the forensic guys recovered some evidence from Doctor Branson or his car." Bex pointed as Neela walked across the parking lot toward them holding a sheet of paper. "Wonder what this is about? Hope it's not your report card from earlier because you'll get low marks on plays-well-with-others."

"Shut up."

Neela approached Bex's side of the car and didn't look at Jordan. Her hand shook as she handed Bex the typewritten note. "I found this on my windshield." Jordan leaned over to read it.

> *Neela Sahjani,*
> *Branson was only the beginning. Stop what you're doing or you'll be next.*
> *I know where you live.*
> *None of you are safe!!*

"Not very specific, is he? This could reference anything—stop my stem-cell research, shopping at Target, eating wheat." Neela's attempt at humor didn't hide the frightened look in her eyes.

"Still think this has nothing to do with you?" Jordan pulled an evidence envelope from the glove compartment and dropped the note inside, using her fingernails.

"Detective, I could care less about myself—"

"Right."

Neela glared at her, and Jordan turned toward the basketball court. Probably best, since she couldn't look at her without thinking about that damn kiss. She had to get off this case, or she and this woman would shred each other. The chemistry between them was too intense.

"As I started to say, I'm concerned this person knows where I live and is brazen enough to put a threatening note on my car in full daylight with the police only yards away. I wasn't really concerned at first, but the other letters were never specifically directed at me. Now my home and my family are being threatened."

The hairs at the back of Jordan's neck stiffened. Neela sounded so damned sincere. Where was all her concern for her family when she was flirting with Rosemary earlier and kissing her?

"I understand. We all want to feel safe," Bex said. "Let's get you home and make sure everything's okay. That's our first priority. Tomorrow I'd like you to park in front of the building, not in the employee lot at the rear, and use only this entrance to come and go."

"Yes, that's fine." As Neela started to walk away, her cell rang. She held up a finger, asking Bex to wait. "Hi, Liz." She shook her head like it wasn't who she was expecting and turned her back. "No, I'm sorry. I can't tonight. I need to go home." She lowered her voice almost to a whisper. "Can we talk about this later? I really have to go." Neela hung up and faced Bex again. "I'll see you at home. And I will be breaking the speed limit."

Jordan shook her foot and stared out the window as Bex tried to keep up with Neela's car on the interstate. "You drive like a grandma. She'll be home, finished with dinner, and ready for bed by the time we get there."

"And then she'll be our relief's problem, won't she? I called the guys and told them to meet us at the house."

They'd been quiet on the ride, which meant Bex wasn't happy with her. "So, who do you think Liz is?"

Bex pursed her lips. "I don't give a happy horse shit, and you shouldn't either."

"I was just asking, making conversation. It certainly wasn't the little woman at home."

"Why do you sound so smug? Is the whole point of this exercise to prove Neela Sahjani is a cheating, lying partner? It's not our business, Jordan. And even if it's true, it has nothing to do with our job. What *is* it with you and this woman?"

Bex was right. It shouldn't matter. Why did the thought of Neela's possible infidelity annoy her? "I tried to get off the case. I told you we wouldn't be a good fit. Our personalities just clash. It happens."

"That's not all of it though. Something else is bothering you."

"It's nothing."

"You can spread that bullshit as thick as you want, but I'm not buying it. You've been irritable ever since you started seeing that therapist, Molly. She's bringing up stuff about your past in the orphanage, isn't she?"

Jordan forced her foot to stay still. She didn't want to appear as rattled as she felt inside. Molly had dug open old wounds, and they never seemed to stop bleeding. Every scab she picked only led to a deeper injury. Jordan was starting to believe the numbness of denial was far better than this constant dose of painful memories and recurring nightmares. "It's all right."

"I don't think so. It's affecting your work and your life. But I won't push it right now. If you ever want to talk, I'm here."

Jordan couldn't imagine talking to anyone else about a childhood that would make even the most seasoned officer cringe. "Yeah, thanks."

Bex pulled in front of Neela's house, but their relief hadn't arrived yet. "We need to make sure the house is secure before we go off duty."

"Yeah. Let's sweep the outside first." They made their way around the brick residence checking windows for security and the ground for disturbance, and then Bex knocked on the front door. When Neela answered, Jordan stopped at the corner of the house and listened.

"Mind if we come in and make sure everything is all right?"

"We?" She looked both ways, and Jordan stepped out of the shadows and up onto the stoop. Neela pulled the door almost closed behind her, leaving only a small crack. "Everything's fine. I've been through the house. No need to waste your time."

Jordan couldn't stop staring. Neela wore a pair of jogging tights and a top that hugged her shapely body. Her breasts were perfectly proportioned to the small waist Jordan's hands had encircled earlier. Her fingers tingled with sensory memory. Without her heels, Neela seemed almost diminutive, but her presence filled the doorway. She seemed fiercely protective of her home and whoever was inside. Jordan swallowed hard, unable to imagine what it would feel like to be the recipient of such concern. But Neela's devotion didn't coincide with her earlier indiscretion.

"We've checked the outside and can't find any evidence of trespassing or tampering," Bex said. "We'll give our relief the information about the note. Sure you don't want us to check inside while we're here?"

"That's really not necessary." Jordan saw a female figure cross behind Neela in the background. She craned her neck to get a better look, but Neela was already closing the door. "Thank you. I'll see you tomorrow."

"Talk about rude," Jordan said as they walked back to the car.

"You're one to talk, mate."

"Wonder why she wouldn't let us in?"

"Why should she? It wasn't a social call, and she was confident everything was okay."

"Did you get a glimpse of the mystery woman?"

"No, but I wasn't trying. Why are you so concerned about who Neela's sleeping with?" When they got back in the car, Bex blatantly stared. "Well? Has she ignited a little interest in your indifferent ass? If so, that's good, but she isn't the kind of woman you want to mess with. She's got a family, a stable life."

"And I'm what, a reject looking for a thrill?" Bex's words stung, but she wasn't about to let the pain show. She'd earned her reputation as a player, but it still hurt when even her best friend couldn't see beyond the façade. So she'd learned to act the part, never show her true self because she was certain that would hurt even more. "I'm just saying I could hit that."

"I didn't say you were a reject. But I get the feeling Neela's the kind of woman you hit once and stick to for life. You just don't seem interested in domesticity right now."

Jordan retreated to the familiar. Bex already thought Jordan was incurably horny, but wasn't every twenty-five-year-old? "You up for the bar tonight?" She really wanted to strip and let the fresh night air peel away the memory of Neela's body pressed against hers and the feel of her lips hungrily returning her kiss.

"We haven't been to the bar since last week. Damn skippy I'm in. I wouldn't miss a master class in seduction Bishop style. Ten o'clock?" When Jordan nodded, she fist-pumped the air. "Sweet."

"Will you drop the note off at the lab? I need to run by the apartment and take care of something." She wasn't about to tell Bex she'd temporarily adopted the stray collie she'd dodged in the road. She'd get a lecture on being a responsible pet owner, which she didn't need. She'd already taken him to the vet to be checked for injuries, shots, and registration, and she'd named him as well—Blue, at least until she found out his real name.

The vet said her new friend was unusual because most collies were mixed colors, not totally white, and larger than Blue. She'd promised to take care of him until his owner could be located. It was the least she could do after almost running over him.

"No problem. By the way, Phil and Harry want to know if we'd alternate some days and nights with them. You up for that, so nobody gets stuck pulling graveyard all the time?"

"Whatever. Just let me know."

Bex stopped beside Jordan's Ducati while she got her helmet out of the backseat, pulled it on, and rode away.

❖

It was three in the morning before Neela settled softly onto the bed next to Bina. The four-day treatment protocol she'd received in Panama three days ago had left her anxious and exhausted, but she was finally asleep, and Neela breathed a thankful sigh.

After the incident with Jordan, her day at work had been packed with meetings and personnel dramas, and at home with personal dramas. She hadn't had time alone to process what had happened between them.

The first part was easier to address. She'd kissed Jordan. *And she kissed me back.* "And she kissed me back." Hearing the words aloud, Neela stared at the ceiling, trying to understand why she'd kissed a woman who'd ignored and insulted her since they met. Jordan Bishop was rude, unprofessional, distant, sarcastic, and judgmental. *What kind of masochist am I?*

Her feelings were much easier to decipher than the reasons for them. The world around her receded until nothing existed except their kiss. Jordan had seduced her with the softness of her mouth and the workings of her exquisite tongue. Jordan had kissed her with undeniable passion, as if searching for something. She would've gladly dragged Jordan into an office, locked the door, and surrendered to her on the worn carpet. She'd ignited like flash paper and just as quickly been extinguished. When Jordan had pushed her away, she felt she'd failed a test and disappointed her in some way. *"That was so wrong."* What had she meant?

When Jordan had walked away, Neela had struggled to catch her breath and restore her equilibrium. She'd always meted out her pleasures in small, manageable servings and buried her ravenous desire under the responsibilities of her life. But the cravings Jordan Bishop conjured in her defied management, and that scared her more than the possibility of caring for her.

In spite of her reservations, reliving their kiss had aroused her. She slid her hand into her pajama bottoms and stroked the tight mass of nerves aching between her legs. Would Jordan be a passionate, assertive lover driven by the demons Neela had seen in her eyes? Or would she submit to the seduction of a gentle woman who could touch her heart? She stroked again and Bina shifted beside her.

She'd made promises to Bina and their life together and needed to concentrate on her priorities. Slowly withdrawing her hand, she rolled over. Sleep would be an elusive partner tonight.

CHAPTER FIVE

The neon lights of the marquee flickered, and the Q Lounge became alternately the Q Long. Jordan had met and subsequently been dumped by several women here while new lovers waited in the wings. She didn't want to be here, but the place drew her in with the promise of mind-numbing drink and free, easy sex. Drastic times required drastic measures, and today had been one of those days. A familiar calling pulsed insistently between her legs, and this was the only place it could be soothed with no questions or expectations.

She took a deep breath and pulled on the heavy metal door. An old eighties disco ball cast glitter light around an otherwise dark room, and ghostly figures danced to a thumping beat. When her eyes adjusted, she spotted Bex at a table already holding court with four other women. Bex's preference was of a type—medium height, feminine, large breasts, and red or auburn hair. The two blondes were obviously meant for Jordan.

Sometimes their pick-ups felt too hetero-meat-market for Jordan, but if the other woman was agreeable, and neither of them wanted anything serious, it worked temporarily. And she only had a short game.

"There she is," Bex said as she approached. She gave her a jock hug, slapped her on the back, and whispered, "I was starting to think you weren't coming."

"Needed some action tonight." Her response sounded like the Jordan Bex expected when they were cruising. She could be a recluse, so her horniness gave her an excuse to appease Bex by being sociable.

"Wait till you see what I've picked for you." Bex pulled up a chair and waved to the women seated around the table. "Ladies, this is my best friend, Jordan. Jordan, meet the girls." They didn't bother with names unless the chemistry was right. If one of them used the woman's name, it meant she was heading for a hookup and not to wait around.

Jordan nodded to the women and perused Bex's choices, impeccable as usual, but tonight she wasn't looking for her usual type. She wanted something different. Either of the blondes would've been fine for an evening, and they both seemed interested, but she wasn't. She scanned the room while half listening to the conversation. The scene was too familiar, the outcome too predictable, and she was too ready for a real change. She leaned toward Bex. "I'm going for a drink. Anybody want anything?" Everybody seemed content.

Jordan had just gotten her vodka tonic and taken the first sip when she spotted her across the room—petite, olive skin, with long, flowing dark hair. She was wearing brightly colored clothes that sparkled in the sea of darks and whites under the black light. Jordan's drink dribbled down her chin and her clit twitched. She wiped her mouth with the back of her hand and stared. *It can't be.* As she stared, the woman walked straight toward her. *It's not.*

"If what you're drinking is good enough to wear, I'll have one, please." The high-pitched voice wasn't what she expected, but she wasn't in the mood to talk.

"Sure." She motioned to the bartender for another. "I'm Jordan."

"Lilly. Do you come here often?"

Jordan hated these trivial games of "let's pretend we want to get to know each other." She especially didn't have the patience for one tonight. Up close Lilly was attractive and her eyes glinted with promise. After a couple of drinks, Jordan would see if she was agreeable to some private time. She chugged her drink and ordered another.

An hour later Jordan waved as Bex left the club with her choice du jour, and she maneuvered Lilly into a back corner near the exit. She raked her fingers through Lilly's long hair, disappointed that it felt coarse against her skin. She'd imagined the lengthy tresses cascading softly over her body, not lashing her into submission.

"You like long hair?" Lilly whipped her head and leaned back against Jordan's chest.

She liked Neela's hair and wondered how it would feel sifting through her fingers. "Yes." Lilly's position was perfect for Jordan's next move. "I like you too." She placed her drink on the end of the bar, grabbed Lilly's thighs, and pulled her ass tight against her crotch. She'd been aroused since this afternoon, and she almost popped. She pumped her hips and ground against Lilly's ass. Her jeans were so tight she could come against the seam with only a few strokes. "You have a fantastic ass." It wasn't as perfectly round as Neela's, but it was hot and responsive.

"Don't come without me, lover." Lilly put her hands over Jordan's and moved them to her breasts. "These are pretty awesome too. Want to see them up close?"

This was going much better than Jordan had imagined. "Absolutely, but I don't have a car."

"That's fine. I have a van in the back lot. I came prepared."

"What are we waiting for?" She couldn't remember the last time she'd been so horny and swollen that walking hurt. She'd replayed that damn kiss with Neela over and over in her mind—that kiss that shouldn't have happened with a woman it shouldn't have happened with—and every time her need became more urgent. She'd tried to handle the situation herself, masturbating before she left home, talking to herself on the way to the club, breathing, relaxing her muscles, but nothing eased the impulse. She needed physical contact.

Lilly guided her around the pool tables and out the back. "I've got vodka on ice, if you want." When Jordan gave her a skeptical look, she said, "Told you I'm prepared. There's not always time for hotel rooms and champagne. Sometimes you just have to get it where you can, and I have a feeling this is one of those nights for you."

"Yeah." She pulled at the seam of her jeans and flinched.

Lilly opened the back of the van and waved Jordan inside. The walls were upholstered with fabric and the floor covered with lush carpet. Perfect fuck pad on wheels.

"Get undressed," Lilly said as she pulled a single sheet from a basket on the front seat. When she'd spread the sheet and turned back to Jordan, she was kneeling in front of her wearing her black boy-cut shorts and sports bra. "Holy shit. You're fucking buff. I bet you're delicious."

"I should probably tell you—"

Lilly held up her hand. "Let me guess. You don't do head."

"I do, but only with protection, and I don't let you. And you can't touch me," she pointed to her crotch, "down there."

"So, I get to be a pillow queen, and you do all the work?"

Jordan's cheeks flushed as she reached for her shirt. "Major turn-off, right?" These were her rules for one-night stands. Not everybody was comfortable with her restrictions. Sex came in many forms, and she wasn't ready for emotional or serious physical intimacy.

"It's not a turn-off for me. I'm great with whatever." To prove her point, Lilly stripped and knelt in front of Jordan. "How do you get off?"

"Don't worry about me." Sometimes it just didn't happen, no matter how much she teased, rubbed, pulled, or poked. She wasn't kidding herself about the possibility of climaxing with this woman. But Neela had left her feeling frazzled, and she needed to feel in control. "Can I kiss you?"

"Of course. You can do anything you want. I have dams, condoms, and lube in that box on the floor."

Jordan moved closer until their bodies nearly touched, closed her eyes, and recalled a snapshot of kissing Neela. She grabbed Lilly around the waist and pulled their bodies together as Neela had done to her. With her eyes closed and the heat from their bodies, it was easy to imagine holding Neela. Lilly's breasts were indeed awesome, but larger than Neela's and didn't tuck as perfectly against her chest. Jordan pressed her crotch against Lilly's and tried to remember if she and Neela had made full body contact. Doubtful. If they had, Jordan wouldn't have been able to stop. She was certain of it.

"Are you going to—"

"Don't talk." Lilly's high-pitched voice threw her out of the moment. She sighed and opened her eyes, reaching for the bottle of vodka in the ice bucket. "Want a drink?" After Lilly took a sip, she chugged and replaced the bottle. "Come here."

She closed her eyes and went through the routine again. This time the body in her arms produced the required results. Fire burned in her gut. She lowered her mouth and relived the kiss that had tortured her all day. With just enough vodka to blur the lines, the lips against hers, the hungry tongue, the soft full breasts and eager torso were Neela's. Neela wanted exactly what this woman wanted. They both gave themselves easily and willingly. Jordan's clit tingled and strained for release.

She dipped and rubbed herself against Lilly's pubic mound. *So good.* She cupped a breast and massaged the tender flesh, and Lilly moaned against her neck. Another stroke. *Yes.* Jordan wedged her leg between Lilly's so she could enter her and straddle the muscle along her thigh. Lilly was wet and ready, and her fingers slid in easily. She pumped faster. *So close.*

"Oh yes, baby. Fuck me with your fingers."

When Lilly spoke, Jordan made the mistake of opening her eyes. The green-eyed woman staring unfocused at her was not Neela. Disappointment shot through her and desire vanished, leaving knots of pulsing pain.

"Don't stop, lover. I'm close."

Just because one of them was in agony didn't mean they both had to suffer. Jordan stroked Lilly's clit, trying to rekindle her own spark with no luck. She pulled her fingers in and out, praying for just a tingle of the desire she'd felt with Neela.

"Yes, that's it." Lilly surged and rubbed against her. "Your hands are magic."

Jordan tried to refocus and make her body respond, but the harder she tried, the more disconnected she became.

"Right there. That's right. I'm coming." Lilly grabbed Jordan's hand and held it inside her until she collapsed, breathing in short rapid spurts. "Holy shit. That was awesome. You're amazing. Again? I know you didn't come. What happened? Did I do something wrong?"

Jordan reached for the vodka again. She wasn't usually such a heavy drinker, but Lilly wouldn't shut up, the images of Neela wouldn't stop, and she desperately needed to come. While she took a few more sips, Lilly talked, about everything and nothing—where she lived, where she worked, her best friend, where she was going on holiday. Jordan ignored the yammering.

The scene with Neela returned with an agonizing jolt, and she rolled Lilly over on all fours. "Is this all right?" This was a part of Jordan that Neela probably wouldn't understand. When lust consumed her and her body refused to cooperate, Jordan resorted to more aggressive and less intimate means of satisfaction, rutting like a wild animal just to get off.

She pulled a condom from the basket, ripped it open with her teeth, and slid it on her middle finger. Squirting some lube on Lilly's ass, she rimmed her anus with the tip of her finger. "You okay with this?"

"Oh yeah, feels great."

Jordan felt a tingle of arousal as she fingered Lilly's anus with her left hand and entered her vagina with her right. "You like this, don't you?"

"I love it. Ahh, that's so good. Harder."

Jordan pressed her crotch against the back of her hand and rode it as she fucked Lilly with her fingers. *Yes.* She was hot and wet again, and her muscles strained against invisible fetters. She closed her eyes and relief built inside. "Tell me what you want."

"Fuck me deeper in the ass. Yeah. Like that. I want it so bad."

Her knees stung from rubbing on the sheet but she couldn't stop humping. She'd never felt so feral and desperate, so in need of something so out of reach.

"More fingers in my pussy," Lilly pleaded.

Jordan slammed her fingers into Lilly until sweat rolled off her forehead. The muscles in her legs trembled as Lilly started convulsing around her fingers.

"I'm coming again. Right now. Don't stop."

The back of Jordan's hand burned like she'd been sandpapered. Her clit was almost numb but she couldn't come. *Damn it.* When Lilly collapsed on her stomach, Jordan pulled out, fisting her own swollen folds as she fell backward. "Fuck. Fuck. Fuck." Her shoulder struck the side of the van and popped out of joint. Pain spiraled down her arm. She jammed her shoulder against the side of the van and felt it pop back into place. It'd hurt like hell tomorrow, but pain during sex was nothing new for her. She closed her eyes against the discomfort and squeezed her clit. Her shoulder throbbed, but the ache between her legs was much more acute.

"Let me help you, lover." Lilly put her hand on Jordan's stomach and slid toward the band of her shorts.

"No."

"But you're in pain."

"I'll do it. Look away." Lilly probably thought she was a freak, but she didn't care. She'd learned to manage by herself a long time ago, especially when she was this vulnerable. Resting her back against the side of the van, she slid her hand inside her shorts and tweezed her clit between two fingers. She was agonizingly hard and almost raw from rubbing, but she milked gently until she was wet again.

"I'd be really happy to do that for you," Lilly said.

"No, just keep your back to me. Just like that." Having anyone watch while she huddled in the corner like a coward made her skin crawl. No one would see her so exposed ever again.

She closed her eyes, blocking out the substitute in front of her, and imagined what Neela would look like with her legs spread, fingering herself to orgasm. The visual coursed through Jordan like a liquid explosion. She pulled harder and tremors started in her toes. Her legs quivered as the climax roared through her. She stiffened and yanked one final time. "Oh. Yes."

As the blessed relief oozed out the bottom of her feet, the red haze in Jordan's mind thinned to a light fog. At least the orgasm had dulled some of the tremendous pressure that had tormented her all day. She had enough difficulty controlling her impulses normally, but being around Neela had ramped up her urges. The only way to deal with the situation was to stay away from Neela completely. If she didn't, she could lose more than her self-control.

When she left Lilly at the bar and climbed on her Ducati to head home, it was almost three in the morning. But she didn't go directly to her apartment. She ignored her own advice and cruised through Hamilton Lakes by Neela's house, surprised to see a light on in a back room. Was she awake? What could she possibly be doing at three in the morning? *Maybe the same thing you've been doing.* Jordan gunned her bike as another shock of arousal registered.

When she opened the door to her sparsely furnished apartment, Blue was waiting. He had plenty of food and water and a doggie door installed by the previous tenant, so she couldn't figure out why he waited so patiently for her to come home. She patted his head, ruffled his fur, and stumbled toward the bedroom. "Come on, fella." When he hopped on the foot of her bed, she pointed to the pile of blankets she'd thrown on the floor for him. "I think you know the rules. Off."

He gave her a pitiful stare with eyes as blue as hers and jumped down. "I promise to get you a proper bed soon." The last thing she heard was something that sounded like a grateful whimper.

The door slammed behind her. She heard the lock click into place and felt cold. He moved toward her, rubbing his pudgy hands together like she was a gift. She backed up until her legs struck the metal table. Nowhere to go. Trapped again. Screaming wouldn't help.

Jordan woke to the sound of her voice echoing off the empty apartment walls. Blue was beside her, nudging her arm with his nose. "I'm okay, fella." The nightmares had returned since she started therapy, images of the past recurring, spilling over and tainting the present. Would she ever be free of them and in control of her life again?

Chapter Six

Jordan and Bex debriefed with the guys on speakerphone while traveling down the interstate at nearly eighty miles an hour. Neela had left home earlier than usual and was apparently in a rush to get to work. Her driving was more erratic than the day before, and Jordan was glad there were fewer cars on the road to navigate around.

"Wonder what's gotten into her today? Either she's anxious to get away from home or to get to work." Bex tried to drink her coffee, but Jordan stomped the accelerator again. "Seriously? I'd like to have at least one sip before we get to Raleigh."

"Maybe she stayed up all night and just decided to go in early." Jordan remembered her cruise by Neela's house and squeezed her thighs together.

"You mean like you? You look like hell and smell like leftover sex. Did you bother to shower this morning?"

"French whore's bath. Got in late, left early."

"Did you sleep at all?"

"It's overrated." After she'd ridden by Neela's and gotten worked up again, she'd opened her bike up on the highway, daring a state trooper to try to stop her. She'd been in the mood to test her limits, but in the cold, lust-free light of day, she was glad it hadn't happened. It had been a stupid move because she'd had way too much to drink. She couldn't afford to lose her license and possibly her job or to hurt someone else.

"So tell me about the girl last night. She wasn't your usual flavor." Bex wiggled her eyebrows and raised her coffee again. This time Jordan tried to make her spill it.

"Variety is the spice of life."

"She looked like Ms. Short, Dark, and Sexy ahead of us. I hope you got her out of your system. If we screw this up, Milton will have our asses walking a beat downtown, barefoot."

If she protested, Bex would know for sure she had a thing for Neela. If she admitted it, Bex would try to play matchmaker, in spite of her own interest. She was that kind of friend. Either way, it was best not to give her any ammunition. "Have we heard anything from the lab on Branson's case yet?"

"Forensics found a couple of hairs that don't belong to him. They're running them for DNA typing, and then they'll check for a match in the system."

"That would be too easy," Jordan said. "I bet whoever did this isn't in the system. The whole thing feels disorganized. The suspect didn't choose a private location for the attack. A parking lot with security cameras seems like an amateur mistake."

"But, of course, the cameras weren't working at the time. Now that would've been easy."

"And Branson's knife wounds look frenzied, like the suspect was just trying to inflict damage without any real knowledge of the most efficient place to strike."

"Yeah, I thought that too. I'll keep the heat on the lab guys. And it'll give me a chance to check out the new crime-scene investigator that I'm pretty sure is on our team."

"Jeez, Bex, is that all you ever think about?"

"You're one to talk. Remember the good old days when you came in hung over with all kinds of sex-induced injuries like rug burns, bondage marks, and spanking welts?"

"Not much has changed." She winced and relaxed her shoulder as she turned the wheel to follow Neela into the parking lot. Neela slid her car into a space and sprinted inside. "Pull up the camera feed," Jordan said.

"I've got it."

Jordan parked between other cars in the lot to look less conspicuous and turned her attention to the tablet Bex was holding. Rosemary was already in Neela's office with papers spread across the small worktable and a coffee pot in the center when Neela arrived. They exchanged a few words, and Neela put on her reading glasses before hunkering over the documents.

"Don't you just love those freaking glasses," Bex asked. "Makes me want to—"

"Focus. This looks serious." She didn't need Bex conjuring up tantalizing images of Neela. Her own traitorous mind did that quite nicely without any help.

"As long as she's not yelling for help or waving us in, it's none of our business. Damn, this is good coffee." Bex sighed contentedly.

But Jordan was concerned about what had put a very noticeable frown on Neela's lovely face so early in the day. Her shoulders slumped forward like she was trying to protect herself, and her eyes had lost some of their usual spark. Bex was right though. As long as Neela was safe, it wasn't their problem.

She watched the interaction between the two women for three hours, straining to pick up every nuance of Neela's movements and expressions. She didn't know enough about Neela's work to speculate about the crisis that had brought them into the office so early. She'd decided not to like Neela before they met, but her body had responded quite differently. She felt off balance. The only way to resolve the issue was to get more information.

When Neela pushed away from the worktable and left the office, she grabbed the opportunity. "She's out of camera range. I'll check on her."

❖

Neela had hoped to be on her way to work before the officers' shift change. She had to focus single-mindedly on work today. Rosemary's call an hour earlier had left her scrambling to get to the office, assess the situation, and do damage control. The last thing she'd needed was a distraction like Jordan Bishop, but every time she'd looked in her rearview mirror, there she was. Bex's comment that Jordan's taste for speed aroused her had flipped through Neela's mind as she'd dodged slow-moving vehicles.

How could she manage today's demands with images of Jordan floating through her mind like frames on an old movie reel? Today wouldn't be like any other day. The governor's agenda was changing, and she had to represent the best interests of the state's health-care community and her subordinates.

When she reached the office, Rosemary had everything she'd asked for ready. She'd scattered House Bill 695 across the worktable and highlighted the segments of interest. Neela dropped her briefcase, grabbed a mug of coffee, and put on her glasses before staring at the three pages of text bleeding yellow.

"How did you get your hands on this? It hasn't been released yet."

"Don't ask. I've been reading it since last night but didn't want to bother you until I was sure we needed to be concerned."

"Tell me," Neela said.

"Nineteen of our *highly regarded* Republican representatives put forth this bill, ostensibly to ensure the state would be safe from the application of foreign law."

Neela shook her head. "What does that even mean, and how does it impact us?"

"I'm getting to that. You better sit down." Neela continued to pace. "Sharia law was the focus of the original bill—an overreaction to fear and prejudice against the Islamic culture. The name of the bill was changed to the Family, Faith, and Freedom Protection Act, and three pages of abortion-related legislation were added. It contains limits on abortion funding under certain health plans, including those of local governments, outlaws sex-selective abortions, and requires the physical presence of a physician during an abortion procedure."

"Jesus, are these people totally insane? They'll set the state back fifty years, not to mention endanger women's lives."

"And create a boom in the sale of wire coat hangers." Neela cringed at the reference. "There's more. The bill would also require clinics certified by the Department of Health and Human Services to meet the standards required of ambulatory surgical centers."

Neela finally slumped into a chair as the ramifications registered. "That would close every abortion clinic in the state except one, and that's not enough to meet the demand."

"Exactly."

"Have our people heard about this yet?"

"I'm not sure, but you know how rumors spread. We should probably prepare them for the worst because I think it's coming."

"If they were just rumors, we might stand a chance. Rose, you know we can't get involved in this directly, but we have to notify everyone with an interest in this legislation. They have to rally their supporters and make a blitz effort to derail this catastrophe before it goes too far—if it hasn't already."

"I'm on it, boss."

This was what she'd dreaded since Matt Lloyd took office. He seemed determined to obliterate the progress made by the former administration and railroad his conservative agenda through regardless of whom it hurt. "I need a minute." Rosemary had seen her on overload before, but right now she had to appear professionally calm and in charge.

She left her office and hurried past other employees along the corridor to the ladies' room. Pulling a drying cloth from the stack, she dampened it with cold water and locked herself in a stall. The temptation to stay in this tiny, isolated cubicle was strong. If she didn't come out, she wouldn't have to deal with the avalanche of unpleasant news and bad decisions teetering at the pinnacle of state government.

Neela sat down and held the cool fabric against her forehead. As her breathing calmed, she thought of the people who coordinated programs with the clinics throughout the state. She'd hosted the department Christmas party for them for several years, attended parties at their homes, and sent gifts for their children's birthdays and graduations. She had no doubt what unemployment would do to their families. Her most important task was to save as many jobs as possible, even if it meant walking away from her own.

With renewed determination, she opened the stall door and momentarily froze. The door smacked her backside and urged her dangerously close to Jordan Bishop, who leaned nonchalantly against the sink. Before she could decide what to say, Jordan moved into her personal space.

"Are you all right?"

She looked up into those azure eyes, surprised by something she hadn't seen there before, warmth. Jordan sounded almost concerned. Or was she curious? Maybe she was simply feigning concern to up the stakes in whatever adrenaline-fueled game she'd decided to play with Neela. "Of course, why wouldn't I be?"

"You were upset when you left your office."

"How could you possibly—" Then she remembered the cameras, but how could Jordan know she was upset just by watching? She'd controlled herself until she was out of Rosemary's sight, which would've also been outside the camera's range.

"Your body language isn't as relaxed and open. The set of your shoulders isn't as confident. You've got small worry lines around your eyes, and—"

"Never mind. Forget I asked." Knowing Jordan had studied her so closely, and seen so much, made her feel vulnerable yet special. She moved around Jordan to wash her hands and felt her watching every move. "Did you need something, detective?"

"I just wanted to make sure you're okay. You were out of camera range, and I volunteered to check on you."

"Why?"

"Because it's my job and…"

Jordan stepped even closer, and Neela's mind filled in the blank. *Because she wanted to see me, to be close to me, to kiss me again.* Her body registered the possibility with a shard of arousal before her mind clicked into gear. "And what?"

"I thought you might want to talk about what happened yesterday— that kiss."

Yes, please. Absolutely not. Oh yes. No! "No need. Let's just say I got carried away, and I apologize. That kind of daring and spontaneity probably happens to you a lot." *But not to me.*

"Actually—"

"Detective, let's not make a kiss more than it was. It happened. It's over. It was a mistake. Now, as you can see, I'm fine, and I really need to get back to work." She tried to reach the trash bin behind Jordan, who didn't budge. As Neela pulled back, she got a whiff of something different—not Jordan's usual musky fragrance—stale sex and booze— and it simultaneously repulsed and aroused her. "Detective Bishop, I can't do this today."

"Do what?" Jordan raked her fingers through her hair and skimmed her hand down the side of her leather jacket, hitching her thumb over her belt. The ostensibly simple motion seemed like an invitation, and Neela's insides quivered. She placed a hand over her stomach and prayed for strength.

"This." She wiggled her finger between them. "I have more important things to think about than whatever game you're playing. People's lives and jobs are on the line, and I can't be distracted." And she was definitely distracted and annoyed with herself for being so weak.

Jordan propped her hands on the counter behind her and leaned back, effectively blocking her access to the bin and the exit.

"Please let me pass." She reached around Jordan again and purposely bumped her right shoulder to get out.

"Ouch. Holy crap." Jordan cradled her arm like Neela had seriously injured her. "Careful."

"What's wrong? Have you been hurt?" Jordan's neck and cheeks flushed a bright shade of pink, and heat rose on Neela's own skin. "Never mind. It's none of my business." She'd already imagined Jordan in the arms of an amorous lover, rough play, and several sensitive body parts. That could explain the bloodshot eyes and faint scent of liquor and sex. "Do you even remember her name?" Her arousal evaporated in a cloud of irritation verging on jealousy that only increased her annoyance.

"Who?"

"The woman who made you so sore this morning." She had no right to ask and hated herself for letting Jordan know she cared enough to do so.

"Lilly, and we're not—"

"I really don't care." Neela turned and slammed the door on her way out. Games. This woman was all about games, and Neela didn't have time for someone so frivolous and shallow.

Jordan followed her down the hall. "I know we got off to a rough start, but how about a walk? The fresh air might help clear your head before you go back in there."

"I don't think so, detective. My head is quite clear. You're the one who could use an airing."

"Call me Jordan." She blocked Neela's path and stood her ground, staring at her with eyes that seemed to devour her. "Please."

She'd never expected to hear Jordan Bishop use that word, and it resonated through her like a cry for help. She should say no. Jordan was always a hair trigger away from her next angry explosion. Whatever her personal circumstances, she was a complication Neela couldn't handle. Her life was already like a ticking time bomb with the governor's agenda, the situation at home, her stem-cell research, and Liz lobbying for more than friendship. But for some unfathomable reason, she didn't object when Jordan guided her with a hand in the small of her back through the exit and out toward the athletic field.

Jordan's energy vibrated against her, compounding the inevitable conflict that appeared whenever she was near. Why was she repeatedly drawn to someone so completely opposite to everything she believed in and cared about? They walked for several minutes before Jordan spoke. "Why are you so upset?" Her soft tone was laced with concern.

Neela couldn't look at her or she'd surrender her troubles in a gush of details. "Just work." She desperately wanted to let someone else assume, if only for a moment, the responsibilities that never seemed to wane. But it couldn't be Jordan. She could barely contain her own temper. How could she shoulder even a fragment of Neela's problems?

"You said people's lives and jobs were on the line. Did you mean that literally?"

"The jobs, yes. Their lives, figuratively."

"Talk to me."

"Why should I, Jordan? You've made it abundantly clear you don't like me or even respect me. Why would I possibly share anything with you?"

"I never intended—I mean, I'm just not good with—" The expressions on Jordan's face changed like cartoon drawings: first confusion, followed by consternation, pain, surrender, and finally humor. "I'm bound by the super-secret code of cop conduct not to repeat anything you tell me in the course of this investigation."

"You've already violated several codes of conduct." Neela laughed as Jordan crossed her heart and saluted in some made-up pledge of silence. She was just as gorgeous as the last time Neela had fallen into her arms and kissed her. Standing so close, she saw tiny strands of dark hair at the nape of Jordan's neck, the only indication, other than those curly lashes, that her thick mop of hair had ever been anything but snow white. Dressed entirely in black and waiting so patiently for her response, Jordan looked suddenly more serious, her motives more sincere. Even if Neela had wanted to, she couldn't refuse her. So, she told Jordan about the proposed bill and the ramifications of its passage to the state, the women seeking assistance, and the people who worked in her department.

Jordan scratched her head, looking oddly like a child trying to come up with the right answer. "I'm confused. You're a liberal, pro-choice, stem-cell-research doctor in a Republican administration. How does that even happen?"

"Are you serious right now? That's the second time you've condescended to me about my politics and position. Are you Catholic or just ignorant?" She couldn't believe she'd even tried to have a serious conversation with this woman. Jordan scuffed her boots into the grass. Apparently one of Neela's accusations had hit too close to home.

"Neither," Jordan said. "And not all Catholics are bad."

"A woman has the right to choose her politics, what happens to her body, and the kind of health care she receives."

"What about her right to choose a competent doctor? I don't object to abortions, just doctors who do them poorly and put people's lives in jeopardy. And I seriously object to administrators who are supposed to take care of the less fortunate and are too busy taking kickbacks to be bothered. This administration seems intent on limiting choices of all kinds, especially for women and the underprivileged."

"Finally, something we agree on," Neela said.

"So what am I missing?"

Neela stepped in front of Jordan and stared up at her, a rare flash of anger rising to the surface. "Obviously someone hasn't done her homework. I worked for the previous governor, a wonderfully progressive woman who cared about the state and its people. I don't support the conservative agenda of this administration."

"What about the regulations assuring a safe and healthy environment in child-care centers and homes? Do you support that?"

"What?" The question seemed totally out of context, but the expression on Jordan's face was pure anguish. "Of course I do. Where did that come from?"

Jordan turned her back and stared out across the athletic field. After a few seconds she faced Neela again, her eyes clear and focused. "If you don't agree with the governor, quit."

Neela wanted to discuss Jordan's previous statement because it had obviously resurrected something genuine and passionate in her, but she had no doubt Jordan would dismiss it as inconsequential. "If only it were that simple."

"Of course it is. Why would you stay if his agenda goes against your beliefs? Do what you want to do."

"It must be nice to live in a world where all you have to think about is pleasing yourself. Some of us don't have that luxury, Jordan."

Tears welled in Neela's eyes and she blinked them back. She had to tough it out as long as possible. The insurance benefits alone, not to mention her salary, kept her and Bina from the poverty level. The demands of work, home, and her research were increasing, and the stress was almost unbearable. It was the worst possible time for this legislation. If she allowed herself even one second of weakness, she might never regain control. "I have to get back. This is no time for a stroll in the park with a…"

"A what? Say it. I know what you must think of me."

"And what is that, Jordan? Since you're so good at reading my mind."

"You think I'm a womanizing player who gets off on risk and adrenaline, superficial and unsettled, with absolutely no interest in commitment or meaningful relationships."

"That sounds more like your opinion. You have no idea what I think." She walked away and headed toward the building. Neela wasn't sure how she felt when it came to Jordan, but whatever it was, she couldn't deal with it now. She needed to end this dangerous flirtation once and for all.

Before she reached the door, she turned to tell Jordan so, but she was entirely too close, the air between them alive with energy. "And another thing. From your wild mood swings, I'd say you shouldn't even be kissing anyone, much less considering a relationship."

Jordan looked as though she'd been slapped. "Is this the pot calling the kettle black? You don't know anything about me."

"That's the second thing we agree on. Though you don't know anything about me either, you've already judged me and found me lacking in some way."

As she reached the back entrance, her cell rang and she pulled it from the pocket of her suit jacket. "Hello, Bina? Are you okay? I'll be right there." She hung up and turned to Jordan. "I need a police escort home. It's an emergency."

"Is she injured? Do I need to have dispatch send patrol officers or an ambulance? They could be there in minutes."

"No, just get me home." This day couldn't possibly get any worse, given the governor's bombshell and Bina's urgent call. She desperately needed to be two places at once.

❖

"And she didn't tell you what was going on?" Bex held onto the dash as Jordan swerved in and out of traffic on the interstate.

"Nope. She got a call from Bina—her partner, I guess. Then she said she needed an emergency escort home. But she said something that might be helpful in the case. You mentioned the possibility somebody wanted to push her out of her job. She's not exactly a Lloyd supporter. At least it's worth a closer look."

"I'll put it back on the list of possibilities, if I live through this trip."

Driving fast was second nature for Jordan, but she wasn't used to someone trying to keep up with her. She constantly glanced in the rearview mirror to make sure Neela was safe in their high-speed game of dodge cars. Their earlier conversation flashed through her mind like the vehicles racing by. Maybe she'd misunderstood Neela, made assumptions about who she was based on limited and faulty information. She didn't support the restrictive and sweeping changes of Lloyd's government, so that was to her credit. But she was a politician, and politicians were notorious for self-serving agendas and underhanded dealings. Why would she stay in a job she hated if she wasn't getting something out of it?

"Hey, sport, this is our exit." Bex grabbed the dash again as Jordan signaled and swerved to make the turn. "Jesus. Did Neela make it?" She tried to look behind her, but Jordan's rapid acceleration kept her pinned against the seat.

"Yeah, she's with us." Jordan wished, not for the first time, that Neela had accepted her offer to ride with them. The trip could've been faster and less dangerous, but she'd flatly refused, saying she needed her car at home. As they slid up in front of her house, Jordan was about to find out what had precipitated Neela's emergency trip home in the middle of the day.

Jordan and Bex bolted out of the car and arrived at the door the same time as Neela. "Let us go in first," Jordan said.

"No! You can't." Neela held up her hands. "Wait here."

"Absolutely not. Our job is to protect you and your family. What if she's in real trouble? We have to go in, Neela."

"Jordan, please. I can handle it. Really. Go back to your car. Thank you for getting me here so quickly. If I need you, I'll let you know." Neela looked at Bex, and Jordan could read the plea in her eyes. "I've got this."

"Fine, but if you don't brief us in ten minutes, I'm coming in."

Without acknowledging her ultimatum, Neela unlocked the door and disappeared inside.

"Goddamn it!" Jordan kicked a pebble from the sidewalk across the lawn. "What a hard-headed woman. How are we supposed to protect her when she won't tell us what's happening?"

"She's got a right to privacy, regardless of the risks or our efforts to protect her."

"Fuck that." As frustrating as it was to hear, Bex was right.

Exactly nine minutes after they arrived, Neela exited the house and walked to their car. She refused the offer to sit, leaning against the side of the vehicle for support. Dark circles rimmed her brown eyes, and the corners of her mouth were tight with worry. "Bina has some health issues that can be debilitating. I've managed to stabilize her. Thank you for your help today." She turned and walked back into the house.

"Well, that told us absolutely nothing," Jordan said. She wanted to chase Neela and demand to know exactly what was going on, but she had no right. Neela was taking care of an ailing partner, trying to salvage jobs for her subordinates, and working in a job she hated. Her earlier advice about Neela quitting her job now seemed insensitive. What did Jordan have that came close to such a level of commitment?

All she'd done the past several months was fuck strangers and wallow in self-pity. She suddenly felt shallow and insignificant compared to this woman who shouldered so much.

"At least they're safe. That's our shift done." Bex pointed as Phil and Harry pulled up.

"I'd like to stay on a bit, just until I'm sure everything's settled."

"The guys will take care of them. You know that. Let's go home."

She could tell Bex was reluctant to leave. She'd behaved erratically and been totally unprofessional toward Neela since they met. She couldn't blame her for being cautious.

"Please, Bex. Can you have the guys drop you off? They can have dinner with their families and catch a nap. Tell them I'll cover until midnight." Jordan wasn't sure where her sudden concern came from, but she couldn't leave Neela yet.

Bex stared at her, apparently trying to guess her motive. "Sure, partner. Just don't do anything stupid. Okay?"

"Yeah, no problem." The way her mind was whirling, stupid covered a lot of territory.

Chapter Seven

Neela checked Bina's pulse and pulled the blanket over her shoulders. The high dosage of pain medicine she'd given her had finally kicked in, and she would sleep until morning. Neela slipped out of her work clothes, showered quickly, and pulled on her terry-cloth robe. Leaving a night-light on beside the bed, she closed the door and tiptoed into the den. This had been one of those days that got progressively worse and never seemed to end. She finally collapsed on the sofa, shivering from hunger, fear, and exhaustion.

Bina's condition was deteriorating and she'd been helpless to stop it. The treatment in Panama hadn't been as successful as she'd hoped. A tear slid down her cheek and she quickly brushed it away. If she started crying, she'd never be able to stop. She should eat something but didn't have the energy to make it. As she pulled the blanket from the back of the sofa over her, the doorbell sounded and she jumped to answer it before the noise woke Bina.

Rosemary stood on her stoop with a pizza in one hand and a six-pack of beer in the other. "Delivery."

"You truly are an angel." She hugged her before pulling her inside. "How did you know I was starving?"

"When you texted Bina was in trouble, I knew you'd forget about everything else, including food. How's she doing?"

"Sleeping. This was a bad one, Rose. I'm scared."

Rosemary deposited the beer and pizza on the coffee table and pulled her onto the sofa beside her. "I know, honey. You're doing all you can."

"Am I?"

"Your salary pays the bills, your insurance helps with her medication and treatment, and you're conducting research to find a cure. What else can you possibly do with only twenty-four hours in a day when you spend sixteen or seventeen taking care of Bina? You've got to find time for yourself soon."

Rose's words confirmed the helplessness and fatigue she wore like a second skin. "Let's eat." She popped the tab on a beer and guzzled it, enjoying the way it fizzed in her mouth and slid down so easily. "This is heaven. I haven't had a drink of any kind in months. If you're not careful, I could get tipsy."

"A couple of beers with a slice of pizza won't get you drunk. Now eat." She slid the box toward Neela as she grabbed a piece, folded it in half, and took a bite. "Isn't there anyone who can help out for a while, just to give you a break?"

The mouthful of deliciously greasy cheese and meat suddenly tasted foul. "I don't trust just anyone with her, but it might be time to consider some part-time assistance, after they're properly vetted."

Neela would love to hand her responsibilities over to someone else for even an hour. She couldn't remember the last time she'd done something spontaneous, until she kissed Jordan Bishop. Her liaisons with Liz had always seemed an obvious side effect of their work. But when she'd kissed Jordan, she'd released everything and gone with her emotions. She'd felt freer than she'd been in years and more turned on than she'd ever been. Heat flushed her body, and she reached for the cold beer again.

"Is there anything I can do?"

"Could you just hold me for a minute?"

Rosemary pulled Neela into her arms and they slouched into the sofa. Rose's old sweatshirt felt soft and comforting as she rocked her back and forth like a mother. "It'll be fine, honey. I'm right here."

But Rose's kind words and comforting hugs made Neela feel guilty. She was so ineffective in the affairs of her life. If she couldn't stop the downward spiral of events, why did she deserve comfort, pleasure, or even kindness? In spite of her best efforts, she just couldn't handle it all.

She pulled away from Rose. "I'm really tired. Thanks for the beer and pizza, but I should probably go to bed."

"Of course, honey." Rose gave her a parting hug at the door. "Call me if I can help. And take the day off tomorrow. Seriously, I'll handle everything."

"Thanks, Rose, but I'll see you in the morning." She closed the door and slumped against it for support. She looked from the pizza to the pile of papers on her desk and then toward her bedroom—sustenance, work, or sleep. Several minutes passed as her mind seemed stuck in a loop of indecision. A sharp knock startled her and she jerked the door wide. "What did you forge—"

Jordan's gaze raked over her body like fingernails on a chalkboard—a look that said she was the last woman Jordan wanted to see, but the only woman she wanted. Lust burned in her cobalt eyes and spilled over on her flushed cheeks.

"What're you...doing here?" The words caught in her throat, but as she spoke, she stepped aside and waved Jordan in.

"I wanted to apologize for earlier today. I had no right to judge you." When their eyes met, Jordan's expression changed. "What's wrong? You're flushed."

"I'm...I need..." Neela couldn't force herself to verbalize what she so desperately wanted so she slid her arms around Jordan's waist and leaned into her.

"You want *me*?"

"What...I..." She tried to argue, but her body betrayed her. She cupped Jordan's ass. "I need you to—"

Jordan shoved her against the door and pressed their bodies together. "I know exactly what you need." Her breath was hot and her words sure. "What about Bina?"

Neela struggled to breathe as her body heat rose and her resistance fell away. "Medicat...drugs...asleep." She edged her knee out of the robe and it opened to her thighs.

Jordan glanced down, thrust her leg between Neela's, and rubbed against her sex. "Is this what you want? Are you sure?"

"Yes." The rough texture of Jordan's jeans against her clit was like striking a match. Panting and clinging to Jordan's shoulders, she stretched up on her toes and slid back down the length of Jordan's firm thigh, craving the quick release that was only seconds away.

"Oh no, you don't." Jordan stepped back, stripping Neela's robe off her shoulders as she moved. Suddenly her hands stilled as her eyes stroked Neela's bare skin. "I've never seen anyone so beautiful."

Neela stood naked in her living room and imagined herself in a porn movie and Jordan the powerful dominant about to claim her. "I thought you were all about fun and pleasure." Neela cupped her sex and slid her finger through the slick folds. "If you don't touch me, Jordan, I'll have to take care of myself."

"Don't," Jordan said. She captured Neela's hand, brought it to her lips, and slowly licked her fingers one at a time.

Neela's arousal doubled. She reveled in the coarse feel of Jordan's tongue as she sucked her fingers into her hot mouth. "Jordan, please."

"Please what? Do you even know what you want?" She draped Neela's robe across the back of the sofa and motioned for her to lie across it.

"What?"

"Bend over," Jordan said.

"Just take me." She was too wound up to care how tactless or slutty she sounded. She just wanted to come. "Can't you just fuck me like you do everybody else?"

Jordan's eyes pinned her like the tip of an icicle as she pointed to the sofa again. "That's exactly what I'm doing. Bend over."

Neela leaned over the sofa, exposing her bare ass and her desperate need to a woman who would probably soon forget both. When Jordan slapped her across the bottom, Neela tried to get up, but Jordan held her in place. "What the hell?"

"Are you mad?" Jordan slapped her again. "Because I want you really pissed off. You want somebody to take charge and give you a seriously hard fuck, don't you?" Slap.

"Let me up." Slap. "Now. I mean it." Slap. "Jordan, I'm serious." Slap. "Jordan!" In spite of her objections, Neela felt a trickle down the inside of her thigh. "Oh, God."

"What's the matter? Getting hot?" Jordan entangled a hand in Neela's hair and pulled like she was riding a stallion until her neck stretched painfully backward. Then Jordan scraped her teeth along the side of her jugular.

Her clit throbbed. "Jordan…" Her voice sounded like a cross between a wounded whimper and a plea for release.

"Not sure what to ask for?"

Jordan was right. She wanted the quick release of an orgasm, but having Jordan dominate her was also a relief of sorts. She couldn't be held accountable for what she felt or wanted or was forced to do while someone else was in charge. She gratefully relinquished control of everything, including her own pleasure.

Jordan slapped her once more and then massaged her stinging cheeks with powerful hands. She kneaded her flesh and teased her tightly puckered anus until Neela relaxed and met each stroke. Neela rubbed herself against the terry-cloth fabric covering the sofa, trying to get off. She was so wet and ready.

"Stop." Jordan's order was husky but firm.

"I need to come."

"I know." Jordan slid her fingers to Neela's opening and stopped. "You have to answer one question honestly first."

"Anything, just hurry." Neela tried to back onto Jordan's fingers, but she pulled away.

"How can you do this with Bina in the house?"

"I need you so much. Please, Jordan."

Jordan's fingers entered her and Neela cried out. "Yes." She gripped the back of the sofa and thrust to meet Jordan's hands. "Harder." Her robe bunched under her and she rubbed her clit against a fold. "Yes, Jordan. Harder."

Jordan hunched over, and Neela heard her labored breathing, felt her heat as she pumped her ass. "You're so hot. Ahhh." Jordan's muscles were hard against the curve of her body as she strained for control. "I want to come all over you, Neela. Oooo." She moaned like she was in pain. "Why do you have to be—"

"Just do it, Jordan. Let me feel you come."

Jordan whispered. "You've wanted this since we met, haven't you?"

"Yes. Don't stop. I'm coming."

Suddenly Jordan pulled out and Neela humped against the back of the sofa, desperate for what had been taken. "Why did you stop?"

"I can't do this. It's not right." Jordan walked out of the room, and a few seconds later the door slammed.

Neela rolled onto the sofa and stroked herself until a sliver of release escaped. It wasn't the huge roiling orgasm that had been building with Jordan inside her, but it would have to do. She'd never been so frustrated or confused.

❖

Jordan leaned against Neela's front door and grabbed her knees. Her insides burned, and every muscle screamed from being so tightly constricted. She'd been so close to coming with her fingers buried in Neela that it had been physically painful to withdraw. Neela had surrendered to her completely. Her neediness and vulnerability had triggered something in Jordan, and she'd imagined for a moment they were lovers so desperate for each other they'd barely made it inside the door. But she couldn't complete the act. Neela was with someone else. Jordan might be a major screwup, but she still had a few standards.

When her breathing slowed and the ache between her legs subsided, she turned and grabbed the door handle. She owed Neela another apology. She'd seen Rosemary arrive earlier and had watched them hug at the door. She remembered her first overreaction to Rosemary's affection and struggled to explain its recurrence. No matter what Jordan's motivation, Neela didn't deserve to be mistreated, and Jordan was in no position to teach moral lessons. Neela was right. She probably shouldn't be having sex or even kissing anyone at the moment.

Nothing about this woman or Jordan's attraction to her made sense. But her problem wasn't really with Neela; at least she knew that intellectually. She struggled so desperately with her dark side that she destroyed anything good in her path. Neela was an open, caring, and trusting woman, who thought about others. She couldn't possibly understand someone like Jordan. Once again she vowed to leave Neela Sahjani alone and pray she didn't complain about her unprofessional behavior. She let go of the door handle and walked toward the street just as her relief pulled up.

After debriefing the guys, Jordan went home and rolled out her bike. Blue watched her from the window, his paws scratching against the glass. Maybe she'd take him out for a run sometime. Dogs liked the outdoors. She waved good-bye and immediately dropped her hand. *You're losing it, Bishop. He's a dog.*

As she revved the engine, she considered the bar, but the possibility of anyone else quenching the thirst Neela had created seemed unlikely. Her cell rang as she started to pull away.

"Yeah?"

"Why don't you come to the police club for a while. It's only midnight. The guys are starting to think you don't love them any more." Bex often launched into her spiel without an introduction.

"They're right."

"Seriously, Jordan. You used to be a lot of fun. We miss that."

"So do I." She had missed spending time with her squad mates. They were her quasi-family, but recently she hadn't been able to deal with both them and her therapy. They asked too many questions in the name of concern and helpfulness. Molly was bringing up enough issues in their bi-weekly sessions, and the emotional overflow made her erratic and irritable. The void in her soul was immense, and every day it rubbed a deeper raw spot. "Maybe another time, okay?" She hung up, rolled her Ducati toward the street, and pressed the starter.

Jordan zipped her jacket and opened the throttle when she hit the interstate heading west. She leaned forward and hugged the bike, the vibrations infusing her with energy as she pushed harder. She'd slow if she crossed a speed trap, because all the officers along this strip knew her. Even with a 160 horsepower engine between her knees, she couldn't outrun a police radio.

As she took the exit onto Old Mill Road and unzipped her jacket, memories of her two encounters with Neela ambushed her. The wind pressed against her chest, reminding her of Neela's body so close the first time they'd kissed. Neela had tried to comfort her, to ease some of her sadness, but with a partner at home, her offer seemed tainted and disingenuous. And tonight, Jordan had been so overcome with lust she'd almost totally succumbed. Their chemistry was as volatile as the gas that powered her bike, but Jordan had to smother it even if Neela was the only woman who'd really excited her in recent memory.

Jordan gunned the accelerator again, feeling the cold and erasing her thoughts. She didn't slow until she pulled up to the place that always seemed to call her back, the defunct New Beginning Orphanage. She dismounted and pulled on the rusted chain wrapped around part of the metal gate, which opened with a grinding objection. Often when her mind wandered on her rides, she ended up at this spot. She hadn't managed to go inside the decaying building, but someday she'd have to.

When she'd walked away from this place seven years ago, she'd sworn she'd never return, so why did she keep coming back? *The only person who never intentionally left me lived here—Amy.* The answer was simple—it was the closest thing to a family she'd ever had. Or maybe the answer was more disturbing. Maybe she came back when she felt vulnerable to remember her outrage and pain, to fortify her walls.

She listened to the calming sounds of tree frogs croaking and crickets chirping, a far cry from the noises she associated with this place. The beautifully landscaped yard that had once camouflaged the deeds committed inside was now more appropriately a gnarly patch of weeds. She shivered from the memories and the damp air that suddenly felt too cold. When the moon shadows started to resemble faces from her past, she mounted her bike and headed home.

Somehow Neela Sahjani had created a fissure in her pristine protective shell. She'd gouged at Jordan's tender underbelly and pushed one of her hot buttons—fidelity. Jordan wasn't sure why it bothered her so much that Neela was a cheater, but it twisted inside her like a scalpel slicing through flesh. Maybe her outrage was the byproduct of something deeper. *There's nothing deeper inside me.* New Beginning had seen to that. Everything in her life had been a mirage to tempt, tease, and torment her, but always with the same result—she ended up alone.

It was nearly two in the morning when Jordan returned home and called Bex. "Hope I didn't wake you."

"Nope, just on my way to bed with a little something, if you get my drift."

"I need to work nights for a while. Can you arrange it with Harry and Phil?" She really needed to stay away from Neela, and this was the best way without alerting the sergeant that she'd fucked up, again.

"But…I'm kind of into something at the moment. I'd like to stay on days."

"Can you see if Harry or Phil will switch with me? Please, Bex. It's important."

"Yeah, sure. We'll cover today and you can start tonight." Bex mumbled something with her hand over the phone and then spoke to her again. "Are you all right? You sound weirder than usual."

"I'm fine, and thanks, Bex. I owe you."

CHAPTER EIGHT

Neela placed her glasses on the desk and rubbed the bridge of her nose, trying to stay awake and focused. When Bina had finally fallen asleep just before daylight, Neela looked out her bedroom window and saw Jordan leaning against the side of her police car. Her hair glowed under the full moon like a signal calling to her. Neela wondered why she hadn't seen Jordan in three days, since their—what had that been—encounter? Jordan had apparently volunteered to work nights, probably so she wouldn't have to see her. Neela's feelings had fluctuated between tremendous relief and gut-wrenching disappointment.

When she looked back on her behavior that night, she realized it had been totally out of character but exactly what she'd needed. She'd allowed herself to be stripped bare, thrown over the back of a sofa, spanked, and fucked from behind. Jordan had known what she wanted without being told and had given it to her without being asked.

Jordan had worked her into a sexual frenzy, but Neela had felt safe enough to surrender. She'd felt light-headed, and then Jordan had just as quickly withdrawn with some cryptic remark about it not being right. Three days later her body still hummed with suppressed energy and burned for Jordan so badly that thinking about anything else had been a challenge.

"Are you all right?" Rosemary stood in the doorway of the office with her afternoon cup of coffee.

"Sure? Why?"

"Don't think I've ever seen you treat your glasses quite so fondly."

Neela was sucking one of the legs, pulling it seductively in and out of her mouth. "Oh." She started to put them on but dropped them as though they were hot, then neatly stacked the papers on her desk. "I'm fine."

"Right. Your face is flushed and you've just combined the financial reports it took our intern all morning to separate by division."

"Shit." She shrugged. Rose knew she was off her game but didn't know why.

"Everything okay at home?" Rosemary placed the cup in front of her and sat down.

"As well as it can be." She tried to avoid Rose's gaze. They'd known each other long enough that their looks spoke as loudly as their voices.

"If you want to talk, I'm here."

"I know. Thanks. So what's wrong now? You have that expression I hate."

Rose pulled her side chair closer and leaned toward her. They didn't talk about anti-administration issues too loudly. Things had a way of traveling straight up the chain to the governor's office. "I've been trying to contact the protest organizers, but we're missing a large component of the group. Since Doctor Branson was hurt, nobody has stepped up to fill his spot. We need his contacts so we can reach out. We can't let this bill go to a vote without some serious opposition."

"Maybe you should visit him in the hospital. I'd go, but I've got to run by the lab on my way home. We've got a promising sample that needs to be checked."

"Are you sure it isn't your lab partner that needs to be checked?" Rose grinned, and Neela shook her head. "That flush on your face and neck when I came in usually means one of two things, anger or horniness. I'm betting on the latter after seeing that display with your glasses."

Neela pointed toward the door in mock anger. "Get out of my office."

"I've seen the fiery redheaded Doctor Blackmon from State. I wouldn't blame you for lusting after her. You *were* lusting just now, right? Admit it." She dodged the paperclip Neela threw at her. "I almost forgot, detectives to see you. Shall I send them in?"

Neela nodded and her body tingled with anticipation until Rose ushered Bex and a male partner into the office. She took an extra minute to calm her nerves before extending her hand to the middle-aged man. "I'm Neela Sahjani."

"Phil Morris."

"How can I help today?" she asked.

Bex seemed content to let Phil do the talking. "Just wanted to give you an update on the case, such as it is. We don't have any leads on Doctor Branson's attacker yet. A couple of strands of foreign hair were recovered at the scene, no results on those yet, and the tests on the note from your car didn't turn up anything. Have you gotten any more threats?"

She shook her head. "Does that mean we can end this charade? It seems a huge waste of time, manpower, and the taxpayers' money."

"I'm afraid that's not our call, ma'am." He looked to Bex for confirmation.

"He's right, Neela. Only the chief can cancel the assignment."

"Fine." She stood and offered her hand to Morris as he left. "Bex, could I have a minute?"

Bex closed the door and waited. The anxious look on her face said she didn't really want to hear what was coming.

Neela had no right to ask, but damn it, she wanted to know. "Where is Jordan?"

Bex's eyebrows shot up. "You don't beat around the bush, do you?"

"It's a waste of time, like this protection detail. Is she avoiding me?"

Bex sat down, her posture rigid, preparing for bad news. "Has something happened between you two? Jordan could get us both in a lot of trouble if she's been...reckless."

"Does that happen often, her indiscretions?"

"More so lately. She's usually very careful, but she's in a bad place right now. You didn't answer my question. Has something happened?"

"Yes, but I'm not sure what. We had a...she...I needed...I have no idea. Seriously, I don't know what to tell you. But I won't jeopardize either of your jobs because of a moment's irresponsibility."

Bex sighed heavily. "Good. I mean, thank you. I apologize if she insulted or upset you. It's not like her to be so unprofessional. At least now I understand why she asked to be on night shift for a while."

"That would make sense in light of…what happened. Do you know why I seem to offend her so deeply? I know she's not crazy about politicians, but that can't be the only reason. It feels deeper, more personal."

"No. I've probably already said too much."

"Of course, I understand." But she didn't understand at all. One minute Jordan acted like she could eat her with a spoon, and the next she avoided her like a case of the clap. "Please don't mention this conversation to her. I was mostly concerned that she was okay."

"I'm not sure she's okay, but at least she's trying to do the right thing and stay away from you. For some reason, you seem to push her buttons, and not in a good way."

The truth of Bex's words hurt. Whatever was happening between her and Jordan obviously distressed her, and distance was probably the best thing, but it didn't stop Neela from wanting to see her and trying to help.

When Bex left, Neela packed her briefcase, called to check on Bina, and drove to the lab. Liz greeted her at the back door and pulled her into a hug just inside the corridor.

"I've missed you." Liz tried to kiss her but Neela turned away.

"Have you forgotten the cameras?"

"Why do you think I accosted you here? This is a blind spot." She ran her hand up Neela's back and tried to pull her close.

"Don't, Liz. We're here to work."

Liz pinned her against the wall and sniffed. "Jesus, you smell great—floral, musty, and…horny. You're aroused."

"Don't be ridiculous." But she'd been horny for three days. Thinking about Jordan earlier, she'd felt her bikinis get more than a little damp.

"I know what you need. Let me make you feel better."

Liz could probably relieve the pressure between her legs temporarily, but she'd never quench the yearning for Jordan that pulsed like a heartbeat. How had she gotten into such a state over a woman she didn't know and who seemed hell-bent on annoying and avoiding her in equal measure? "Can we just evaluate the specimens, please?"

Liz followed her into the prep area where they changed in silence. The night's work progressed quickly. When they kept their hands out of each other's pants, they made a formidable research team. They were poised to make a breakthrough in the use of stem cells in spinal-cord injuries in animals, if their recent specimens produced the results they were hoping. And if they provided enough evidence to support their research, their efforts could help Bina and countless others with a wide range of illnesses and injuries.

It was almost one in the morning when Neela wrapped up her specimens and joined Liz in the hallway outside the lab. "What do you think? Are we any closer?"

Fingering her red hair in a gesture Neela associated with calculated thought, Liz said, "I think our blank-slate cells are starting to take on characteristics of the surrounding tissue. But that's only what I think. We can't know for sure yet. We've gotten this far before and been disappointed when they deteriorated. We'll have to be patient." She held the door for Neela and followed her to her car. "Which is something I am not where you're concerned."

Liz guided Neela to the side of her car and pressed their bodies together. "Come home with me. I want to be with you."

Neela edged away and reached for the door handle. "Not tonight." Liz started to kiss her good night, but before their lips met, Neela felt a rush of cold air.

"Get the fuck off her. She said no." Jordan shoved Liz away and positioned her body between them. "Get in my car." Jordan called over her shoulder, and Neela was so stunned she obeyed without question.

Liz regained her balance and started toward Jordan. "Who the hell are you?"

"I'm the police officer about to whip your ass if you don't get in your car and leave right now." Liz raised her hands toward Neela in question. "I said now."

Neela mouthed *sorry* as Liz walked to her car and drove away. She sat in Jordan's vehicle shaking with adrenaline and disbelief. When Jordan got in, Neela didn't speak for several seconds, determined to sound calm when she did.

Jordan gripped the steering wheel so hard her knuckles were white and the muscles along her strong jaw clenched and flexed.

Neela finally asked. "What just happened?"

"It's my job to protect you. I didn't know who she was. It looked like an assault."

"Really? We came out of the building together. If she wanted to assault me, don't you think she would've tried inside, in a confined space?"

"Are you fucking her?" The question was almost inaudible, and Jordan looked as though it pained her to ask.

"I'd be careful what I said right now if I were you, detective. You're not exactly in a position to throw stones." Neela couldn't resist the barb. She'd been annoyed or perhaps jealous when she realized Jordan had been so enamored with another woman that she'd injured herself while having sex. *Lilly.* She shook her head to dislodge the image.

"I thought she was forcing you. But since you seem to like that, I should've known—"

"Don't presume to know what I like based on how you treat women."

Jordan stared and her nostrils flared. "How I treat women? I would never—you wanted exactly what you got the other night. Or am I mistaken?"

Why was she even trying to explain anything to this infuriating woman who'd just made a spectacle of herself in front of her colleague? Neela was at least a decade older than Jordan, but it seemed more. Jordan was like an emotionally undeveloped teenager. She should leave and stay well away from Jordan Bishop, but she couldn't. Something powerful and compelling drew them together like a force of nature, but they clashed like fire and ice.

She sat quietly until she could respond without sounding like an immature brat as well. When her emotions were so convoluted, Neela relied on what she knew best, the truth. "You're half right. I did want you. But you were too busy putting me in my place, whatever that is by your standards, to see what I really needed."

"And what was that?"

"To relax and let someone else be responsible."

"Responsible for what?" Jordan really looked at her for the first time, and her eyes said she was actually interested.

"Helping me forget my problems and feel real pleasure for just a few minutes."

"And what about Bina?"

"What's my mother got to do with this?"

Jordan's alabaster skin seemed to pale. "Your *mother*?"

"Who did you think she was?"

"Your partner." Jordan's voice was almost a whisper.

Suddenly Jordan's comment from three nights ago made sense. *I can't do this. It's not right.* "I see. You're not a home wrecker and you don't have sex with cheaters. Am I close?" Jordan looked away, but Neela saw her bottom lip tremble. It was the first indication that anything besides anger pulsed in her emotional veins. She slid across the seat, cupped her chin, and made Jordan meet her gaze. Her blue eyes were pools of pain, tears close to overflowing. "I'm not like that, Jordan."

"Everyone causes some kind of pain," Jordan said.

"No, we don't." She edged closer and briefly pressed her lips to Jordan's. Pulling back, she looked into Jordan's eyes again to be sure she hadn't imagined the vulnerability. Why hadn't she paid closer attention to the hurt and pain hidden there? She stroked her thumb across Jordan's upper lip. "Where did you get the scar?"

"Motocross accident."

"No, really."

"Really. I was twelve."

The image made Neela cringe and she kissed Jordan again, trying to absorb the scar and erase the damage. The softness of her mouth melted against Neela's and made her ache. Jordan turned slowly, slid from under the steering wheel, and scooped Neela onto her lap, their mouths never parting. Neela threaded her arms around Jordan's neck and pressed against her. Their connection was tender and gentle, nothing like the rough claiming of before. Neela hardly recognized the woman in her arms. The beast seemed suddenly tranquil and pliable.

As Jordan explored her mouth, Neela slid her hands under Jordan's shirt and up toward her breasts. The firm muscles of Jordan's chest rippled under her hands, and Jordan rubbed against her in an excruciating rhythm.

"I want to make love with you, Jordan."

Jordan's body tensed and all movement stilled. "I can't."

She leaned back and searched Jordan's face. "Why? We've both wanted this since we met. Now that you know I'm not a home wrecker, what's stopping you? Is there someone else, this Lilly person?"

"No, it's nothing like that."

She skimmed her hand up Jordan's thigh. "Then, please."

Jordan dumped her off her lap. "I told you. I can't."

"What's the matter? Do you want to be in charge? That's fine with me. I just need you. That was enough the other night." Neela couldn't believe she was practically begging one woman to have sex with her when she'd just turned down another. She'd never thrown herself at anyone before. Why was it so important that it be *this* woman? If she knew the answer, maybe she could walk away.

"Talk to me, Jordan. Can I touch you? I've never wanted anyone so badly." She reached toward Jordan's belt and tugged on the buckle.

"Don't, Neela."

"Fine." Neela raised her hands in surrender and reached for the door handle. "See ya. I don't really have to beg for sex."

Jordan grabbed her arm. "Wait."

"What? One minute I can't touch you and the next I can't leave. I'm not sure what to do here, Jordan. You have to help me."

Jordan breathed in irregular bursts, and the muscles in her thighs flexed and relaxed. She grimaced as she stared at Neela, her eyes begging her to understand something she couldn't say.

"What is it, Jordan?"

"I want you so badly my whole body aches, but I can't."

She traced the curve of Jordan's mouth with her fingertips, feeling her tremble under her touch. "Why? Your eyes say you want me. Your body says you need me." Suddenly another thought occurred to Neela and she dropped her hand. Maybe Jordan couldn't handle the intimacy of sex and needed to depersonalize her conquests to enjoy it. Maybe their last encounter had been exactly what got Jordan off. She'd try anything to connect with her. "Will you finish what you started the other night?"

"What do you mean?" At least she had Jordan's attention again.

She reached for the hem of her blouse and shucked it over her head before unsnapping her bra and letting it drop. Jordan's gaze shifted to her breasts.

"You're so gorgeous, almost too much." She reached toward Neela but stopped.

"Touch me, Jordan." She massaged her breasts and watched as Jordan squirmed in the seat. "Please." When Jordan bit her lip but didn't respond, Neela unzipped her slacks and rolled them and her bikinis off. "I'm asking you to have sex with me. I thought you lived for this." She placed her blouse over the back of the seat and bent over, exposing herself as Jordan had demanded at her home.

"Fuck." Jordan practically breathed the word, and Neela felt her shift on the seat behind her. Jordan leaned over her back and pressed her clothed crotch against Neela's naked ass. "Are you sure about this?"

"I'm sure. Do whatever you want. Just finish me this time."

Jordan brushed Neela's hair aside and rimmed her ear with her tongue, her breath hot and erratic. She massaged Neela's breasts while rubbing their bodies together. "You feel so good." She brought her right hand to Neela's mouth and pressed her middle finger inside. "Wet this. I'll fuck you with it."

Neela moaned as she sucked on Jordan's finger and imagined it sliding in and out of her. Jordan rocked against her in rhythm with her sucking. When Jordan pulled her finger out, Neela almost came. "Take your clothes off, Jordan. I want to feel your skin on mine."

"Shush." Jordan spread Neela's legs farther apart with her knee and slowly filled her completely, firing heat and sensation through her.

Neela instantly gripped Jordan's fingers and the contractions began. Jordan reached around and squeezed her slick folds around her clit. "Not yet. I want to be inside you longer. You're so wet and hot… and soft." Jordan was gentle with her, but Neela felt her straining to hold back her own responses. What was she afraid of?

Neela tensed to stave off her building orgasm. "I'm so ready."

Jordan took Neela's hand and placed it where hers had been, holding her sex. She resisted the temptation to stroke herself to orgasm. Then Neela heard Jordan unzip her jeans and turned to see her fold the waistband over and slip her hand inside. *I want to touch you.*

Neela hung on, trying not to come until given permission. She couldn't resist much longer. "Jordan, please. Can I come now?"

"Not…yet."

Jordan's thrusts into her were firm yet tender, but she wildly clawed herself as if sex had to hurt to be pleasurable or maybe to be acceptable. "Oh, fuck." Neela looked over her shoulder, wanting to meet Jordan's gaze when they came. Jordan pumped frantically as she fingered Neela. "Now. Come now."

Neela surrendered to the heat scorching her, the juices running down her legs, and the rasping sound of Jordan's breathing against her neck. She rode Jordan's fingers up and down until ripples of pleasure gripped and squeezed and her knees gave way. "Oh my God, Jordan." She clung to the seat back as she spilled into Jordan's hand. Struggling for breath, she enjoyed the final spasms of release as Jordan slid her fingers from her.

Jordan fell back against the seat with her hand still inside her jeans. The pain on her face was almost unbearable. She curled up like an injured animal, frightened and defensive. Neela reached for her but Jordan pulled away.

"Are you all right?"

"Yeah." Her guarded tone was back.

"No, you're not. Let me help you." Neela knelt between Jordan's legs on the floorboard and pulled Jordan's hand from her shorts. "You smell delicious. I want to taste you." She licked her fingers one by one as Jordan watched. Her hand quivered against Neela's lips, and fire still burned in her eyes. "Jordan, please let me satisfy you."

"Jesus, Neela. You're making me crazy."

"Why?"

"You're just so damn sexy and…"

"Horny?"

"Uninhibited. But I can't." Jordan straightened her jeans and tucked her shirt in, every movement near her crotch causing a visible flinch. "You need to go."

"But we're not finished. You're in pain."

"I'm fine. It's late and Bina is alone."

The statement was like a cold splash of reality, and the accompanying guilt was almost dizzying. Neela immediately started pulling on her clothes. "I really don't understand you. One minute you're angry because you think I'm cheating on a partner and the next you're worried my mother is home alone. Are you trying to push me away?"

"I'm not—I don't know what you want me to say. It's best if we just forget about this. Move on with our lives. We both wanted this to happen again, but I—"

"Oh yes, I forgot. This is just another game for you, another conquest. Well, congratulations. I was so desperate I allowed you to screw me in a car like a teenager. Your friends will get a kick out of that. Too bad you don't have pictures." She really didn't want Jordan to respond because she feared the worst.

As she finished straightening her clothes, she paused, reluctant to leave her anger between them. Bina's health issues had taught her to express her feelings, especially if it might be her last chance. "I'm sorry. This is what it is. I knew exactly what I was getting into with you. I don't necessarily *want* you to say anything. Just talk to me. I can't explain why I care, and I certainly can't understand this chemistry between us. I'm just interested in you."

"You wouldn't be if you knew who I really am. Go home, Neela. This was a mistake." Jordan reached across, opened the door, and waited for her to get out. "And please don't speed on the interstate. I don't have the energy to chase you tonight."

On the way home Neela wondered if Jordan was right. Could she go back to life as usual? Would she be content with her normal routines and an occasional vanilla orgasm with Liz? Or had Jordan breeched her physical and emotional barriers so completely she'd never be the same? Equally important, why was she attracted to Jordan—a reckless, rude, conflicted being who wouldn't allow herself to be touched or satisfied by a partner—a woman who made her abandon all sense of decorum? But Neela's instincts told her there was more to Jordan than she'd been allowed to see, and that insight intrigued her and pulled her deeper into Jordan's emotional quagmire.

Chapter Nine

Jordan crossed her ankles and shook her foot until her chair vibrated as Sergeant Milton paced back and forth in front of her and Bex. They'd been summoned to an eight o'clock meeting after Jordan's sexcapade with Neela. After a steady round of pacing and a coughing fit, Milton finally stopped in front of Jordan.

"Do you know a woman named Elizabeth Blackmon?"

"No."

"That's interesting because she says you assaulted her last night outside the Veterinary School of Medicine on the State University campus. Ring any bells?"

"Oh, her." Bex's sideways glance indicated she didn't appreciate being blindsided.

"Care to elaborate, or should I just take her word for it and suspend you now?"

"We hadn't been briefed about this woman. I didn't know her connection to Doctor Sahjani, so when she grabbed her in the parking lot, I reacted. And I didn't assault her. I pushed her to create distance and assess any further threat potential."

"Jesus, I can tell you've been in Internal Affairs a few times. You've got the lingo down pat. But is that really what happened?" He looked at Bex.

"I don't know, boss. I wasn't there."

"You're her damn partner. Where were you?"

Jordan couldn't let Bex take the heat for her. "I asked to work nights for a few days, so Bex switched with Harry Styles."

"And where was Harry during this non-assault?"

"He called in sick."

"What a clusterfuck. All I have is your word against that of an upstanding doctor with impeccable credentials and no criminal history. Was a time that would've been enough, but not lately. I never know what you'll do next."

Had Neela asked Elizabeth Blackmon to complain so Jordan would be removed from her protection detail? Or had Neela complained? It really didn't matter because she absolutely needed to be replaced. Things between her and Neela had gone too far, and she couldn't undo what had happened.

"Sarge, if I screw up, I take responsibility. I told you what happened, but if you need to suspend or replace me, I get it."

"Today must be your lucky day, Bishop. Doctor Blackmon doesn't want to pursue formal charges. She just wanted to know why the police were watching Doctor Sahjani. I told her to talk to her friend."

Jordan's foot stopped shaking and she relaxed slightly. She knew Milton well enough to know he wasn't finished yet. He directed his attention to Bex.

"Get your schedules back together and manage this walking disaster, or I'll transfer you both to evidence control. You're senior detective, and I expect you to act like it. Harry and Phil have split their shifts so the two of you can have the day off. This assignment isn't over until the chief says so, and I don't want any more screwups. Now get out of my sight before you spoil my good mood."

Bex didn't speak until they were in the parking lot and Jordan was astride her bike. "We need to talk. I mean really talk. Can you do it sober, or do we need to reconvene at the bar?"

"I've got something else to do."

"Take care of it and meet me later. I can't be your partner or your friend this way, Jordan. You've got to help me."

"Fine. See you there at two."

Jordan rode for hours trying to clear the thoughts and images of Neela enough to figure out what to say to Bex. She'd crossed the professional boundaries days ago and put both of their careers in jeopardy. She'd also stretched their friendship to the limit too many times recently not to give Bex an explanation.

She'd refused help from anyone for a long time and had become angry and reckless. The therapy sessions with Molly were bringing everything to the surface, but it wasn't just the memories. Her problem went deeper and she wasn't anxious to share it with anyone. It was a wound that never seemed to heal, a rejection that underscored her worthlessness as a human being. And that was a deficiency she couldn't reveal to her work partner. The job required she at least appear to have her shit together, but since Neela had come into the picture, she'd failed miserably.

She didn't want to examine her behavior with Neela last night too closely either. Neela had been open and willing to satisfy Jordan's needs, no matter what they were, while she treated Neela like just another conquest. She'd wanted to give Neela more and was disgusted with herself that she couldn't.

Neela's kindness had been too much for Jordan. She couldn't look at Neela or let Neela touch her while they had sex. And even though she'd been physically aching, she couldn't come with this gorgeous creature writhing against her. Neela had seen that she was without substance, sensitivity, or the capacity to truly love. So she'd run like every other time before. Jordan had to get a grip on her life before she destroyed everything.

She took a chance her therapist might be available and sent her an emergency text. She'd disregarded Molly's encouragement to spend a bit more time in counseling before entering into another relationship. Her interaction with Neela wasn't really a relationship, but it was certainly complicated. Molly's advice only seemed to make sense after the fact. Any fool could see now what she'd done was wrong, but in the heat of the moment, all she knew was how badly she wanted Neela. Why couldn't she purge her demons and move forward? When Molly called, Jordan summarized her latest digression and asked for advice.

"So, let me see if I understand what you're telling me, Jordan. You're interested in someone. She's also interested, and you've already had sex."

The long pause was Jordan's signal that Molly didn't approve but was trying not to say so. "I know you said I should wait until I sorted my feelings and dealt with my past, but she just happened, out of the blue. I certainly didn't plan any of this. As a matter of fact I've been fighting it—except for the sex."

"Do you care for this woman—more than just a sexual partner?"

Jordan wasn't sure she could answer truthfully. How would she recognize the line between sexual need and emotional caring with no clear definition of love or boundaries in her past? "How will I know?"

"You'll know you care when sex isn't enough. When you're not okay just getting off and walking away."

She'd already started questioning her past lifestyle, but did that mean she was in love?

"Jordan, do you remember the training rule about using deadly force?"

"Yeah. When in doubt, don't."

"Exactly. I'll go a step further. Slow down. Think about what you're doing *before* you do it. And when the past comes up, don't let it drag you down. Figure out what you want now and work toward that. If you're not sure about your feelings, that's okay for the moment. Just be honest with this woman. It's all you can do, and it's the greatest gift you can give her. You're making progress, Jordan. Be patient and be kinder with yourself."

"Thanks, Molly. I'll try."

When she walked into the bar at two, Bex had already ordered their first round of drinks, another thing her therapist had suggested she avoid for a while. She strode to the secluded table in the back and guzzled half of her vodka tonic before sitting down. Would she ignore the rest of Molly's advice too? "I'm sorry."

"I know, but I need more," Bex said.

"You've been a good friend, better than I deserve lately." She finished her drink and waved to the bartender for a refill. Closing her eyes, she waited for the welcome buzz that would dull some of the pain. "When my mother left—" The words hung in her throat, choking off further explanation.

"I can't imagine, Jordan."

"It wasn't just losing *her*. She took everything. I grew up with no sense of family or belonging to anything good." Jordan cringed as visions of the orphanage resurfaced. She took another big gulp of her drink, unable to meet Bex's gaze. "Do you have any idea what it's like to be in an orphanage? I don't remember many happy times, just an overwhelming sense that something was missing. The younger children were herded into a room with one attendant, not much interaction, while the bigger kids went outside to play. We mostly fought, and whoever was bigger and tougher got the toys. When I had a growth spurt and was shuffled out with the older kids, I was always bottom dog—the punching bag, fetcher, and blame-taker for whatever they did. I never seemed to fit in, always felt misplaced, temporary, and basically a problem to be dealt with." Bex's eyes filled with tears. "For God's sake, don't pity me. I can't handle that."

"It's not pity. I'm trying to imagine how incredibly hard it was for you to be in a place like that. How long were you there?"

Jordan had imagined telling her story so many times and suppressed the feelings for so long it rolled off her tongue with little emotion. It had been easier to tell Molly because she was a stranger. "My mother dropped me off on the doorstep of New Beginning when I was only a few days old, and believe me, it wasn't a new beginning. It was hell, from what I remember. I'm probably the only baby in the history of the state who wasn't adopted. What's wrong with me?"

Bex shook her head. "I didn't know. I always thought you were older."

"I didn't want to face that look in your eyes I see right now. I didn't want you to use the past as an excuse for my messed-up behavior. And I certainly didn't want you to think less of me because of the missing pieces. Nobody wanted me and I didn't develop very well. I've made mistakes and I've taken responsibility for them. I should've gone to jail several times, but one youth detective and a sympathetic judge took an interest when I was caught joyriding in a stolen car. If it hadn't been for them, I'd be a felon now instead of a police officer."

"Jesus. It's a wonder you can function normally at all."

"I'm not sure I do." She finished her drink and shouted to the bartender. "Double vodka, straight up."

"Maybe you should slow down."

"I can't do this sober, and if I don't get it out now I never will. Just listen, and if you want to walk away, I'll understand." She couldn't imagine having this conversation with anyone but Bex. They'd been friends a long time but didn't have the intimate connection lovers shared. Lovers expected more, were more easily disappointed and quicker to use the past as a weapon when things went wrong, or at least that's how she imagined it.

Bex took a generous sip of her drink and smiled. "I'm not going anywhere, partner. No matter what." She sat back in the booth and waited until Jordan was ready to continue.

"I've got some challenges, to say the least. Anger management, duh, impulse control, and intimacy, to name a few. Big surprise, right? The orphanage had rules for everything and against everything but no explanations for them. My Catholic keepers weren't good at being questioned. I'm not saying they were all horrible people, just uninformed in the ways of the world and how to raise a rebellious kid. And other shit was going on too. You can imagine how I became such a cornucopia of psychological dysfunctions. I rebelled, acted out, and eventually ran away. When I joined the police department, I needed structure and real discipline, not just domination and control. I'm still trying to fit in."

"And that wild streak we all know and love became one of your defense mechanisms." Bex said it like it made perfect sense.

Jordan shrugged. "I guess. When I reached puberty, I was told my feelings were wrong, that sex was bad and intended only for procreation, not pleasure and never with women."

"You knew you were a lesbian?"

"I knew I was different but didn't know exactly what that meant. With such a fanatical upbringing, I had a lot to shovel through."

"That explains your aversion to health-care professionals who're supposed to take care of the young and needy," Bex said.

"You think? It's hard to accept that nobody knew what was going on or tried to fix it."

"I can understand that. But you need to remember this was years ago, long before Neela was health director."

"But does an organization ever really change, or are the attitudes of complacency and apathy systemic? It's not her I object to. It's the societal failure to protect children who can't protect themselves and the politicians who won't change the situation."

"I'm with you there, partner." Bex took the remainder of Jordan's drink and downed it in a single shot. "Look on the bright side. You seem to have gotten over the sex-for-pleasure part."

Jordan chose not to correct Bex's inaccurate assessment. "I've tried to overcome the imprinting, but sometimes it flares up. Most kids brought up in a really strict environment go to one extreme or the other, saint or sinner. My pendulum swung heavily to the sinner side."

"And what about relationships?"

Jordan raised her hand for another drink to steel her for what came next but changed her mind and waved the bartender off. "I've never actually had one."

"Really? You always hung with me in the bar and had your share of women."

"Sex is easy, at least the doing part. Relationships require intimacy, sharing, and trust—all the things I suck at." She could tell by the look on Bex's face she wasn't grasping the full meaning of her words, and Jordan wasn't sure she could tell her more.

"I'm sorry, Jordan. I'm glad you're talking to Molly. I mean a professional, somebody who can help. God knows I'm crap at it."

"But I don't always follow the plan, you know? Don't always listen. And you're right. Our sessions are why I've been so on edge lately. I think I'd rather go into a gunfight with only three bullets than deal with some of the stuff she's digging up." Jordan pushed her empty glass away. She'd told Bex more than anyone, but she couldn't tell her everything.

Jordan hadn't gotten past her physical barriers. Her casual partners seemed content with being pleasured and not having to reciprocate. But most women tired of a rough exterior and feral rutting and eventually wanted tenderness and intimacy. All of her liaisons had sought that in the end. She thought about Neela and the liquor in her stomach churned. What had she been thinking, involving Neela in her disaster of a life? What had Neela thought about her pathetic sexual displays? She shook her head, trying not to imagine.

"Hey, at least you're working on it. That means a lot. So, want to tell me what happened last night, with the Blackmon woman?"

"She was all over Neela. I had to peel her off."

Bex waited until Jordan looked at her. "But what happened with you?"

"I lost it. I don't know what's going on between us, but it's making me crazy. I've never felt anything like this, and I don't know what to do about it. I feel possessed. I have to have her, but I don't deserve her and can't give her what she needs."

"What did you *do*, Jordan?"

"I had sex with her in my police car in the university parking lot." Bex's jaw tightened and she didn't speak for several seconds. "Say it. Don't handle me with kid gloves because I've told you all my shit."

"What were you thinking? I know what you were thinking with. She has a partner. She's a classy woman who deserves to be treated properly."

"She doesn't have a partner. Bina is her mother."

Bex's surprise didn't overshadow her irritation. "And that makes it all right that you fucked her in your squad car?"

"No, I didn't mean that. She wanted it…I mean…I told her to go home."

"After the fact, I'm sure. Jordan, she's caring for an ailing mother, trying to save her subordinates' jobs, and working on a cure for God knows what, and you're offering her a quick hookup. She deserves somebody who loves her, who can share her burdens and offer her happiness. And I'm not saying that to be cruel. You're just not where she is right now."

Jordan winced. Bex was right, and hearing the words aloud that she'd already told herself stung. She was a fallow field compared to Neela's abundance.

"What should I do?"

"If you can't give her what she deserves, then leave her alone so she can find someone who can."

Jordan buried her face in her hands. "I'm not sure I can stay away from her."

"Then you better deal with your issues and figure out how you feel about her. Be as honest with her as you've been with me. That would be a great place to start."

"You sound like Molly."

"I obviously give good advice and without the charge." Bex elbowed her in the ribs, eyed a group of women who'd just entered the bar, and scooted toward the edge of her chair.

"Before you go, I should probably tell you something else."

Bex leaned over the table, her expression set for the worst. "What?"

"I've got a dog."

"You're lying."

"Nope. The one I almost ran over the other night."

"And you're…taking care of him?"

"Well, he certainly isn't taking care of me. It's only temporary until his owner comes forward. He's sort of cute and sweet. I call him Blue because in the moonlight his white coat looked totally blue and his eyes are the same color as mine."

"Great, a canine version of you. Aren't you dog enough? Okay, now I really do need to get drunk. If you'll excuse me, I've spotted the love of my evening. See you bright and early tomorrow morning. We're back on days."

"And you call me a dog? You're the biggest one in the kennel."

"Seriously, though, thanks for talking to me. I know it wasn't easy."

Jordan watched Bex work her magic with her woman of the hour. At least she realized she was playing a game and knew how to stop when she met someone of quality. Bex's previous relationship had lasted fifteen years before her partner left for a younger woman. Jordan wasn't certain she knew how to stop pretending and just be herself, whoever that was.

Bex pointed to a particularly luscious blonde who would normally have pushed all Jordan's sexual buttons, but tonight she didn't touch the ache for Neela that had become a constant. She shook her head and left the bar, choosing to take a cab back to her apartment.

"What troubles you so, Beta?" Bina brushed her gnarled hand across Neela's forehead. The intimacy of the gesture and the pain she was certain it caused made Neela's heart ache.

"Nothing, Mama. I'm fine. Did you take your medicine tonight?" Bina's rheumatoid arthritis had grown progressively more painful in the last year, and the inflammation had made even some of the simplest tasks impossible.

"Do not change the subject. I am fine, but I worry for you. You never go out. You work always. This is not the life your father and I imagined for you."

"You and Papa did everything for me, coming to a country you didn't know, working menial jobs so I could go to good schools, denying yourselves the simplest pleasures. The least I can do is make your life more comfortable now. Please let me."

"But you are only thirty-six. A young woman needs a life, a lover, joy."

Neela's mind flashed to Jordan, hunched over her back, trying desperately to come, and her body heated. "I don't have time for love." But she'd make as much time for sex as Jordan wanted. Neela enjoyed things with Jordan she never thought she would and felt more deeply than she imagined possible. Maybe her life had simply been too bland and Jordan had shown her variety. If Jordan could only offer a few minutes in a public toilet, she'd take it.

"Your eyes say different. Do not try to fool an old woman. Is it because of me?"

"Don't talk crazy, Mama. I love being here with you. You keep me sane."

"And single, I think. It is hard to live with an aging, decrepit mother. Maybe I should go to one of those assisted-living places. I could make new friends, and you could have a real life."

Neela's inside recoiled at the thought of losing her mother even temporarily. They'd shared everything since her father died, and being without her would be too painful. She took Bina's hands. "Mama, I don't want you to go, ever. If I'm to have what you call a real life, it will be with someone who understands the meaning of family and who loves and adores you as much as I do. Okay?"

Bina's eyes filled with tears as she nodded.

Neela helped her finish dinner and prepared her for bed. She seemed to be having a good night, so maybe she could sleep in her own bed for the first time in a week. "Your place or mine?" She never wanted Bina to feel like a burden. The weight of it pressed against her like a stone.

"My room. I feel brave." Bina hobbled beside her until they reached her bedroom filled with brightly colored fabric and pictures of her departed father. The room reminded Neela of her roots in the Indian culture and the philosophies she still held sacred, such as karma, reincarnation, and the concept that no religion is superior.

"Are you sure?"

"Yes, Beta. Now go." Bina kissed her cheek and shooed her away.

"Call if you need anything."

Neela left the bedroom door ajar so she could hear if Bina called. She couldn't remember the last time her mother had a good night, and she looked forward to a peaceful evening of reading and relaxing. After a quick shower, she pulled on her old terry-cloth robe and thought about the last time she'd worn it. Jordan had ripped it off her just before taking her from behind. The memory was so powerful she clutched the doorframe for support.

Neela had known she was in trouble as soon as she met Jordan, but that night she'd gotten a glimpse of just how reckless and intense Jordan could be, and it excited her beyond reason. Last night Jordan's wildness seemed a cover for something else. She'd pulled away when Neela tried to touch her intimately, and Neela worried her difficulty went much deeper than the physical. Why hadn't she listened more closely to what Jordan said and to what she struggled so desperately not to say?

She settled into her old leather recliner beside the fireplace with a cup of green tea and picked up *Life of Pi* and her glasses. She'd been trying to find time to read it for months. As she opened to the acknowledgments, the front picture window shattered and glass raked over her like sharp razors, leaving trails of blood. She stared at the streaks of red running down her arms, too stunned to realize what had happened. Before her mind kicked into gear, someone was pounding on the door.

"Police. Open up."

The scene finally registered, and Neela flung open the door before racing to Bina's room. Her mother was still sound asleep. *Thank God. If anything happened to you, I wouldn't survive.* She stroked Bina's forehead with a quivering hand and returned to the family room.

"You're injured." Phil Morris stood in the doorway gesturing to her cuts. "I'll call an ambulance."

"No. They're superficial. I'll clean and bandage them myself if necessary." Her voice sounded too clinical. She was probably in shock. "Who? Why?"

"I don't know. Harry's looking for him. He came out of nowhere and disappeared in the bushes. The sergeant will have our asses, not to mention Jordan. She's very protective of you and your mother."

"What am I supposed to do about this?" She pointed to the gaping hole that used to be her family-room window.

"We have a repairman on call. He could bring some plywood and secure it until you get a glass man out tomorrow."

"Thank you. If you'll excuse me." She went into the bathroom and looked in the mirror. The left side of her face was red from a bleeding wound near her hairline, and her arms looked like she'd been running through a briar patch. She mechanically removed the first-aid kit from the cabinet and cleaned the scratches, relieved that all but the one on her forehead had already stopped bleeding. She applied a Steri-Strip and returned to the cacophony of activity invading her family living space.

Phil was taking pictures of the damage and a huge rock with his cell phone. A piece of paper was secured around the stone with a rubber band, and he carefully removed it with his gloved fingers. The note was similar to the first one but more threatening.

I told you we know where you live.
Stop what you're doing before it's too late.
This is your last warning.

Neela's stomach churned. This sick, anonymous bastard had violated her home and her family, and she had no idea what she was supposed to stop doing in order to appease him. He had struck twice with the police only yards away. Her confidence in the protection detail took a nosedive.

After Phil finished the report and the repairman left, Neela rolled her yoga mat out beside Bina's bed. She couldn't leave her alone after what had happened, and since she wouldn't sleep, she wanted to be close. She could fight for herself and Bina when she was here, but what about when her mother was alone and more vulnerable? Whatever it took, she'd see that Bina wasn't harmed.

CHAPTER TEN

When Bex pulled in front of Neela's house the next morning, Jordan was out of the vehicle before it stopped, running to the door. The huge sheet of plywood across what used to be the picture window spelled trouble. The night-shift guys had obviously dropped the ball, and she'd deal with them later. She just hoped no one was injured. She pounded on Neela's door and kept pounding until she finally opened it, dressed for work. Jordan stopped her fist mid-air when she saw Neela's scratched arms and bandaged forehead.

"You're hurt." She wanted to touch Neela, to make sure she was okay, but she couldn't force her arm forward.

Neela took Jordan's hand and pressed it to her cheek. "I'm fine. See. Still warm and no permanent damage." How did she know what Jordan was feeling, what she needed, when she wasn't sure herself? And how did she touch so easily and so gently when Jordan struggled with anything beyond sexual groping?

Neela's skin was so warm and incredibly soft, but visibly scarred. Her brown eyes were wide and held a glint of something she hadn't seen before, fear, maybe, or confusion. Jordan breathed deeply and her anger rose. "Goddamn it. Somebody will pay." She turned toward the detectives across the street.

Neela grabbed her arm. "Stop. It's not serious, and it wasn't their fault."

"It's their job to see nothing happens to you or…is Bina okay?" She brushed past Neela and scanned the hallway and adjoining areas within sight. As she started going room to room, a short, slightly stooped woman came out from the kitchen.

"And who is this come here to save us, dear Beta?" The rolling r's and long consonants of the rich Indian accent dissolved some of Jordan's anxiety, and she stopped.

Bent and slowed by her twisted joints, a silver-haired woman wrapped in a bright-orange sari moved toward Jordan with determination. Her inviting smile was the same as Neela's, and Jordan was instantly drawn to her.

She raised her hand and pointed a crooked finger at Jordan. "I see you." Bina surveyed her up and down, her head tilting from side to side and her smile never wavering. Raising her arm with obvious effort, she touched Jordan's white hair. "We have both lived hard." She motioned toward the kitchen. "You two come." She turned and led the way, obviously expecting them to follow.

Jordan didn't want to resist as Neela looped their arms, and they followed Bina into the kitchen. "I need to tell the guys—"

"I think they'll figure it out," Neela said. "When Bina Sahjani summons you for a cup of tea, you don't keep her waiting."

"I see that." Jordan glanced around as they walked toward the back of the house. Each room was filled with soothing colors, family pictures, and soft surfaces to ease aches and encourage intimacy. Even the air smelled like a home—breakfast cooking, coffee brewing, and freshly washed clothes. Huddled in her bunk at the orphanage, she'd often imagined how a real family lived. This was it. Her chest ached for what she'd missed.

Neela squeezed her forearm. "You okay?"

She could only nod.

"Neela, our guest needs coffee." Turning to Jordan, Bina motioned to a circular table beside the window overlooking a flower-lined lawn. Jordan pulled a chair out for Bina and she sat. "A hero with manners." She smiled appreciatively and offered her hand. "I am Bina."

"Jordan Bishop, ma'am. It's a pleasure to meet you." She hadn't meant anything so sincerely in months. Bina had captured her with only a smile and a few kind words. How simple she made it seem. "Are you all right? It must've been scary last night."

"Slept like a baby. When I awoke Neela was on the floor beside my bed so I knew something was wrong. But we are safe, and that is all that matters." Her lilting cadence and precise English seemed formal but fit her sophisticated manner.

Neela handed Jordan a cup of coffee, Bina a tea, and sat across from them. "Yes, just a little commotion, but at least Bina wasn't disturbed." Her tone was guarded, and Jordan took the hint not to discuss the incident further in front of her mother.

"So, Jordan, how do you know my Neela?" Bina's brown eyes drilled into Jordan and heat rose up her neck.

"We met at work," Neela said. "Detective Bishop was asking about an acquaintance."

"I see," Bina said. "She is a genius, my daughter, but she works too hard and has no life."

"Mama."

Bina ignored Neela's warning tone. "I want her to be happy, find someone to love. She spends too much time taking care of me. Do you not think a woman needs love?"

"Mama, *please.*"

Bina waved her hand dismissively and directed her next question to Jordan as well. "Do you have someone?"

Neela raised her hands in resignation. "That is *so* inappropriate, Mama."

Bina continued as if Neela hadn't spoken. "Attractive women such as yourselves should have someone." She smiled that arresting smile again and looked back toward the front of the house. "What are we to do about the window? It is too chilly for an open living space just yet."

"I've called the glass company, Mama. They should be here shortly. I'll wait until they've repaired the window before I go to the office."

"Let our Jordan speak, please." She shook her head when Neela offered more tea and returned her attention to Jordan. "Tell me about yourself. Where is your family? Do you live nearby? How many siblings do you have?"

Jordan felt the shame of her past crawling over her like a sickness. "I don't—"

"Bina, stop. Jordan isn't here to be interrogated."

Neela's words sounded protective and Jordan was grateful for the intervention. Bina's questions would've been quite harmless to anyone else, but each one pierced her like a blade, reminding her of the missing parts of her life and the void in her heart. She had to refocus on work because Bina was skirting too close to her pain.

"Neela, can I talk to you for a minute outside?" Jordan didn't wait for a reply. She rose and said to Bina, "It was a pleasure to meet you, and I look forward to seeing you again soon." She stepped onto the back deck and waited for Neela.

"You haven't told your mother about the threats, have you?" Neela shook her head. "What does she think happened to the window?"

"Vandals. Why would I upset her? She's dealing with enough already."

"I appreciate that. I really do, but she needs to know, especially when she's home all day alone. We need to take more precautions."

"We?"

"I think it's time to reconsider those cameras you were so dead set against. And I'd like to install sensors around the boundary of your property."

"Forget it."

"You don't even have an alarm system or a dog, and Bina is by herself a lot. Don't you care what happens to your mothe—"

Neela's brown eyes burned as she stepped into Jordan's body space and lowered her voice. "You don't get to question my life, *especially* when it concerns my mother. Are we clear?"

Jordan's customary anger vanished as the hurt in Neela's eyes turned to tears. She'd crossed the line, but she couldn't imagine having someone who loved her as fiercely as Bina loved Neela and not protecting her in every possible way. She reached out but Neela backed away. "Please." Neela stopped, her shoulders slumped, and Jordan pulled her close. "I'm sorry. I know you'd do anything for Bina. I just want to help. Please let me."

"Why?"

Neela's voice was muffled against her T-shirt, her tears soaking into the fabric, and she'd never felt more needed. "It didn't take long to realize what a special person she is and how important she is to you. I couldn't bear it if something happened to her."

"You're serious, aren't you?"

"Totally."

"Why is this so important to you, Jordan?"

The feelings Bina had stirred in her were new but reminiscent of the way she and Amy had bonded in the orphanage. Amy had accepted her immediately and completely, never questioning her basic goodness. "She reminds me of someone…I cared about deeply."

Neela looked up, surprised and searching Jordan's face as if to confirm she hadn't misheard this small glimpse of her soul Jordan had revealed. *I see you.*

"Then I guess we better get busy building a little fortress for Bina. Call your tech guys while I explain the situation to her. External cameras only, but the boundary sensors and alarm sound like a good idea." She started back in the house but paused. "And thank you."

"Just doing my job, ma'am." Jordan tried to be cavalier though she felt anything but.

"Not just for that, but for speaking from here," she placed her hand over Jordan's heart, "for the first time."

Jordan couldn't breathe for several seconds as her heart pounded under Neela's hand. For just an instant she'd let her guard down and her feelings about Amy flooded out. She smiled as she walked around the house, happy and also slightly concerned that Neela had felt her sincerity.

As she approached Harry and Phil, they edged closer to their car, readying for her wrath. "What happened last night, guys?" She was surprised how cool her voice sounded. When she arrived, she'd been so angry she was ready to take them both on. But Neela's assurance that she was okay and her calming influence had soothed her. "Any leads on the suspect?"

Phil shook his head. "Sorry. He came out of the bushes in a flash and was gone just as quickly. He smashed the window on the fly and scaled the fence next door like a ninja. No way we could catch him." Harry and Phil looked like they'd let down their side, and that was probably punishment enough.

"Doctor Sahjani has agreed to cameras around the house. We'll also put sensors on the perimeter and alarm the house. Hopefully, all of that will be in place when you come on tonight." The guys drove away and Bex shook her head. "What?"

"I wouldn't have believed it if I hadn't seen it for myself."

"What are you talking about?"

"I expected you to chew both of them a new asshole for letting this guy slip through their fingers. Could you be mellowing?"

"Shut up."

"Are Neela and her mother okay?"

"They will be. Neela has a few minor cuts from flying glass, but Bina slept through the whole ordeal. She seems so frail and crippled she can barely move, but she doesn't let it get her down." Jordan admired Bina's determination because she'd been unable to overcome her comparatively minor emotional problems.

"You really like her, don't you?"

"She's what I always imagined a mother should be—" Her voice cracked, and Jordan turned her back to regain her composure. "You mind shadowing Neela today while I supervise the camera and alarm installations?"

"No problem. How long before she's ready to leave?"

"Not sure. She's explaining the situation to Bina right now. Why don't you grab some breakfast? I'll text you when she's ready to go."

"My day's looking better all the time, breakfast and a little one-on-one time with the doctor."

The picture of Bex and Neela that flashed through her mind made Jordan cringe. "Bex—"

Bex slapped her on the back. "Don't worry, partner. I was only kidding. You're obviously hooked."

"Seriously, shut up." As she walked back to the house, Jordan wondered about Bex's comment. Was she falling for Neela? Ridiculous. They were like feral cats, fighting one minute and fucking the next. Had a couple of groping tangles been powerful enough to tame her dark side? *More like the first look at her.* "Shut up." Even if she was attracted to Neela, she didn't know how to show her. She didn't do sweet, kind, and loving.

Neela met her at the front door again with her finger pressed to her lips. "Bina has gone back to bed. She tires easily and takes frequent naps. Is everything in order?"

"The tech guys and the alarm company should be here in a couple of hours. What about the glass company?"

"Same."

"I can wait for both. No point in holding you up." Jordan was simply being practical, at least that's what she told herself. In reality, she wanted to help Neela and Bina beyond the basic requirements of her job. The reason wasn't as clear as her need.

"That's very kind of you, but I thought I'd stick around for a bit, in case Bina needs anything when she wakes up. Is that all right?"

"Sure." Jordan tapped the side of her leg and tried to figure out how to say what had been bugging her since her less-than-chivalrous behavior in the university parking lot. "Can we talk?"

"Never thought I'd hear you say those words. Of course, come in." Neela led Jordan into the family room where they'd had sex. Not Jordan's ideal spot for an apology, since she'd been less than gallant in here as well. Neela rubbed her arm reassuringly and waited.

"I just wanted to apologize for the other night, in the car. Not my finest hour in many respects." She still hadn't figured out why she always had such a visceral response to Neela and how to contain or at least direct it in a more appropriate way.

"Can you tell me what's going on?"

"Trust me. You're better off keeping your distance from me."

"Maybe I don't want to keep my distance. Maybe I enjoy your charming personality and challenging conversation."

"We haven't had a real conversation."

"So you see why it's challenging." She grinned and slid her hand across the back of the sofa. "I got my first spanking as an adult right here."

Jordan glanced at the brown leather and quickly looked away as heat gathered in her middle. "I remember. Sorry about that too."

"Don't be sorry. I didn't realize I enjoyed being spanked." She leaned against the sofa and tried to pull Jordan between her legs.

"What are you doing, Neela?"

"Trying to seduce you. Am I that bad at it?" She rose on her toes, then licked Jordan's lips and probed for access. Her eyes sparked with sexual hunger.

Jordan tried to swallow. "Bina is—"

"Sleeping soundly. I really need you right now, Jordan."

Neela licked the scar over Jordan's lip and then kissed her so fiercely that Jordan gasped. Neela radiated a mixture of passion and barely contained fear.

"You're just feeling the effects of the trauma, the adrenaline rush."

"I don't care." Neela grabbed the hem of Jordan's T-shirt and tried to pull it over her head. "I need you. No strings."

"It's not me you need."

"Who cares? It's just sex, right?" Jordan tried to pull away, but Neela cupped her crotch and squeezed. "You want this, don't you?"

She brushed Neela's hand away.

Neela straddled Jordan's leg and rubbed against her thigh. Her eyes were wild, asking for something Jordan didn't have and seeing someone who didn't exist. "I can't do this." When she pushed Neela away, the expression in her eyes was pure agony.

"What is it with you? Can't you accept what's given freely? Or do you have to take it?" Neela shoved her and ran down the hall. Jordan followed into a small bedroom. "Get out."

"I'm sorry." She didn't know what else to say.

"Really? What are you sorry for this time? Because you weren't turned on when I threw myself at you? Because you're not attracted to me? Because I'm not enough of a challenge? You started this game, Jordan. Let's play." Neela grabbed Jordan's belt and pulled her toward her.

"Neela, you don't understand."

"I thought you liked aggressiveness, or is it just yours that gets you off?"

Neela's words were like strokes across Jordan's sensitive clit. She was wet and aching. "Neela...please."

"Please what?" She tugged again before releasing her grasp and plunging her hand into Jordan's pants. "Jesus, you're soaked. Look at me, Jordan, while I make you come."

Jordan's mind spiraled into memory, and all she saw was someone else groping for something she couldn't give. She jerked Neela's hand from her pants and spun her around, ripping at her slacks and blouse.

"Take me, Jordan."

When Neela was naked, Jordan guided her onto all fours on the bed and plunged three fingers into her.

"Yes, oh God, yes," Neela said, rocking against her hand.

Jordan pumped hard and fast until she lost track of time and was suddenly in another place—a place where she was being forcefully entered with no concern for her pleasure. She was drenched in sweat, no longer aroused, and Neela wasn't responding. "Is this what you wanted?"

Neela's response was soft, almost sad. "No, darling. It's what you wanted."

She froze in mid-stroke, withdrew her fingers from Neela's body, and slumped to the floor at the foot of the bed. Covering her face in her hands, Jordan tried to block out where she was and what she'd done. How long had it been since she'd actually made love, not just taken what she wanted like an animal? *Never.* She didn't belong in the same room with Neela, much less in her home with her mother nearby.

"Jordan?" Neela was sitting beside her on the floor, still nude and making no effort to cover up. She was the most beautiful creature Jordan had ever seen and not just physically. Her goodness radiated from her. Why had she never really looked before? She'd been too consumed with possessing the unattainable, proving she could, playing her games, and moving on before anyone saw what she was really like.

"Jordan, please talk to me."

"What do you want me to say?"

"First, are you all right?"

"Why do you always try to take care of everybody? I'm fine. Did I hurt you?"

"You've never hurt me. You haven't done anything I didn't want you to do. But I need to know what's going on between us. If this is just fun, tell me. I can handle anything as long as I know what it is."

"Neela, I can't give you what you want."

"How do you know?"

"I prove it every time we're…close, like this. Don't you see? I can't do it?"

"Can't do what, Jordan?"

She put her hands on Neela's breasts and caressed the tender flesh until her nipples puckered and Neela moaned. "How does that feel?"

"Fantastic."

"I mean how do you feel inside?" She tweaked Neela's nipples between her finger and thumb, pressing and releasing as Neela rose to meet her touch. As Neela's breathing increased, Jordan's body heated.

"I feel soft, hot, wet, like I'm melting and like my nipples are attached to my clit. I'm desperate to touch you and be filled by you. I want all of you, now."

Jordan's hunger raged. "Know what I feel?"

"Tell me."

Neela's voice was languid with need, and Jordan put one hand between her own legs to slow the torment throbbing so painfully it almost blinded her. "I feel like a volcano full of fire and fury. I need to ravage something, to tear it apart. And it's…so hard…to come. I want to so bad it hurts. But I've never felt that soft, sweet stuff you do. I'm not…normal."

Neela stretched out on the floor and pulled Jordan down beside her. "Normal is overrated. The only one who gets to decide what's normal in my bedroom is me, and my lover. What do you need, Jordan?"

Neela wouldn't understand what she needed, and if she did, it would only disappoint her more. Something inside Jordan tightened like a pulley about to break. If it snapped, she'd fly apart. She pushed away from Neela, fastening her jeans as she rose. "I need to go."

Neela stood in front of her, naked and glowing as she flushed with emotion. "And God knows it's all about what *you* need, isn't it, Jordan? What about what *I* need right now? Isn't it bad enough I have to beg you for sex? This time I thought you'd understand. I'm scared and crawling out of my skin. I know it's the adrenaline. I'm a damn doctor. But I *need* to do something with these feelings."

She'd been where Neela was. The surge of energy that coursed through her was like fire and ice, simultaneously searing and numbing. Jordan could relieve her sexually, her body was drenched with wanting her, but she couldn't allow Neela to depend on her emotionally. She'd only disappoint her, so she said the first thing that came to mind. "We're not in a relationship." She regretted the words the instant they left her lips. A physical slap probably wouldn't have affected Neela as profoundly.

"You're exactly right." Neela stooped, picked up her ripped clothes, and walked calmly toward the door. "Thank you for reminding me of the rules of the game. I won't forget again. If you'll excuse me, I need to re-dress for work."

You total fuckup. But what else could she do? She had to keep Neela at arm's length or she'd only be hurt much worse. Jordan found a bathroom, then splashed cold water on her face and washed her hands before texting Bex. She waited on the front porch until her partner pulled up outside. "Nice breakfast?"

"Great. Uh-oh, you've got that look. Did you upset Neela? You in the doghouse again?"

"When am I not in somebody's doghouse?"

"True." Bex shoved a file toward her. "I reread these over breakfast. Take a look and see what you come up with. We'll compare notes later."

"What did you find?"

"I'd rather talk later. Maybe nothing, but if we agree, could be something."

Neela exited the house once again dressed for work and looking only slightly less gorgeous than thirty minutes ago when she'd been naked and sweaty. "You don't have to wait here, Jordan. Bina can handle the window man, and I'm sure your professionals are capable of installing cameras and an alarm without supervision."

"I'd like to make sure they know where everything goes, if you don't mind."

"Suit yourself." She waved to Bex, who got into her car and began to pull out of the driveway.

"Yep, definitely in the doghouse." Bex took off behind Neela's speeding vehicle.

Behind Jordan the front door opened and Bina motioned her in. "We have more tea."

She took Bina's arm and walked with her to the kitchen, placing the file Bex had given her on the table. "Shall I make the tea?" Bina nodded and gave directions from her chair. Jordan never realized how complicated making a cup of masala chai tea could be, but she lost herself in the task and prepared for Bina's questions.

Jordan poured the steaming milk concoction into a child's sippy cup and set it on the table in front of Bina. She hooked one of her swollen fingers through the handle and attempted a toast. "I guess it is true that we all return to our childhood. Thank you."

"You're welcome. Can I get you anything else?" Bina shook her head. "I guess Neela told you what's going on."

"Yes, but I do not understand why anyone would want to hurt Neela. She is so good."

"Try not to worry. I'll do everything I can to keep you both safe."

Bina patted her hand. "I know, brave one."

"I don't feel very brave."

"But I see you. Inside you have the heart of a warrior, but you try to hide. Something has made you fear your power. You and my Neela are both protectors. She protects the heart and soul, and you the body. It is hard work alone. Maybe you can help each other?"

Jordan didn't have anything to offer Neela, and if Bina was as wise as she sounded, she'd understand. "I don't know how I can help. Neela seems pretty independent."

"You speak of external things. I speak of what is in here." She placed her hand over her heart. "You like my Neela."

Jordan thought about her answer. So far she'd been concerned only with the chase and having Neela sexually. She hadn't seriously considered if she liked her as a person. After she'd found out Neela wasn't a conservative, disengaged politician or a cheater, it had been easier to spend time with her. Neela was a classy woman with good values and a sense of dedication, but did she *really* like her, or just admire her? "Yes, she's an amazing woman. I do like her."

"More than a little, I think."

Jordan tapped her fingers on the table like she was pounding a typewriter. Was Bina asking about her sexuality or her intentions toward her daughter? Did she know about Neela? How was she supposed to answer questions like this from someone's mother? "I—"

"I am old and crooked, Jordan, not blind and insensitive. I see things only those of advanced years can see. My daughter's soul is tired. Your heart is wounded. Perhaps you can help each other mend."

"I'm not sure I know how to—"

"You can do anything, brave one. Trust yourself and my Neela." She finished her tea and slowly rose as the doorbell rang. "Will you see to the workmen? I must sleep again."

"Of course. I'll leave something on your bedroom door when I go. Don't hesitate to use it. Is someone coming to be with you?"

"I will be fine. Lock the door on your way out. I feel much safer just knowing you are my hero." She kissed Jordan's cheek and shuffled toward her room. As she walked away, Jordan's heart ached from the simple gesture and Bina's unconditional kindness. She didn't know anything about Jordan's history, yet she knew her well.

While the workmen went about the repairs, Jordan read the file Bex had left. The reports detailed Ed Branson's and Neela Sahjani's family, education, and work histories. Bex had a reason for digging up all this information so Jordan searched it carefully. Their backgrounds were impressive in their own ways, but they shared nothing in common until medical school. They'd worked on several research projects and had even been part of the same study group and two professional organizations—connections, but nothing that red-flagged them for retaliation.

Jordan flipped to the most recent page of organizational affiliations and skimmed down the list on Branson's side. He'd been a founder and avid supporter of the Guilford Citizens for Equality protest group since medical school. Neela's list showed no such association. She made a note to ask her about it. Vocal groups like these were sometimes the catalysts that spurred fanatics on the opposing side to violent action.

Five hours later, the workmen were packing their tools to leave. She reviewed the camera and alarm operation with the tech guys and tested the connection to her tablet. Next, she scribbled a short note, wrapped it around the remote panic button, and hung it on Bina's bedroom doorknob.

As she reassembled the papers and returned them to the file, Jordan wondered if Neela's protection detail was coming to an end. If so, she wouldn't have any reason to see or contact her. Before closing and locking the door, she looked around the cozy house she would probably never be inside of again.

She'd definitely miss Neela when the assignment ended. She'd opened up to her about her sexual problem—and they weren't even in a relationship—a testament to Neela's compassion and understanding. But she hadn't gone into why she couldn't let go with anyone. Neela probably already thought she was a freak. Why would she want to hear any more? Did it really matter?

What they had was only a hookup, and after her behavior this morning, that was probably over as well. She hadn't enjoyed exposing her shortcomings and vulnerabilities to Neela, and she'd feel embarrassed facing her again. Who'd want to have sex with a woman who whined about her problems after only a couple of romps? She'd be better off going back to barhopping—fewer complications, more straightforward sex, and less emotion.

She was about to call for a ride home when she saw Neela's car coming down the street with Bex's vehicle and another one following close behind. Bex sped around Neela and slid to a stop in front of the house before Neela pulled into the drive.

"Let's go, partner. The guys are on the way."

"What's the hurry?"

"It's quitting time. Let's hit the bar on the way home."

Bex was giving her the bum's rush so she purposely slowed her pace. She'd just reached the passenger side when the two cars stopped in the driveway, and Neela and Liz Blackmon got out and walked toward the house. Neela's briefcase was slung over her shoulder, and Liz carried a small overnight bag in one hand. Neela didn't look at her, but Liz waved and smiled, placing her hand in the small of Neela's back as they entered the house.

Jordan started across the lawn, but Bex grabbed her arm. "Don't."

"Let go of me."

"What are you going to do? Piss on the doorstep to mark your territory? Fight her for humping rights? It's not your call, Jordan."

"She's fucking with me." Jordan tried to pull away but Bex held fast.

"No, she's not, and that's the problem, isn't it? She gets to choose who shares her bed."

She'd never shared Neela's bed. They'd fucked over the back of a couch and in a police car and humped on a floor, but never anywhere that indicated their connection had meaning—because she hadn't allowed it. A sick feeling overshadowed Jordan's anger because she'd driven Neela into another woman's arms. But Neela wouldn't have sex with this person while Bina was home. *She did with you.*

"Damn it." Jordan jerked her arm out of Bex's grasp and got in the car. "Explain the alarm system to her and then get me out of here before I do something more stupid than I've already done."

Chapter Eleven

Neela nuzzled close to the warm body in bed beside her. *Jordan.* But when she slid her arm across the full-figured woman next to her, she remembered.

"Good morning, lover," Liz said, and spooned her back. "How are you?"

"Fine."

"Fine? That's all you can say after the night we had? It was exceptional. You've never been quite so…ravenous."

Neela tried to roll away but Liz scooched closer. "Instant replay?"

"Can't. Early meeting, and Mrs. Scott, Bina's friend, is dropping her off at home shortly." She pecked Liz on the cheek, grabbed her robe, and locked the bathroom door behind her. Turning the hot spray of the shower on full blast, she stepped in and finally considered what she'd done.

After her encounter with Jordan yesterday, she'd been frustrated and confused. She'd surrendered completely every time Jordan had needed her, submitted to her assertive couplings, and enjoyed the raw physicality of sex with her. Neela had been consistently patient, which had finally paid off when Jordan opened up to her. Neela had thought they were making progress until Jordan once again rejected her touch, completely disconnecting. She understood sexual dysfunction and preferences of all types. She'd paid attention to the courses in medical school, but when it came to someone she cared about, she seemed ill equipped.

Maybe Jordan didn't want help. Sharing those kinds of intimate details had to have been unbearable for someone so guarded. She was probably regretting it already. Her heart ached for Jordan, but yesterday her need had been paramount. Jordan should've understood the desperation that such a frightening ordeal caused. But she seemed incapable or unwilling to comfort her. The realization had been a wake-up call. She'd been trying to mold a fuck buddy into a partner. Jordan couldn't be molded.

When Liz called mid-day and suggested a review of their research over dinner, Neela had accepted. She hadn't planned to have sex with Liz, but after their business was complete, Liz had quickly picked up on her vulnerability. Their night had satisfied Neela's physical need and she'd been more adventurous with Liz, but her passion had been for Jordan. The eventual relief was a poor substitute for what she really wanted. She should've known better. She'd given Liz encouragement that their tryst could be something more by bringing her home, and Jordan now knew they'd slept together. Not a proud moment. She'd abandoned the guidance system of her life—honesty.

"Hey, save me some hot water." Liz knocked on the door. "I'd love to join you in there."

Neela turned the water off, slipped into her robe, and wrapped a towel around her unruly hair. She unlocked the door and finished brushing her teeth. She'd used Liz, but now it was time to set the record straight. When she wiped the steam off the mirror, she gasped at the big purple bruise on the side of her neck. "Damn it, Liz."

"What?" Liz stood behind her naked with her arms spread in an innocent gesture.

"You know what. Look at this ungodly thing on my neck. We're not in high school."

Liz came up behind her and pressed their bodies together, resting her chin on the opposite side of her neck. "Guess I got as carried away as you did. Would you like one for this side? I'd be happy to oblige."

Neela stepped out of her embrace. "Liz, you know I—"

Liz held up her hands. "Oh no, please don't give me the I've-slept-with-the-wrong-woman speech. Honey, we've been having sex for a while. Don't you think I know when you're not really making love to me?"

Neela shook her head. "I'm sorry. I didn't mean to hurt you."

"I'm not hurt. That was the best sex I've had in years. And unless I've completely lost my ability to read people, you like that cop a lot. If she was the inspiration behind last night, I want to shake her hand."

Neela felt the blush creep up her neck. "I wouldn't advise it." Jordan's default emotion was anger, and if she thought she had any claim on Neela, an encroachment on her turf could lead to unpleasantness.

"No shit. I'm the one she attacked the other night. And the look she gave me yesterday afternoon when we came home—she's got it bad. If my little beauty mark provides her with some incentive, all the better."

"This isn't some kind of game, Liz."

"Really? Does she know that? I've been checking up on Detective Jordan Bishop. She's got a string of conquests as long as—"

"I don't want to hear it."

Liz turned Neela so she could look in her eyes. "So, she's not the only one with a bad case. You're playing with hot coals, Neela, and this one bursts into flame with a slight breeze."

"And how do you think this little love bite will help?"

"Maybe she needs to think she's got competition."

"Liz, you're not athletes vying for a medal."

"No, we're lesbians vying for the same woman—that's much worse. The stakes are higher, the game more dangerous, and the reward immensely more satisfying."

"Get in the shower. I've got to cover this damn thing up and get to work." She popped Liz on the ass with her towel. "And thanks for last night, really. I needed it."

"Any time." As Liz stepped in the shower, she said, "I've been meaning to ask, would you be interested in going into business with me?"

Neela stopped fluffing her hair, not sure she'd heard right. "You don't have a business."

"I've been thinking about opening my own research lab. The grant we have can't last forever, and who knows what the university will do when it runs out. Actually, I've already made preliminary inquiries with some research facilities and have some promising leads. I really want to see where our work is heading. And I want out of the restraints of academia. The sooner we can be on our own, the better. Interested?"

"Definitely, but where would we get the money? I have to make a living, you know." Neela had never considered a full-time job as a researcher, even though she loved the work.

"A couple of the facilities I've approached are interested in backing us, plus I have some seed money. Stem-cell research is the next big thing, and if we get in early, we could write our own ticket, especially when we make a breakthrough…and we will. Just think about it."

"I will. Thanks, but you understand—"

Liz stuck her head out of the shower. "Yes, I understand it's not a personal arrangement. My offer is strictly business because you're a brilliant researcher. Just be ready. You know me. When I set my mind on something, I don't waste time."

"You're good for my ego. I should've married you a year ago."

"Too late. My dance card is extremely full." She grinned and popped back under the shower spray.

An hour later, she and Liz were on the way to their respective jobs. Neela hadn't acknowledged her protection detail across the street. She didn't need to see the expression on Jordan's face to know she was angry. She'd seen that look every time Jordan was aroused, like she was to blame for the pain and her inability to release it. The time had come for Jordan to step up if she was interested in, and capable of, anything beyond sex. Neela had drawn a line in the sand.

Rosemary was waiting in her office with an Excel spreadsheet clutched in one hand and a cup of coffee in the other. "What've you got, Rose?"

"Nothing as exciting as *that*." She pointed to Neela's neck and feigned shock, her tiny frame shaking with suppressed laughter.

"Do you miss anything?"

"Not when it's the size of a small state. Who's the proud artist—doctor or supercop?"

"Rose, put that stuff down and help me hide this thing. I don't need to be the center of gossip in my own office."

"Too late for that." Jordan's voice rumbled through her like a train barreling down the tracks, and Neela practically fell into her chair. She forced herself not to look up. The only saving grace was that Bex stood beside Jordan, hopefully gripping her short leash very tightly.

Rosemary did her best to arrange Neela's scarf to hide the hickey, while Neela tried to appear dignified and unaffected. Rose whispered, "Guess it wasn't her."

"Thank you, Rose. Leave those spreadsheets and I'll look them over." She nodded as Rosemary dodged an unmoving Jordan Bishop and closed the door behind her. "Detectives, good morning. Have a seat, please." To her surprise, her voice was calm and professional, unlike the turmoil swirling inside.

Jordan remained standing and Neela could feel her staring at her neck, while Bex took a seat and handed her two sheets of paper. "We have a couple of questions about your association with Doctor Ed Branson."

"Of course, anything to help." Neela put her glasses on to examine the documents. Jordan groaned but she didn't look up. The sound was far too provocative. "What does a list of my professional organizations have to do with Ed's assault or the threats?"

"That's what I'm hoping you can tell us. Have you ever been associated with the Guilford protest group?"

Neela took her time removing her glasses before she made eye contact with Bex. If she admitted an association with the group, her job could be over. These people were philosophically and very publicly opposed to Governor Lloyd's policies on almost every issue— education, voter regulation, abortion, and same-sex marriage, to name only the most hotly contested.

"As I'm sure you're aware, the Guilford Citizens for Equality group is committed to keeping many of Governor Lloyd's campaign initiatives from becoming legislation during this term."

"Spoken like a true politician," Jordan said, "but it doesn't answer the question."

Neela kept her focus on Bex. "Can we talk somewhere else, please?"

Bex seemed to grasp her dilemma. "Sure. Why don't we go for a walk?"

She followed Bex out the back door and toward the athletic field, acutely aware that Jordan was very close behind.

"Okay, you've got your private audience. Answer the question." Jordan either had no idea of the situation these answers could create or just didn't care.

"Ed Branson and I started the Guilford Citizens for Equality group in our medical-school days. We saw the need even then to give pro-choice proponents a voice in the political arena. The effects of bad legislation on women and children, especially in poor communities, were evident. The group was a very small version of the conglomerate of today. Ed was much more vocal and took a more active role in the organizational aspects. I supported him with advice and funding, particularly after I became involved in politics. We agreed I could do more good wielding a pen behind the scenes than waving a sign on the street. And my parents had risked too much for me to be blackballed from medicine before my career got started."

"And you didn't think it was important to mention this when we asked about your connection to Doctor Branson?" Jordan's tone was accusatory, but Neela chose to remain professional and not challenge her for once.

"It seemed unlikely that anyone would find that particular link and even less likely it would be connected to his assault and the threats against me."

"And you've been an investigator for how long exactly?" Jordan was trying to provoke her, and it had nothing to do with the case.

"Jordan, not helping," Bex said. "Neela, we're not sure if it is the connection, but we have to consider every possibility since the notes have been so vague. Abortion opponents usually want their actions to be noticed and are diligent about making them public. This feels different."

"You understand why I can't be publicly associated with this group. The governor is already looking for ways to fire me. This could be his ammunition."

Bex placed her hand on Neela's shoulder, and Jordan cleared her throat rather emphatically. She was like a pit bull guarding her master. "Can you get us a list of the current initiatives?"

"Sure, it's all online, but it's extensive."

"We just need a summary of the most controversial ones, and you'd know more about that. We'll work our way through them and look for anything suspicious."

"Bex, you're talking about political initiatives. They're all suspicious. And besides, the initiatives themselves aren't necessarily the problem. It's the unrelated riders politicians attach to innocent bills." Neela laughed when Bex scratched her head and nodded.

"Are we done here?" Jordan asked.

"I think so. Thanks for your help, Neela." Bex started back to the car but stopped when Jordan didn't follow. "Jordan, let's go."

"I need to talk to her." She nodded toward Neela.

"Maybe she doesn't want to talk to you." Bex looked at Neela, and she indicated that it was okay. "Fine. I'll just wait over there." She pointed to a picnic table a short distance away.

"I don't need a babysitter," Jordan said.

"No, you need a rabies shot." Bex laughed and took a seat with her back to them.

Neela wanted an apology for her abrupt dismissal yesterday, or at least an acknowledgment that it had been hurtful, but she didn't expect it. Jordan kicked at a clump of grass with the toe of her boot before finally speaking.

"Neela, look at me."

She took a deep breath to brace herself for Jordan's anger and verbal onslaught. When she looked up, she swallowed a gasp. Jordan's eyes were glistening and her face was a mask of anguish.

"Why did you sleep with her?" The rich timbre of her voice had become a raspy whisper.

All the professionalism Neela had vowed to maintain and the strong line she'd drawn in the sand vanished, and she spoke from her heart. "I needed comfort. I wasn't trying to hurt you. And as you've pointed out, we're not in a relationship."

"Are you in love with her?"

"Liz is a wonderful person. We're the same."

"The same as what?" Jordan stepped closer and Neela searched for the fire that fueled her, but the angry energy had shifted into the misery of defeat.

"Ordinary women who want a life with a woman we love."

"Neela, you'll never be ordinary." Jordan's gaze slid to her neck and her nostrils flared. "She damaged you, but I guess I did too. I'm sorry about last night, about everything. You're probably getting tired of my lame apologies, especially when I just turn around and do more stupid stuff. I won't bother you again." She walked toward the patrol car.

"Jordan—"

"Neela." Rose was running across the lawn frantically waving her arms. "Neela."

"Not now, Rose."

"But—"

"Rose, please. Jordan, wait." Rose was never upset, which meant something was seriously wrong. But this could be the most important conversation of her life, and if she let Jordan walk away, they might never have it. She had to figure this woman out, solar one minute and polar the next. "Jordan."

"*Neela.*" Rose was insistent. "I'm sorry, but the governor will be here in five minutes."

"What?" Neela watched Jordan get in her car, helpless to stop her. She walked back toward the building with Rose, leaving a piece of her heart behind. "How many ways can this man mess up my life?"

"I'm sorry. I didn't know what else to do. His assistant said the governor had to speak to you personally. It must be bad if he's coming to see you. He's never been here before. Wonder what it's about? Have you heard anything? You don't think he'll fire us, do you?"

"Take a breath, Rose. We'll deal with it when it happens." Like she should've done with Jordan two days ago. She'd glimpsed Jordan's vulnerability and should've cherished and nurtured it, not walked away from it. But she hadn't just walked away. She'd run into another woman's arms. No wonder Jordan had written her off.

"What do you want me to do, boss?" Rose was practically hyperventilating beside her.

"Check my cell phone and make sure I have a lot of battery time. If not, give me yours. I want everything this man says recorded."

"You've got it."

They'd barely gotten back to the office and set up the phone when Governor Lloyd walked in. He stood about six feet tall with straight brown hair that stuck out at odd angles. A man in his position ought to be able to afford a decent barber.

"Neela, how nice to see you again. I hope my visit hasn't interrupted your day too much."

Like you really care. "No imposition at all. I'm always glad to see you, sir, but I'm sure this isn't a social call. You're much too busy."

"That's one thing I've always admired about you, Neela. You're a smart girl, and you're exactly right." He pulled her desk chair into the middle of the room and sat down. The arrogant ass always had to be the center of attention. "As you know, these Guilford Citizens for

Equality protestors are smoking my ass every week about one damn thing or another. You and I haven't always been on the same page, but you've done a good job for me since I took office. I need to ask a big favor."

He had a lot of nerve asking anything of her after calling her a girl. Her immigrant parents had clawed their way up the socio-economic ladder to provide for her. She had fought every prejudice of her upbringing to become an esteemed scholar in her field, even securing public office and helping set policy that affected people's lives. Having Matt Lloyd call her a girl was disrespectful to her parents' struggles and her accomplishments. She bit back a sarcastic retort and waited for him to drop the bomb. "How can I help?"

"That's the spirit. I want you to attend a meeting for me day after tomorrow."

Neela felt a sick roiling in her stomach as she asked, "What kind of meeting?"

Lloyd grinned like he was presenting her with a gift. "These protestors want to ask a few questions about the abortion-related portion of the Family, Faith, and Freedom Protection Act bill. I figured you know more about it than anybody, since you used to advocate for that sort of thing and now you work for me."

She tried to swallow the foul taste in her throat. He wanted her to represent him and his degrading legislation to a group of people who opposed it—a group she actually supported. If she refused, he would probably fire her on the spot and her staff as well. If she agreed, she'd be going against everything she believed in and betraying a lot of people she'd worked with and respected in their fight against men like Matt Lloyd. And she had to consider Bina. What would happen to her health coverage and her expensive medicines if Neela lost her job? *When all else fails, go with the truth.*

"Governor, as you've already pointed out, we have some basic philosophical differences. Do you really think I'm the best person for this particular assignment?"

"Damn, girl, you're the only person for the job. If they see you're on board, it'll take some of the wind out of their sails."

He wanted an answer, and she needed to stall. "Could I have some time to review the bill before I commit? I obviously wasn't one of the authors." She knew the damn thing by heart, but it was all she could come up with on the fly.

"You've got two days to review the bill and get your presentation ready. I expect you to be there to support our administration. My assistant will email you the location details." He stood and shoved her chair back toward her desk with his foot. "Have a nice day, Neela."

When the governor's car pulled out of the lot, Rosemary was back in her office. "Jesus, we're in deep shit now, boss."

"Well, one of us certainly is."

"How can I help?"

"I can't ask you to get involved in this, Rose. If there's any way to save your job, we have to take it. I'll handle this myself."

Rosemary put her hands on her hips and stared at her over the rim of her reading glasses. "First, you're not asking me to get involved. I volunteered. And second, I wouldn't work here for one second without you. Now, what do we need to do?"

She hugged Rose and guided her toward the small corner table. "You really are my rock. Remember the Excel spreadsheet you gave me with Ed Branson's Guilford Citizens for Equality contacts on it?" Rose nodded. "We need to call every person on the list and have them spread the word. Round up a few volunteers to help us make the calls. We can meet at my house tonight. Then find a quiet community center, a place our redneck governor wouldn't be caught dead."

"And then what?"

"We'll hold one hell of a pep rally tomorrow."

"What the hell are you thinking?" Bex followed Jordan to the car, asking questions with every step. "What have you done? Did you just walk away from *that*? Are you crazy?"

Jordan got in the car and slammed the door. "She made her decision."

"Did she? Or did you make it for her?"

"She slept with that woman, that Liz. She's made her choice, and I can't blame her. I don't have anything to offer."

"You mean besides your pleasing personality and charm? Who can blame her for running in the opposite direction, but that's what you wanted all along, isn't it?"

"What are you talking about, Bex?"

"You treated her like just another fuck so she wouldn't care about you. That's one of your defenses. If she's not scared off by your recklessness, she certainly won't stick around when you treat her like crap. You keep everyone at arm's length, and if they try to get close, you push them away first. Keeps you from being left again, doesn't it?"

"Shut up."

"That won't work this time, partner. Neela is a once-in-a-lifetime woman. She cares about you in spite of yourself. Can't you see that?"

"Then why did she screw another woman?"

"She went through an ordeal the other night. You know what it's like to be scared out of your mind and have the adrenaline driving you crazy. It's got to go somewhere. Did she ask you to help her? She doesn't pull punches."

Jordan couldn't face Bex. She'd been too absorbed in her failings and her ego to consider Neela. Even after Neela had asked for help, Jordan had been unable to let go of her fear. She didn't deserve Neela. "Yeah, I freaked because I couldn't give her what she needed—the comfort, the intimacy. She deserves better than me."

"So you'll slink off and have your little pity party and let that redheaded vixen steal the girl? Really?"

Jordan's anger rose and she turned toward Bex, ready for a fight. "What the hell else can I do? Didn't you hear what I just said? I'm not good at intimacy. It wasn't exactly a priority in the orphanage."

"Nobody's naturally good at it. It's not in your genes at birth or something you get a diploma for in college. We all have to learn in our own time, in our own way. You're just a little slower than most." She nudged Jordan's shoulder. "It's not a death sentence that you're not a genius at it. You just need somebody like Neela to help you along. She's perfect."

"How do you know?"

"It's been obvious since the first day in her office. Her employees love her. I bet any one of them would fall on a sword for her. She's great with her mother and would do anything to protect her. She talks to

people and really listens. She shows she cares because she's not afraid
to put herself out there. I bet she's totally uninhibited in bed—"

"Hey."

Bex held up her hands in defense. "I'm just saying. She's a really
caring person."

"That's why she needs someone who deserves her."

"That's why you need to give her a chance. Did you ever think
maybe she needs someone exactly like you?"

"What, a total screwup?"

"Maybe you offer her something she's never had, something she's
missing."

"Bex, you're starting to worry me. You sound like Oprah or my
therapist."

"Okay, okay, enough of the therapy session." She turned her
attention to the monitor and waited until the governor left. "I'll check
with Rosemary and see if she has that list of initiatives printed out for us.
I've got a feeling we're on to something with this Branson connection."

"Make sure Neela's okay. She doesn't look too happy with the
governor."

"Why don't you come ask her yourself?"

"I'll wait here."

"Chicken."

"Just hurry so we can go home. I've had enough of this day."

When she got home, she took Blue for a run around the park.
She'd stopped by and collected Mrs. Cherry's terrier as well. She
finally figured out why Blue waited so patiently by the door every
night. He loved to run and herd other dogs and just be outdoors. And
she found mumbling to him under her breath about her day as she
ran quite cathartic. The way he nuzzled her hand and leaned against
her when they stopped seemed almost affectionate. He was a perfect
companion—never talked back, asked her questions she couldn't
answer, or demanded things she couldn't give. Maybe this dog-owning
business wasn't so bad.

CHAPTER TWELVE

When Jordan and Bex pulled alongside Harry and Phil the next morning to debrief, Neela's street and driveway looked like a used-car lot. "What the hell is going on?" Jordan asked as she handed over two fresh cups of coffee and hot doughnuts.

"Thanks, Bishop. We got no idea what's happening in there, but it's pretty calm," Phil said. "People have been coming and going all night like it's Grand Central Station."

Jordan felt a flash of anxiety. "Have you seen an ambulance? Maybe something happened to Bina. Did you check?"

"No ambulance or emergency personnel, just a few real lookers and a mini League of Nations. Everybody seemed seriously focused." They air-toasted their coffees and drove away.

"We need to find out what's up," Jordan said and walked toward the house with Bex close behind. She knocked, and a few seconds later, Liz Blackmon opened the door.

"Well, good morning, detectives." She lounged against the doorframe in a pair of silk pajamas. Jordan clenched her fists and tried to keep down her coffee. She nodded for Bex to handle the situation and stepped away but stayed within earshot.

"We were concerned, with all the cars, that maybe something had happened with Bina or Neela. Is everything all right, Ms. Blackmon?" Bex's tone was ingratiating, almost flirty. Jordan watched her rake her fingers through her hair and square her shoulders, both clear indications of attraction. Liz was exactly Bex's type—feminine, busty, and redheaded.

"Get on with it," Jordan mumbled. She wanted to be anywhere but standing outside Neela's house with Liz Blackmon inside.

"Come in, detectives. I'd love to, what do you call it, brief you." She stood aside, and Bex passed closer than necessary on her way in. "Detective Bishop?"

"I'll be in the car."

"Suit yourself, but Neela has whipped up a full breakfast spread— waffles, bacon, eggs, and fruit on the side. She's really quite the cook. Sure you won't join us?"

Jordan walked toward her vehicle without answering. *Us* indeed. Now her best friend had been lured into the vixen's web. She'd probably come out grinning, freshly fucked just like Neela. *Stop it.* Torturing herself with images of what was happening and what never could would only shred her and fuel her frustration and sadness.

She focused on the ducks paddling effortlessly on the lake across the street and on a couple of runners looping the water. When the car door opened and the seat beside her shifted, she assumed Bex was finally back. "Did you get what you wanted?"

"Not yet, but hope springs eternal."

Neela's sultry tone curled around her heart and squeezed until Jordan couldn't breathe. She was almost afraid to look, fearing she might be a mirage. When she turned, Neela was next to her wearing the same jogging tights and form-hugging top as the first time Jordan had stood on her doorstep. Neela offered her a foil-covered plate and utensils wrapped in a paper napkin.

"Bina insisted you taste my world-famous breakfast."

Jordan's throat was so tight she had difficulty speaking. "W— world famous, huh?"

"Well, at least in Mumbai and Greensboro. Bina thinks that is the world."

"How is she?" Jordan balanced the plate on the dash.

"I think you've bewitched her. She talks about you all the time now, which is a bit disconcerting considering how we left things."

"I need to get out of the way so you can move on with..." She nodded toward the house.

"Jordan, Liz and I are—"

"You don't have to explain. I'd prefer not to hear the details."

"There are no details. Liz and I are friends who occasionally—"

"Please, Neela." Jordan's blood churned as the picture of Liz making love to Neela, the way she hadn't been able to, surged through her like poison.

"What I'm trying to tell you is I'm not interested in Liz like that, and she's not the reason we're not together right now." Neela touched Jordan's arm and she flinched. "That is."

"I can't change…things that have happened to me."

"But you can change how you deal with them. Jordan, look at me."

How could she look at Neela when all she wanted was to take her again, mark her in some way that told the world she was off limits? But Neela didn't want to be taken. She wanted to be loved. "I'm not sure I *can* change. Just when I think I've got a handle on things…maybe I don't have it in me."

"It's in you, Jordan. I see it. Bina sees it. Won't you please—"

"Neela." Liz called from the front yard.

Neela closed her eyes and shook her head. "Really? When is it my turn?" She buried her face in her hands, and her heavy sigh ended in a choking sob. "Why is everything else suddenly so important? And why won't you at least try to meet me halfway?"

Jordan couldn't bear seeing her so distressed. She reached across the seat and pulled Neela to her. Her hair was still damp and she smelled of soap. The outfit she wore was so tight that Jordan felt her nipples harden against her chest. She struggled to focus on Neela's emotional needs and not her physical ones. "It'll be okay."

"Will it, really?" Neela relaxed against her and nuzzled the side of her neck. "Sometimes I get a little overwhelmed. I feel like everybody wants a piece of me—to solve their problem, to look after them, or… I'm sorry. I sound incredibly selfish. I owe many people for the life I have."

"You couldn't be selfish if you tried."

"Neela!" Liz yelled again. "Rose needs to talk to you on the phone. It's important."

"So is this," Neela said almost inaudibly, then called out the window to Liz, "Tell her I'll call her back."

Neela slowly moved out of Jordan's arms. "Guess I better take care of this new crisis. I hope you enjoy the breakfast."

As she reached for the door handle, Jordan hugged her again and whispered, "Can we talk later, please?"

"What? Twice in two days. That's got to be a record." She kissed Jordan's cheek. "I'd like that, but you need to know what I'm intending to do tonight." She gave Jordan a rundown of the governor's ultimatum, their all-night strategy session, and her plan for the evening.

"I don't like it. You'll be in the spotlight, and this crazy person might come after you."

"Then we'll be done with this mess and life can return to normal, whatever that is."

"Will you at least let us put some extra security in the area around the community center?" Jordan had an unsettling feeling that rallying the protesters was a very bad idea.

"I'd rather you didn't. I don't want the governor to hear about this from some politically motivated police officer. Besides, with all the volunteers here and the other folks joining tonight, he'd be crazy to try anything. I'll be fine. Don't worry. I trust you." She quickly kissed Jordan again and opened the door. "See you tonight."

Neela and Bina both thought she was brave. What did they see that she couldn't? She'd always considered herself a risk taker, but only for the thrill, not necessarily brave, and certainly not noble. Maybe it was time she earned the designation. After the rally tonight, she'd have a long and, she hoped, intimate talk with Neela—tell her everything—and see where it led. Anywhere was better than the gaping void of her life and the exhaustion of being constantly angry and on guard. She wanted more, but the concept was so foreign that she had no idea where or how to start toward a meaningful relationship.

Jordan and Bex spent the remainder of the day watching over Neela and wading through the ton of controversial initiatives before the legislature while Neela and Rose worked the phones, contacting as many people as possible for the rally. Jordan rubbed her eyes and glanced at the tablet that monitored Neela's office.

"She hasn't moved since the last time you checked five seconds ago. Do I have to finish reading all this crap by myself?"

Jordan ignored her. They'd hardly spoken on the drive to Raleigh as Jordan consumed the amazing breakfast Neela had brought her, but Bex wasn't the strong, silent type. Something was on her mind.

"Well?" Bex finally said.

"I'm trying to read."

"Let's just get it over with."

She gave Bex a casual glance and returned her attention to the pages spread across her lap. "Get what over with?"

"Elizabeth Blackmon, Liz, that's what, or should I say, who."

"What about her?" After Neela said she had no interest in Liz, Jordan could care less about anything else. "You like her."

"For somebody who doesn't do intimacy, you sure as hell notice every little thing."

"Observation is a skill best performed at a distance, or weren't you paying attention during that part of the surveillance class?" She was playing with Bex and it felt good. She hadn't been in a joking mood for months, and it had affected their work and personal relationship.

"Very funny, but yes, I like her, probably more than a little if I'm honest. The minute I saw her close up I was…just…"

"Completely and totally screwed." Jordan laughed and Bex rolled her eyes.

"Is that all you ever think about? And no, it's not even about that, though I imagine she'd be something else. Sorry. You probably don't need that visual."

"As long as it's the two of you, I'm fine."

"So…you'd be okay with me dating her?"

Bex was serious, but Jordan couldn't resist one final poke. "I'd be grateful if it keeps her out of Neela's bed."

"I hope to keep her out of anyone else's bed except mine, at least for a while."

"Seriously? You just met." Bex nodded. "You're a goner." She bumped fists with Bex. "I'd really like to see you happy. Maybe it's time for both of us to change our evil ways."

"Speak for yourself. I plan to be all kinds of evil with this woman and then—"

"La-la-la." Jordan put her hands over her ears. "TMI. Get back to work. We've got less than two hours before the rally, and I'd like to have some answers before then. I tried to get Milton to approve more security on the QT, but he wouldn't go for it."

"It'll be fine. We can stay late and double up with the guys until it's over, if you want."

"I was counting on it, partner, but I have a feeling your motives aren't entirely unselfish."

"If you must know, I'm having a drink with a certain redhead after the event."

Jordan had to smile. She hadn't seen Bex so excited about a woman in a while. "I can tell you'll be absolutely insufferable if you fall for Liz."

"I certainly hope so. It's the best feeling ever. Trust me."

Jordan thought about her feelings since she'd met Neela. They'd been all over the place, tainted by anger, frustration, and her uncontrollable impulses, but she'd also felt really alive for the first time in recent memory. She caught movement out of the corner of her eye and motioned to the tablet. "They're getting ready to leave. Have you told the guys where to meet us?"

"Relax. I've taken care of everything."

"I won't relax until this rally is over and Neela is home safely."

The line of cars following Jordan down the interstate was longer than a funeral procession. So much for covert surveillance. If the suspect was watching, Neela was painted as clearly as a sniper's target. Once they arrived at the community center, Jordan wouldn't have a chance of spotting him in the sea of diverse individuals. He'd be hidden in plain sight, and Neela would be vulnerable.

The Windsor Community Center's location on the corner of East Lee Street and Benbow Road made Jordan feel a bit more comfortable. The two busy streets guaranteed a steady flow of traffic and less chance anyone could approach unseen, since there was only one entrance and one exit. Harry and Phil were waiting at the back in the parking lot.

She tossed a bag through the open driver's window. "Don't say I never gave you anything."

Phil ripped the bag and practically salivated over the four Yum Yum hot dogs. "What did you bring Harry?" His partner grabbed for the bag and the ruckus was on.

"Can you boys fight over the food after we're in position?" Bex detailed the coverage plan she and Jordan had discussed. The guys would cover the south side of the interior, and she and Bex would cover the north. After the event, the guys would shift coverage to the exit onto Lee Street, and they'd watch the entrance off Gorrell Street into the parking lot. They agreed on the plan and moved into position.

Jordan stepped into the back of the gym and stood against the wall. Her heart rate kicked up and her palms felt damp. Three hundred people packed the gymnasium chanting and cheering like they were watching a sporting event. She wasn't surprised to see Neela onstage with several other people, apparently the organizers of the event. But when Neela moved to the microphone, Jordan suppressed an urge to shield her. She didn't like Neela being so exposed, so visible. She scanned the room for high perches a shooter might favor and, seeing none, tried to profile the roomful of attendees. Shifting positions constantly, she checked every corner. Hopeless. If the suspect was here, she'd never see him until it was too late. She was annoyed yet relieved that she hadn't spotted anything unusual all evening.

"Thank you all for being here, and we'll see you tomorrow evening when we meet with the governor's staff." One of the organizers motioned for Neela to rejoin him at the podium. "And to close our gathering tonight, I'd like to thank Doctor Neela Sahjani, the North Carolina State Health Director, for organizing this event. I understand she'd like to make a few remarks. Doctor Sahjani."

"Good evening." Neela's voice was like hot chocolate on a cold night, warming and soothing. She wore a muted red suit and white blouse that fit her snugly and made Jordan want to shred it with her teeth.

"I really appreciate all of you taking part in this event. This is an important, I'd even say critical, time for state government. Our leaders have lost their way. They're no longer in touch with the majority and seek to serve only the wealthy. I've tried to work within the system to improve our lives as citizens, but I'm finding that increasingly difficult. So, if I may, I'd like to read something that will be delivered to the governor tonight and appear in tomorrow's paper."

She pulled a sheet from a folder and put on her reading glasses. "This is addressed to Governor Matt Lloyd. 'Governor, as you know I served under your predecessor for many years in various positions and considered the work we did to be some of the most progressive in our state's history. Unfortunately, that trend has not extended to this administration. I have significant differences of opinion with many of the policies and administrative directions currently in the North Carolina Department of Health and Human Services. These differences make it impossible for me to be effective in my current role. I hereby tender my resignation effective immediately.'" The room grew eerily quiet as Neela's amplified voice faded but a few seconds later erupted in applause.

The moderator moved to Neela's side and said, "I hope this means we can count on your continued support in our efforts to be heard in Raleigh."

"Absolutely." Neela's response caused the hairs on the back of Jordan's neck to prickle. She wasn't sure if Neela's resignation would exacerbate or alleviate the threats against her, but either way, she'd just put herself firmly in the headlines. Jordan hoped, in the process, it had taken her out of the crosshairs.

As she waited to escort Neela back to the vehicle, Jordan marveled at what an amazing woman she was. She'd just quit her job for the sake of her beliefs and vowed to help others without a voice. Jordan hadn't been able to forego even her own pleasure or emotional comfort for Neela. How could she fit into a life of such depth and compassion with a woman who gave so much so freely?

"You all right?" Bex asked.

"Neela just quit her job. Either this assignment is over or she's just painted a big bull's-eye on her back."

The parking lot cleared quickly until only half a dozen vehicles remained. When Neela emerged, people surrounded her as they walked toward their cars. One by one the others reached their vehicles, said their good-byes, and drove away.

Jordan rested against the side of her patrol car while Neela hugged Rosemary. As Neela and Liz started toward her, a black SUV careened into the lot and barreled toward them. The passenger's window slid down, and the glint of metal barely registered before Jordan shouted. "Gun. Get down."

Jordan pushed off the side of her car and threw herself in front of Neela, shoving her backward. A sharp pain ripped the air from her lungs. *Neela.* She didn't have the breath to call out. She struggled to focus as she gathered her last ounce of strength and turned her head to where Neela should be. She was slumped against a car, blouse covered in blood. Oh God, no. She'd been too late.

CHAPTER THIRTEEN

Neela tried to open her eyes, but an insistent pounding zigzagged across her forehead. She squeezed them shut to block out the light seeping through her eyelids, but the pain surged again. The pungent smell of alcohol and antiseptic cleaners burned her nose, and her stomach churned.

"Neela, can you hear me, honey?"

Rosemary. Close and loud. "Shush. Headache. Have to vomit." She felt Rosemary's arms around her shoulders and the press of cold plastic against her neck.

"Go ahead. I've got you."

She hated throwing up and tried to breathe through it, but the hammering in her head was too powerful. Bile rose in her throat and sprayed out her nose and mouth. She retched again, the foggy memories more nauseating than the pain. When her heaves produced nothing more, she leaned back against the pillows. As Rosemary wiped her mouth and forehead with a cool cloth, she pieced together what had happened. Jordan had shielded her from a bullet.

"Jordan?" Though she was whispering her voice rumbled in her head.

"Neela, you need to rest."

"Rose, where's Jordan?" She had to see Rose's face. She squinted against the light and wished she hadn't. Rose's furrowed brow and the tight lines around her mouth foretold bad news. "Please tell me."

"I don't know. I haven't been here long. She was hurt, but I'm not sure how badly."

Neela swung her legs over the side of the bed and screamed as her right one banged against the metal railing. "Jesus." She held her hand to her mouth, breathing through the returning nausea. "What the hell?"

"You have a hairline fracture. I told them you'd behave if they used the soft cast."

"You were wrong. I have to get up. Find Jordan. Now."

"Neela, please. Relax. You also have a concussion." Rose's voice climbed a couple of octaves, a sign that she was reaching her stress max.

A burly nurse, all spit polish and authority, swung open the door and gave Neela a smile. "Are you the one making all the noise in here, Doctor Sahjani?"

Neela tried to recall the woman's name but her mind was fuzzy. "I need to find my friend, Jordan Bishop. She's a patient? How badly is she hurt?"

"Doctor, you know I can't tell you anything about another patient."

With Rose and the nurse's help, Neela eased back on the bed, resigned to being stonewalled at least until she could move without throwing up. Then another thought made her sick again. "Bina. Has anyone told her?"

"The police said they would notify her," Rose said.

Rose stroked her arm, the warmth comforting but unable to curb her rising panic. Jordan was injured, and she had no idea how badly. Bina would be frightened and unable to get to the hospital. "Oh my God, she'll be traumatized. She can't manage on her own."

"She won't have to."

Jordan's low-pitched tone echoed inside her, and some of the tension immediately eased. When she looked up, Bina stood in the doorway pale and shaky, leaning heavily against Jordan. The left side of Jordan's shirt was bloody, and a huge bandage was visible under her collar. She reached out, unsure which one of them to grab first.

Bina moved toward the bed. "You are so pale, Beta." Another step and she started to fall.

Jordan rushed to her side and eased her into the chair next to Neela. Jordan's face distorted into an agonized mask as fresh blood seeped through the bandage and soaked her shirt again. Neela fumbled for the call button, and the hefty nurse from earlier appeared.

She took one look at Jordan and started guiding her toward the door. "Your dressing has come loose. I told you leaving was not a good idea."

Jordan looked from Neela to Bina. "But I need to—"

"You need to come with me, now." The nurse wasn't letting up.

"Thank you, Jordan. Thank you so much." Neela tried to relay her appreciation with a final, lingering glance, but Jordan deserved so much more after what she'd done for her and Bina over the last twelve hours.

Bina pointed a misshapen finger as the door closed behind Jordan. "Our hero."

Neela smiled at her mother, took her hand, and collapsed into exhausted sleep.

Jordan gritted her teeth as the nurse stabbed a needle into the gunshot wound on her shoulder. She wouldn't complain. She deserved to hurt a little. If she'd moved just a second faster, Neela wouldn't be in the hospital with a concussion and fractured leg, and Bina wouldn't be upset and worried. Some hero she was. She looked at the flickering light above her bed, worrying about Neela, while the doctor probed and cleansed her injury.

When she'd come to on the pavement, Neela was unconscious beside her with a huge patch of blood on her chest. She'd panicked, certain Neela had been shot. All she remembered from that point was struggling to get free and help Neela. She didn't find out she was the one who'd been shot until she woke up in the hospital groggy from drugs. The bullet had missed anything vital, passing cleanly through the flesh above her collarbone. The doctor said she'd been lucky. She didn't think so. Lucky would've avoided the whole incident and caught the suspect before shots were fired.

As the doctor finished his examination and left, Sergeant Milton's raspy voice sounded at the end of the hall, coughing and hacking, getting louder as he approached. Now the real pain would begin—second-guessing and analyzing the actions she'd already begun to dissect.

"Where are you, Bishop?" Milton jerked the curtain around the exam table back and blatantly stared at her partially covered breasts. When his eyes finally wandered to her injury, he said, "Just a flesh wound." He rolled a stool to the foot of the bed and took out a notepad. "I need details."

"You need to get the hell out of my exam area," the nurse said. "This woman has been shot and needs rest. She has a head injury that requires overnight observation. As a medical professional, I can't in good conscience allow her to be interrogated until I'm sure she's in control of all her faculties."

Jordan almost grinned. So Ms. Grumpy Britches has some redeeming qualities after all. When she looked up, the nurse winked.

Milton snapped the notepad shut and huffed out of the room.

"Thanks for that."

"Don't thank me. I don't like pencil pushers or perverts who leer at women's breasts. And besides, you saved Doctor Sahjani's life and that's good enough for me. You deserve a medal, not a grilling."

"Thanks again…" She searched for a nametag.

"Heather." She finished cleaning the area around Jordan's wound and applied a bandage. "Do you need something for pain?"

"I'd rather not, but thanks. Was it true what you said about a head injury? I don't feel like I hit my head."

"No, but you must've when you hit the pavement." She winked again. "Let's keep that tidbit to ourselves, shall we? By the way, there's another officer out there. Said she was a friend, Bex or something like that. She was here earlier."

"Yeah, if you don't mind, could I see her when you're finished?"

"Sure, hon. Relax and don't leave this area until I bring your discharge papers. Promise?"

"Promise." She pulled her shirt on as someone eased back the curtain to her cubicle.

Bex peered through the crack. "Can we come in?"

"Depends on who we is." Bex drew the curtain aside a bit more and Jordan saw Liz beside her. "Sure."

"How you feeling?" Liz's voice sounded sincere and a bit awestruck. "That was an amazing piece of footwork out there, detective."

"Just not quite good enough. If I'd been a little quicker—"

"Are you fucking kidding me right now? You took a bullet for Neela. What more do you want?" Liz stared at her and shook her head.

"For her not to be hurt at all." As Jordan spoke, the truth of her words registered. When had she shifted from viewing Neela as an assignment and a sex buddy to someone she really cared about protecting? As she spoke again, she had to force herself not to break down. "I don't ever want her to be in pain again."

Bex cleared her throat and wiped her eyes with the back of her hand. "Well, she'll be okay. I hope we didn't hurt you out there."

"What do you mean?"

"Phil and I had to restrain you when the ambulance attendants loaded Neela. You were fighting us like a madwoman, trying to get to her. You're freaking strong, Bishop."

"That's all a bit hazy."

"You were losing a lot of blood. I'm surprised you could still stand."

"Thanks, I guess. And I appreciate you going with me to get Bina. I couldn't have gotten her here without your help."

"It's okay. We're partners. When are they springing you?"

"Soon, I hope, but don't tell Milton. He wants a statement, but my nurse convinced him I'm in no condition to give one, something about a concussion."

"Is there someone to look after you when you leave?" Liz asked.

"No, but I'll be fine at my apartment."

"You mean that vacant place that never has any food?" Bex asked.

"That doesn't sound like a very good plan to me." The curtain parted and Neela rolled a wheelchair to the side of the bed, with Bina following closely behind. "You're coming home with us. We have matching concussions. We'll have to look after each other."

"What are you doing out of bed?" Jordan asked. "You should be resting and staying off your leg."

Neela pointed at the contraption beneath her. "I'm in a wheelchair, Jordan."

"Bina, can't you control your daughter?"

"She has a strong will, like you. But she is right. You must come home with us. We take care of each other."

Jordan's throat tightened as she fought back tears. "I can't."

Bina waved her hands in the air. "No more talk about it. You are coming with us."

Bex grinned and took hold of Liz's hand. Jordan mouthed, *Shut up.* "We have things to talk about, like leads on the shooter and those documents we were reviewing yesterday."

"Milton's got another team working the shooting, but we can talk about the rest tomorrow," Bex said. "In case you hadn't noticed, we've spent over eighteen hours here, and we're off today. I'm taking advantage of my free time since you don't need me." She gave Liz a puppy-love look, and Jordan couldn't help but smile.

She motioned for Bex to come closer and whispered, "Would you mind going by the apartment and checking on Blue? He's got a doggie door, so just make sure he's got food and water until I get home."

Bex started to punch her shoulder but drew back just in time. "Sure, you old softie."

Two hours later, Bex and Liz dropped Jordan, Neela, and Bina off at the Sahjani home in Hamilton Lakes. Jordan started toward the house, trepidation building. Maybe this wasn't such a good idea. She'd only been in Neela's home a couple of times and not for entirely noble purposes. Now she was a houseguest until Bina was convinced she was well enough to function on her own. Perhaps Bina needed her help because Neela was injured but was too proud to ask. As she assisted her precious charges up the sidewalk, Jordan decided she was good with that.

She unlocked the front door and helped Bina and then Neela inside. They looked like mismatched bookends, each hobbling like a wobbly toy into the large family room. Bina settled into her favorite recliner and raised the leg rest. Jordan guided Neela to the sofa and pulled an ottoman under her legs. "Are you comfortable?"

Neela held onto her hand when she tried to pull away. "It's perfect, but you're not here to wait on us. You're injured too."

"I'm fine, really."

Neela placed a hand on her stomach and her skin paled. "Would you mind passing me that trashcan over there. All the jostling on the ride home has my stomach acting up again."

"Could it possibly be the concussion, Doctor Sahjani?"

Bina chuckled. "Clever girl."

Jordan placed the trashcan on the floor beside Neela and looked around the room. She suddenly felt out of place. The first time she'd been here, she'd practically forced herself on Neela over the back of this sofa. The second time, Neela had tried to seduce her against the same piece of furniture. Now Neela lounged across the rich leather helpless and needy, and Jordan felt something entirely different, more understated. She shook her head and refocused. "Can I get either of you anything?"

"Masala chai tea," Bina said, "and my medicine. Then I will need a long nap."

To anyone else, Bina's requests might have sounded demanding or even presumptuous, but to Jordan they felt comforting and inclusive. She had a purpose for being here, and these two women trusted her to care for them. But could she? She couldn't even care for a dog properly. Bex always said her nurturing skills wouldn't register on a meter. But she owed these women. She'd failed them twice and wasn't letting that happen again.

"How about you, Neela? Coffee? Water?"

"Not right now, but thank you."

Jordan boiled Bina's tea in milk just the way she liked it and poured it into her sippy cup, placed the cup and her array of medicines on a serving tray, and balanced it in her right hand as she walked into the den. "Here you go."

Bina's eyes blinked open and she sighed. "Maybe just my medicine. I am suddenly very tired. Could you help me to my room, please?"

Jordan opened the twist bottles and distributed the pills into Bina's outstretched hand and then waited for her to wash them down. A few minutes later, Bina was settled in her large master suite one room away from Neela's and sound asleep. Jordan tiptoed back to the family room.

"You're really good with her. She doesn't let many people see her frailty, and I don't trust just anyone with her care. I don't know how to thank you for what you've done for us. You saved my life last night."

Jordan didn't want to have this conversation. She kept reliving the things she hadn't done that led to Neela's injury. She looked around the room, shifting her weight from side to side.

"Oh my God, you're feeling guilty about this, aren't you?"

She motioned to Neela's leg and the large bump on her forehead. "You could've been killed. This lunatic invaded your home and then tried to shoot you while I've been…" She started to say unable to find a single lead, but it was worse than that. Time for some real honesty. She raised her eyes to Neela's. "While I've been playing games and fucking you at every opportunity. How pathetic is that? I've been risking your life while pretending to be a detective and a protection officer."

Neela reached out to her, but Jordan backed away. The only people who had ever reached for her were the ones who meant her harm. Her response was involuntary, but the feeling wasn't the same. Part of her wanted, no, needed, to be touched. Neela tried again. "If you don't come here, I'll get up on this fractured leg and come get you. I'm serious."

Was Neela actually trying to comfort her when she was the one who'd messed up? Jordan's heart swelled, and the look in Neela's eyes made her ache for her in a way that exceeded anything sexual. She stepped to the side of the sofa, and when Neela pulled her down beside her, she didn't resist.

Neela took Jordan's face in her hands and forced her to meet her gaze. "You, my wonderfully brave and tormented hero, are the only reason I'm alive right now. You sacrificed yourself for another human being. You couldn't have been any less selfish."

"But I failed…again." Jordan felt the tears welling and looked away.

"What do you mean again?" Jordan shook her head. "Tell me, darling."

"I'm here to help you and Bina, not to burden you with my crap."

Neela swung her good leg around Jordan and pulled her back between her legs. "That's the thing about caring for someone. It goes both ways."

With her back pressed against Neela's chest, Jordan felt her steady heartbeat and anchored herself in the constancy of it. She'd never told anyone about this part of her life, but she'd never imagined wanting to. "I had a friend, Amy White. She was only a year younger but very petite and frail. The bigger kids picked on her and I…" She swallowed hard.

"You looked after her."

"I tried, but one night they got to her while I was in the hospital with pneumonia. Three of them...raped her and beat her almost to death."

"Oh my God, Jordan." Neela's arms tightened around her, and she held on.

"She got pregnant and...the abortion...went wrong. I never saw her again. She...died." Jordan couldn't stop the tears as she finally allowed herself to cry for Amy. She'd held back all these years, afraid of relinquishing the feelings that held her together. The abyss of grief shrank a little as her tears washed some of the hurt away.

Neela's chest heaved against her back as she sobbed with her. "I'm so sorry, Jordan. So very, very sorry."

"I failed both of you. The only difference is you're not—"

"And that's because of you. You didn't fail either of us. You couldn't have fought for Amy. You were just a child, with pneumonia. And you sacrificed yourself completely for me last night. Failure isn't in your makeup. You're one of the bravest people I've ever known."

"I don't feel brave. I feel like a coward who hides behind the past and uses sex to get by."

"Not many people would sacrifice themselves for somebody else, even if it is their job. And it took courage to tell me about Amy. I know it wasn't easy, but now I understand you a little better and your aversion to professionals who are supposed to protect others." She kissed the side of Jordan's neck. "I'm sorry about your friend."

"Benjamin Brownworth was a hack abortion doctor and self-proclaimed counselor. He was responsible for a couple of deaths and the sterilization of several young women, not to mention his other vile acts. By the time I could do anything about it as a cop, he was dead."

"And you're still fighting to help people. I'd say that makes you courageous and noble."

Jordan pressed the back of Neela's hands to her wet cheeks and absorbed their warmth as more tears fell. "Amy accepted me immediately, like she saw something no one else did. I feel like that with Bina."

"It's scary how wise she is sometimes. She sees the good in everyone, and she wouldn't be so fond of you otherwise. You don't seem to see what's obvious to us."

Jordan tried to believe Neela's words and let them seep into the wounded places in her soul. She hadn't cried in years, and the release was like opening a pressure valve on a system ready to explode. For the first time, she felt truly cared for and supported. She had no idea how long they cried and rocked in each other's arms, but when she opened her eyes again, the mantel clock read almost two in the morning.

"Neela. Neela, wake up. You need to go to bed."

Neela tightened her arms around Jordan. "Only if you come with me."

"Let's go." She had no intention of sleeping with Neela, but she had to persuade her to lie down and rest. She helped Neela to her room and waited while she brushed her teeth and settled under the covers.

"Come here." Neela motioned for Jordan to join her in the king-sized bed.

"I'm not getting in."

"Why? Afraid I'll attack you? Because if you are, I think you're safe, for the moment. Our injuries are on opposite sides but not conducive to romping just yet. Come on. I just want to be close to you tonight."

Jordan hungered for Neela yet craved the comfort of holding her as she'd done earlier. Perhaps that was what intimacy was all about, sharing without expecting anything in return, giving without being asked, and caring when the outcome was uncertain. She didn't deserve Neela's sex or her intimacy, not yet. She'd taken too much and given too little in return. And she'd almost lost her. The thought was unfathomable.

"I can't. Not tonight. But I will sit with you until you fall asleep." She pulled a chair alongside the bed and took Neela's hand. "Sleep."

"Tell me a story."

"About what?" All Jordan's tales were bad ones, nothing conducive to sleep.

Neela skimmed her finger over Jordan's top lip. "Tell me how you got the scar."

She breathed a sigh of relief. That one wasn't too bad. "I was twelve and totally into anything remotely daring. I fell in love with motocross. I guess you could say it was my first mistress—exciting, demanding, challenging—and did it ever turn me on."

"So you really have always been a speed demon."

"Guess so. At first I just enjoyed the rush, but then I became good at it and made a little money." She didn't tell Neela how the orphanage had prostituted her skills and stolen her money. "This one race, I was whipping over the course, leading the pack. The guy in second nudged my back wheel with his front when we were going around a curve and sent me spinning. I lost control and presto. Instant beauty mark."

"It sure is, beautiful, like everything about you. Watching you tell that story, I could almost see the innocent little kid with so much enthusiasm." Her voice was soft and dreamy.

Jordan's leg shook in a nervous rhythm. She'd never been an innocent kid, and the enthusiasm Neela imagined was nothing more than fear, a desperate attempt at self-preservation, and a young girl dreaming of escape.

Neela leaned over and kissed her lightly before snuggling Jordan's hand between her breasts like a pillow. "Good night, my brave hero, and thanks for the story." She was asleep a few seconds later.

CHAPTER FOURTEEN

Neela rolled over and felt a heavy thump against her left leg, followed by a dull throbbing in her right. Hairline fracture. Jordan was no longer beside her bed or even in the room. She pulled on her robe, tightened the soft cast on her leg, and started down the hall to check on Bina. She didn't get far.

Outside the bedroom between her suite and Bina's, Jordan sat propped against the closed door wrapped in the worn blanket from the sofa. A couple of decorative pillows supported her left arm, and under her right leg, Neela saw the butt of her service weapon. From her position, she had a direct line of sight down the hallway to the front door and easy access to the back of the house. Tears filled her eyes as she stared at Jordan's lovely face so unguarded in sleep juxtaposed with the weapon of battle.

"Like the sun and the moon," Bina whispered. She stood beside Neela, apparently seeing the same thing in Jordan's face that she had. "We must help her sun burn away the darkness."

She hugged Bina to her side. "I'm not sure she'll let us. She's been deeply hurt."

"We must try, Beta."

Neela thought about the few minutes of intimacy she'd shared with Jordan the evening before. Until now the only indication of Jordan's passion was her ravenous hunger for sex and uncontrollable anger. Last night, she'd seen emotions she'd begun to doubt existed in her tormented bodyguard. Jordan had dropped her defenses, shared the loss of her friend, and allowed herself to be comforted as she cried—

something Neela bet didn't happen very often. The only downside was now she wanted more.

Jordan's left arm dropped off the stack of pillows and she jerked. She jumped to her feet and grabbed her weapon at the same time, the serenity of a few seconds ago replaced by an almost primal look of protectiveness. "What's wrong?" She moved between them and the door. "Are you all right?"

Neela raised her hands to signal surrender. "We're fine, just getting up. We didn't mean to disturb you." She nodded toward the gun Jordan held raised shoulder height.

"Oh, sorry." She tucked the weapon in the back of her jeans. "How are you both?"

"Ready for morning tea," Bina said, taking Jordan's arm and leading her into the kitchen. "Why did you sleep on the floor? Did my daughter not offer you a bed?"

A tinge of pink colored Jordan's cheeks, and Neela said, "Mama, don't start."

"Jordan is our guest. She should not sleep in the hall like a guard dog."

"Oh, God. I have to go. I forgot." She kissed Neela and Bina on the cheek and started toward the door."

"Stop." Bina's voice was so authoritative even Neela turned from the coffee-making to look. "Where do you think you are going before breakfast? Nobody leaves my house without coffee or tea, quality time, and food, in that order."

Jordan stood in the doorway looking back and forth between her and Bina. "But, I have…a dog. I need to check on him."

Bina's face lit up like an excited kid's. "A dog? What kind? What color? How long have you had him? Where did you get him? May I see?"

Neela started laughing. "Can you tell my mother is fond of dogs? She's been bugging me for years to get one, but I'm not home enough to help care for him. Guess that won't be an issue now." Then she remembered in all the excitement she'd forgotten to tell Bina she'd quit her job. She wasn't sure how she'd take it. "Why don't you have Bex bring him when she drops off your clean clothes? He can stay with us, as long as you're here. You wouldn't have to worry about going back and forth to check on him, and he wouldn't be alone."

"And we have a big backyard with a fence. He could run and play all day," Bina said.

Neela watched a series of emotions play across Jordan's face—surprise, disbelief, confusion, and finally a hint of happiness as the corners of her mouth curled up.

"Are you sure? I feel like I should go home. You don't really need me."

"But we do." Neela feigned falling over and grabbed a chair, and Bina exaggerated trying to pick up a fork and let it drop. "See, we're hopeless." She pointed to Bina. "And would you deny this nice lady the pleasure of playing with your dog?" Bina posed a very sad face.

Jordan held up her hands. "Okay, but you're both horrible actors." She called Bex while Neela finished the coffee and then joined them around the small table. "So what is quality time?"

Neela nodded for Bina to explain. "When my husband was alive our family gathered at this table every morning. No papers, books, television, radio, or phones allowed, just us. And we talked or just sat quietly. It was a special time reserved for family. If the world fell apart afterward, at least we had spent quality time together. After my husband died, Neela and I continued the tradition. As long as you are a guest in our home, we would like you to join us, if you want."

Neela saw Jordan swallow hard before she responded. "I'd love that. Thank you."

As Bina told stories about her childhood and teen years in Mumbai, Neela watched Jordan's reactions. She absorbed the sagas like a child hearing fairy tales for the first time. Her cobalt eyes sparkled, her eyebrows rose in astonishment, and her gorgeous lips curved into a smile, often. This softer, more attentive side of Jordan was one she'd seldom seen, but it suited her. She could've hugged Bina for temporarily lifting the cloud that seemed such a permanent fixture in Jordan's life.

"Did you ever do anything so crazy as a teenager?"

A veil of sadness dropped across Jordan's features. She shifted uncomfortably and looked toward the small bathroom at the front of the house. "No, not really. I should check this bandage. Excuse me." She put her cup in the sink. "Thank you for my first quality time."

When she was out of earshot, Bina said, "The key is in her childhood. Twice she has paled at the mention of family. Go to her, Beta."

Neela wasn't sure Jordan would welcome her intrusion, but she couldn't stay away. She wanted to be near her, whatever her mood or need. The desire was like a calling. She tapped on the bathroom door, waited, and tried again. "Jordan, let me help you."

When Jordan opened the door, her eyes were red and watery. "This hurts more than I thought."

"Let me." Jordan's polo was half on and half off. She shrugged, and Neela grabbed the hem and pulled it gently down her injured arm, dropping it on the floor. With her fingernails, she eased the taped edges of the bandage off and gasped when she saw the extent of Jordan's injury. Her entire shoulder and the skin leading down to her breast were one ugly purple patch of bruising. The bullet hole and tearing along her flesh were ragged and raw. Suddenly all her years of medical training seemed inadequate. She wanted to heal the mangled flesh marring Jordan's body and leave no trace of it, but her medicine wasn't that strong.

"I—I had no idea how bad this was." The room suddenly felt incredibly small, and Jordan was incredibly close, gorgeous, and injured. She felt light-headed and slumped onto the side of the bathtub.

"Neela! Are you all right?"

She nodded and pressed her head between her knees. The image of Jordan's scarred body, the anger at the suspect, and the need to heal and comfort her were overwhelming. "Just a little dizzy. Maybe my concussion is acting up again." A lie, but Jordan didn't need to deal with her emotions right now. "Sorry. I'm okay now. Let me clean and re-dress that for you. Sit." She pointed to the toilet and lowered the lid.

"I can do it, really. It might be better if I…if you didn't…"

"Jordan, darling, I have to touch you. It's a medical necessity at this point." She wanted to tell Jordan it was just as excruciating to touch her and not be able to have her as it was for Jordan to be touched and have to restrain herself. She wanted to ask her if she had any idea how much she wanted her right now, if she knew how much she'd love to help fight her demons. She wanted so many things with Jordan, but now wasn't the right time.

She pulled the first-aid kit from the cabinet and took out the supplies she'd need to clean and dress Jordan's wound. "Come here." She pulled Jordan to the edge of the seat and gently cleaned from the center of the wound outward. Her terry-cloth robe suddenly felt too warm with Jordan's legs tightening on either side of hers. "Am I hurting you?"

When she looked up, Jordan's gaze was fixed on the front of her slightly gaping robe. Her skin burned under Jordan's stare and her hands trembled as she taped the bandage over her wound. As she pressed the last piece of tape in place, Neela traced the bruising until it dipped into Jordan's sports bra. Jordan's skin dimpled beneath her fingers and her breath hitched.

"Neela, please."

"Please what? Stop? Don't stop? Please touch me, let me touch you?"

"I want you so much—"

Neela pressed her fingers to Jordan's lips and then kissed her before opening the bathroom door. "That's all I need to know right now." Between her leg fracture and the pain of wanting Jordan so badly, Neela could barely walk. She lumbered back to the kitchen and started making breakfast.

Jordan clung to the sink as desire rippled through her, eclipsing the ache in her shoulder. She'd barely been able to contain her urges with Neela so close, smelling of sleep and sex. She'd brazenly ogled Neela's olive breasts and dark nipples, imagining her lips sucking and pulling them to puckered points of pleasure. And when Neela had pushed her legs between Jordan's, she'd had to concentrate on the pain of her wound to distract her from Neela's robe slipping farther up her thigh. But she hadn't even touched Neela.

She stared in the mirror and tried to understand what was happening to her. A few days ago, she would've fucked Neela against the door, in the tub, or even on the toilet seat with her mother and a roomful of people right outside, but today had been different. Her hunger had been as strong, if not more so, but she'd controlled it somehow—not because she had to, but because she'd wanted to. Why?

She'd told Neela about Amy and finally released some of her grief. She'd even allowed Neela to hold her and hadn't freaked out, but one night of cuddling and a good cry couldn't reshape a lifetime of subjugation and defiance. What had shifted inside her? Had the injury simply dulled her normal defenses?

She splashed cold water on her face until her temperature leveled and she felt in control enough to be in the same room with Neela and her mother.

Bina's face flashed through her mind, filled with animation and excitement as she told the stories of her childhood. Jordan imagined herself in those scenarios, feeling the innocence of youth, the joy of play, and the certainty of safety and love. But when Bina had asked about her childhood, she'd retreated. She couldn't splatter the ugliness of her past through a place that housed so much love. She'd chosen not to share her secrets, but this time she felt a dusting of regret.

She looked at her reflection again. She'd been wrong about her early dislike of Neela. That she'd considered Neela part of the conservative government, an insensitive health-care professional, and even a cheating spouse hadn't been the problem at all. It was this—this love and compassion she wore so comfortably, so caring and concerned about everyone and everything around her. No matter how hard she tried, Jordan would never deserve a woman like Neela Sahjani.

Drying her face and hands, Jordan looked at her watch and prayed Bex would arrive soon with fresh clothes. She considered hiding out in the bathroom until she arrived, but chided herself for being such a coward and rejoined Neela and Bina in the kitchen.

"Bex and Liz will be here in five minutes," Neela said as she flipped a waffle with each hand. "I'm making breakfast for everyone."

"Shouldn't you be off your leg?"

"I am." She raised her robe to reveal a small stool tucked under her knee. "Where there's a will, there's a way." She gave Jordan an evil grin. "Unless you want to take over."

Jordan backed away. "I'm gifted in many areas, but cooking is not one of them."

A few minutes later Bex's signature double-tap sounded at the front door. "I'll get it." Bex and Liz walked in hand in hand, and Jordan rolled her eyes while reaching for her overnight bag. She gave Blue a quick pat and ruffled his white fur. "I'll be back in a few. I need these clothes badly. Would you mind introducing Blue to everyone and getting him settled in the backyard?"

"Sure, and I'll share the headlines with everybody over coffee." She waved the morning paper as they headed down the hallway. "Neela's public resignation was eclipsed only slightly by the shooting. Not sure it's appropriate breakfast reading though."

Jordan had a quick shower and slid into clean underwear, bra, and another pair of black jeans and a T-shirt with RUN on the front. When she rejoined the others in the kitchen, Neela was just putting the food on the table.

Liz pointed to Jordan's T-shirt. "Exercise statement?"

"Warning."

Liz raised her hands and wiggled her fingers. "Wooh, I'm scared."

They gathered around the table and started reaching for food. "Aren't we waiting for Bina?" Jordan asked.

Neela pointed in the direction of her bedroom. "She's taking a nap. She had a quick bite while I was cooking and then played with Blue for a few minutes. You've ruined any chance I have of ever living without a dog again."

"Did you tell her about your job?" Liz asked as she forked a waffle.

Neela nodded. "I think she's actually happy I quit, aside from the fact I won't have a steady income anymore and no insurance."

"Does that mean you'll be my partner?" Liz sliced off a chunk of ham and was about to bite down when she looked up.

Heat started low in Jordan's gut and roared up as she stared at Liz across the table. Images of her and Neela coming out of the house after their night together sliced through her. Jealousy gouged her insides. She envied the closeness Liz and Rose shared with Neela.

"No—no, detective." Liz sputtered.

"Not like that, Jordan," Bex said.

Neela rubbed Jordan's arm and settled her cool hand on the back of her neck. "Liz is talking about a business partnership, about opening a lab together."

Jordan took a long drink of water before trusting herself to speak calmly. "How will that help your income and insurance situation?"

Liz explained. "My investors already have an established company. They'd finance our work as an umbrella under their business. That way, we get salaries and insurance but still maintain autonomy over our stem-cell research."

Jordan gave Liz credit. It sounded like she knew her stuff and was serious about the work, but she still wasn't sure how she felt about her and Neela working together every day, given their history. "Sounds like a cushy deal for you, but what do the investors get out of it?"

"A percentage of the proceeds from our research, and that will be significant." Liz popped a piece of toast into her mouth. "Pretty sweet idea, don't you think, detective?"

Jordan leaned toward Liz, her stare never wavering. "I have two things to say. First, don't mess with Neela, in any way…unless she wants you to. And second, if you're dating my best friend, I'd prefer you call me Jordan." A collective sigh eased the tension around the table, and Liz nodded.

Bex's grin was one Jordan had seen before, relief mixed with mischief. She already had her and Neela setting up house. "Does this mean you and Neela are together now?"

"No, Bex. It doesn't." Neela's voice was calm and matter-of-fact, her smile warm and open. "It means Jordan cares about my welfare and my mother's. And to answer your question, Liz, yes. I'll be your *business* partner. Get the ball rolling. I need to work."

Jordan worried briefly that she might've overstepped, but Neela hadn't objected when she'd cautioned Liz. Still something felt off. Had it bothered her when Neela had declared they weren't together? What did "together" mean anyway? She'd never understood how women met, had sex, and then settled down so quickly. Obviously, her injury and blood loss were affecting her emotions and her ability to think. "Bex, did you bring the case notes or have you been too busy?"

"Can I finish my breakfast first? This is fantastic." Bex shoveled more food into her mouth and winked at Jordan.

"Fine, but soon. I think I might've found—" Jordan's cell phone vibrated in her pocket and she fished it out. "Hello?"

"Milton, here. Get your ass to my office ASAP to debrief on this clusterfuck. Internal Affairs and the CAP detectives need a statement."

"Yes, sir, on my way." She hung up and looked at the small group around the table. She didn't want to leave Neela alone, even with Bex nearby. Her friend was too fixated on her new lust buddy to remain focused on work.

"Go," Bex said. "I know what you're thinking, and I'll take care of Neela. Besides, we need to go in shifts. I'm sure I'll be called in after you."

Jordan didn't want to verbalize her next thought, but Neela needed to know what to expect. "Since you've resigned, your protection detail may be over. You're not a high-profile state employee anymore, and even with the threats against your life, the department might not be willing to continue the expense of full-time coverage."

Neela placed her hand on Jordan's forearm. "Don't worry. I'll be fine. Go. Do what you have to…and come back to me."

Jordan couldn't move for several seconds. She'd never had a place where she felt the possibility of a real future and a home. But Neela and Bina represented the essence of home. And Neela *wanted* her to come back—to her. She leaned forward to kiss Neela but drew back when she remembered Bex and Liz.

"Go on, kiss her," Liz urged her.

"Yeah, you big softie," Bex said again.

Neela just grinned, obviously waiting for her to decide if she wanted to make that statement in front of their friends.

She pulled Neela against her and kissed her until everything else disappeared. She dissolved into the heat and softness of her lips, the teasing of her tongue, and the hot press of her body. When she finally pulled away, she was wet. "I'll…soon…see. Mean…see…soon."

Neela kissed her again and nudged her toward the door with promises of more. "Hurry."

She closed the door and Jordan stood on the stoop, never wanting to be away from her or this place, too comfortable with both. Her resolution to leave Neela alone, only a short while ago, had vanished. Shaking her head, she ran toward her car and a few minutes later walked into Sergeant Milton's office.

"The chief is crawling my ass. How did you manage to let this woman get injured?"

"I asked for more protection. I wasn't comfortable with the large gathering and only four officers."

Milton glowered at her. "It's not your job to second-guess my decisions, only to protect one little woman."

Jordan flashed to the image of Neela on the ground, blood covering her chest and the uncertainty of whether she was dead or alive. "In case you didn't notice, I took a bullet for that woman. I'm not sure what else you'd expect me to do under the circumstances."

Milton shuffled papers on his desk but didn't look up. "Get out. The detectives are waiting to take your statement."

She didn't need to be told twice. "What about the detail?"

He shook his head and glared at her like she was stupid. "As you so aptly put it, you took a bullet for her. If we called off the assignment now, we'd be crucified in the press if something worse happened to her. We've established an expected standard of care, so we're stuck with the detail for the time being, but obviously you're no longer on it."

Jordan released her grip on the doorknob. "What do you mean?"

"Look at yourself. You're shot and your arm is in a sling. How can you protect anybody like that, even yourself? A few days ago you were bitching to get off the detail. Now you want to stay?" She started to answer, but he raised his hand. "Don't. I'll consider reinstating you when you're back on full duty. In the meantime, you're riding a desk. Let me know when the doctor releases you for light duty."

Assigning a police officer to a desk was like caging a wild animal. Being so confined reminded her of the orphanage, unable to go anywhere or do anything without permission. Her skin itched, and she scratched to relieve a discomfort that burrowed beneath the surface.

As she headed back to Neela's house, she vowed to find out who was behind the attempts on Neela's life. She refused to entrust her safety to anyone else entirely, not even her best friend. When she pulled into the driveway and saw a stranger's car instead of Bex's, she sprinted toward the door. The two officers in the vehicle out front appeared preoccupied.

She knocked on the door but didn't wait for Neela to answer. Trying the handle, she twisted and turned until her palm grew sweaty. She pounded again. When the door finally opened, Bina and another woman stood on the opposite side with overnight bags and purses.

"Ah, Jordan. You are right on time." Bina pointed to the woman behind her and kept walking toward the driveway. "My friend, Mrs. Scott. This is our bingo night. I will spend the night with her, maybe two. Neela is in the shower. Make her rest…and you too. And take good care of our Blue." She waved good-bye as they pulled away.

Jordan stood in the hallway feeling self-conscious. She'd been so certain Neela needed her that she'd practically broken down the door, responding like an overreacting rookie on her first call. What now? Should she wait quietly in the family room until Neela returned? Should she let Neela know she was in the house? Or should she go away and let the other officers handle the case?

She'd almost lost Neela, and that had uncovered feelings she couldn't identify. When she looked in Neela's eyes she saw possibilities she'd never imagined—hope, home, and real love. One thing was certain: it would be hard to contain all the emotions she'd suppressed much longer. Seeing Neela again injured, but alive and *alone*, would test Jordan's limits.

Chapter Fifteen

Jordan paced back and forth in the hallway, debating whether to wait for Neela to come out of the bathroom or go to her. If she caved to her desires and barged in, that would be typical Jordan. If she waited, she'd stretch her patience and restraint to the max but might make a positive statement. She took deep breaths, released them slowly, and willed her muscles to relax just as Molly had suggested. Each exercise seemed to only exacerbate what she tried to control. The pull of Neela naked, wet, and alone in the shower was too great, and she was weak.

She stood just outside the glass enclosure straining for a better look at the gorgeous body shrouded in steam. As she watched Neela rub her body and stroke between her legs, Jordan's crotch dampened and her throat dried.

"Are you watching or joining?" Neela opened the shower door and waited.

She was magnificent. Her long, dark hair hung down her back in shiny waves. Sheets of water cascaded over her body, and droplets clung to her nipples and to the tuft of hair at her middle. Her brown eyes glimmered as she licked her lips and held her arms out. Just seeing her was more than some could hope for in a lifetime.

Jordan turned away, afraid of the raging need inside her. "I'll wait out here."

"Jordan, please."

"I can't."

"Yes, you can. You have my permission. I want you to join me."

Jordan forced herself to leave the room and then collapsed on the floor at the foot of Neela's bed. Blood pulsed in her ears and she counted the hard pounding of her heart, trying to calm it. She pressed her hand against her wounded shoulder to distract herself from the wanting.

"Don't hurt yourself." Neela knelt beside her, naked and still dripping from the shower, and pulled her hand away from the injury.

Jordan tried to stand, but Neela pressed her body closer, her breasts and thighs hot and inviting.

"What do you need?" Neela kissed her so tenderly Jordan barely felt her touch.

"Don't want to disappoint you again." Neela's kiss deepened and she rolled them onto the floor, her injured leg on top of Jordan's thigh.

"Neela, please."

"You have no idea how much I need you." She slid on top of Jordan, pressing her leg between Jordan's jean-clad thighs.

Jordan gently rolled to dislodge Neela, but she clung to her neck. "Not right." She needed to rub against something hard and fast. Neela was too tender, her needs soft and normal.

"Jordan, look at me. Look at *me*."

She opened her eyes and saw Neela's passion burning so close to the surface. She wanted to please her, but she knew only one way.

"I want to touch you, Jordan."

"No touching." Neela rocked against her and thrust her knee hard into her crotch. "That's good. More." She pulled her arm out of the sling and placed her hands on Neela's full hips, pushing and pulling until Neela ground against her crotch and her clit stiffened. "Yeah, that's it." She cupped Neela's breasts and kneaded them in her hands, pumped against her leg, and watched Neela's eyes fill with tears. How could someone so beautiful cause so much turmoil inside her?

"Don't stop, Jordan. I'm so close. You make me come so fast." Neela arched into her hands and climaxed in convulsing waves. "Oh, Jor—dan." Neela collapsed on top of her, kissing the side of her neck and working her way down her body.

"Neela, don't."

"I want to taste you, to make you come."

She grabbed Neela's shoulders to pull her up, but Neela bit down on the crotch of her jeans, catching her clit in the folds. A flash of memory accompanied the pleasurable pain, and she struggled to free herself. It felt good, but she didn't want it. She moved again, more pain, more pleasure. She was about to come. "Oh. My. God."

Neela blew on the fabric and tightened her grip again.

"Ahhh." Jordan was soaked and so close. But this felt wrong. She forced her weak legs to move and rolled Neela onto the floor. When Neela's mouth left her crotch, Jordan doubled over from the loss. Her need for release was an all-consuming pain. She clutched herself and winced.

Neela lay on her back panting. "You wanted to come. I felt it. Why didn't you let me finish you?"

Jordan stroked herself and looked away from Neela. "I can't."

"Can't *what*, Jordan? Can't be pleased, touched, what?"

"Any of that." Jordan searched Neela's gaze for the inevitable look of disapproval, but it wasn't there.

"I'm pretty good with my hands." She wiggled her fingers, and Jordan would've laughed if she hadn't been hurting so badly.

"I have to do it." She unzipped her jeans and slid her fingers into her shorts. "But you could help."

"Whatever you need. I'm here." Neela's gaze followed the curve of Jordan's arm to her hand, where it rested between her thighs.

"Do it with me? Touch yourself. Unless you think I'm pathetic." Jordan looked at herself, hand buried in her shorts like thousands of times before, clawing for relief that never came easily. But this time Neela sat only inches away, willing to do whatever she needed, and Jordan didn't know how to let her. What kind of freak was she? "I understand if you think—"

"I think you're an amazing person with very special sexual needs, and I'm just the woman to satisfy them."

Jordan exhaled and some of the tension drained from her body.

Neela leaned back against the bed between Jordan's outstretched legs and draped her knees around Jordan's thighs. Jordan's body pulsed hard and insistent as Neela spread herself wider. Her creamy mocha skin glistened with arousal, and she dipped her fingers before stroking the tip of her engorged clit.

"Tell me what you like, Jordan." She wet her lips and her eyes never left Jordan's.

"Two fingers, down the sides of your clit. Slowly." Jordan did the same, but the pleasure doubled as she watched the effect on Neela's face.

"So hot and slick. Are you as wet as I am, darling?"

"Wetter." Jordan panted as the pressure grew. She watched Neela breathe into each stroke as she touched herself, undulating like an exotic dancer. "Faster, Neela."

She followed Jordan's directions and the tip of her clit turned bright red. Jordan couldn't take her eyes off Neela's slender fingers and the flesh that grew between them.

"Jordan, you're gorgeous. Your face is flushed and your nipples are so hard. Looking at you makes me hurt. I need more pressure. Please."

"Not yet. One finger inside but no rubbing." Neela licked her middle finger, slid it into her opening, and thrust to Jordan's rhythm. It was almost like her finger was inside Neela, making her writhe and moan. "With your...other hand...ahh...rub your clit. Hard, but tell me before you come."

Jordan pumped against her hand and her hips slapped the floor. She wanted to come so badly. Neela was about to climax and she needed to join her, to prove she was at least semi-normal. *Please let me be normal.* She squeezed her eyes shut as the pain built, and another image—a harsh, twisted face—replaced Neela's beautiful body. She grabbed her folds and twisted. *Damn it. Please.*

Neela's encouraging voice broke through her haze. "Jordan, look at me." She forced herself to gaze into Neela's eyes and saw her arousal and compassion. "I'm coming, Jordan. Stay with me."

She eased her grip and watched as Neela's back arched. "Can I touch you?"

"What about your shoulder?" Neela asked.

"Don't care. Come here."

Neela slid closer and placed Jordan's free hand between her legs. "Do what you're doing to me too. I want to know what you're feeling."

Jordan felt another flood between her legs as she squeezed Neela's slick lips together and heard her moan. She worked their flesh in unison like two parts of the same body, ignoring the tinge of pain in her shoulder. Neela pressed into her hand and Jordan matched her pace.

"Make us come, Jordan."

She wedged her hand deeper into her shorts until she could penetrate and rub at the same time. She fingered Neela's clit with her thumb and entered her, rocking back and forth as she grew hotter. "Come for me now, Neela."

When Neela's orgasm hit, she threw her head back and groaned deep in her throat, bearing down on Jordan's hand. "Yes, Jordan. Yes." She couldn't look away from Neela's clit as it jerked rhythmically in her grasp. She'd never seen anything so beautiful or felt its effects so immediately in her own body.

With Neela's first contraction, Jordan's own release began. As Neela pulsed around her fingers, Jordan's climax ripped loose. She tugged her turgid flesh and strained to force the pent-up energy out. Her spasms milked her over and over until she was breathless and weak. When they finally stopped, she slumped forward with her head on Neela's breasts and her hands still buried between their legs. "Neela, what're you doing to me?"

She held Jordan and rocked back and forth until her breathing returned to normal. "I'm teaching you to share, my darling."

Jordan had never combined sex and humor, but Neela made it seem natural. She'd never let anyone so close while she pleasured herself, but Neela seemed to fit. Neela didn't make her feel broken or inadequate or even a little weird. They were sharing even though she hadn't allowed Neela to touch her intimately. "What could possibly be next?"

"I'm thinking sex without clothes, for both of us." When Jordan started to object, Neela said, "When you're ready, of course. I'm in no rush. This slow, getting-to-know-you stuff is agonizing but so hot."

"How can you be so patient and understanding? You don't really know me."

Neela pulled a blanket off the bed and snuggled closer into her arms. "But I see you."

"Bina says that to me. What does it mean?"

Neela touched her arm, her tone soft and soothing. "It's a saying in our culture that means I see beyond the physical. I see your goodness, your soul."

"You can't…you don't understand."

"Then tell me. I'm not going anywhere."

Jordan wanted to believe that was true, but could she? No one had ever been there for her. Her cheeks stung and she brushed away the wetness. For the second time in two days Neela had reduced her to tears. "I'm not sure I…have a…soul."

Neela didn't look shocked. She simply pulled Jordan closer and kissed her forehead. "My darling, everyone has a soul. Yours has been terribly bruised, but it will heal with time. I'd like to help, if you'd let me."

Thinking of her soul as injured made Jordan feel less self-conscious and defensive. Maybe she wasn't damaged goods, just unhealed. Trust Neela to put a positive spin on a life of distrust and doubt. "That might be a pretty big task."

"I've taken on the governor and the legislature of North Carolina. You'd be a walk in the park, when my leg heals."

Jordan hugged Neela tighter. She couldn't remember the last time she'd held a woman even briefly after an orgasm. Once she'd climaxed, she was usually on to the next orgasm, the next job, or the next thrill, but with Neela, this sated period of rest felt right. Maybe she'd just never felt safe enough to rest anywhere. Molly's words flashed through her mind and almost took her breath. *"You'll know you care when sex isn't enough. When you're not okay just getting off and walking away."*

"Neela…" She had no idea what to say, but the moment called for something other than *that was great* or *I'll see you later*.

"Could we just lie here quietly for a second, please. I'd really like to listen to the beat of your heart." Neela placed her ear against Jordan's chest and closed her eyes.

Once again Neela seemed to know exactly what she needed though she had no clue. Jordan relaxed into their embrace and for the first time wondered if she might actually have a chance with this woman.

"I love what we just did," Neela said. "It was so hot and sexy but also intimate and trusting. I felt almost like I was touching you, bringing you to orgasm with me. Thank you."

"Umm." Jordan had already disengaged, started second-guessing her feelings. Neela's words were like stone pillars between them— intimacy, trust, touch—could she really be everything Neela wanted and deserved? Her heart ached for the connection, but Neela would have to accept her as she was. Could she ask that of anyone? Or would Neela simply accept her idiosyncrasies temporarily and resent them when she couldn't change? Jordan's skin dimpled as a shiver of uncertainty and fear claimed her.

"Are you cold, darling?"

She moved out of Neela's embrace and reached for her clothes. "No. I just remembered I have something to take care of."

"Right now?"

"Yeah. You'll be all right. The guys are outside."

Neela reached for her, but Jordan rose and straightened her shirt. "Can't you stay a few minutes? I really enjoy holding you, especially after—"

"I have to go. I'll see you later." Jordan bent and kissed Neela's forehead, just as she'd done to numerous lovers in the past, and walked out without looking back. Her stomach roiled like a sickness and she wasn't sure why. She needed fresh air and a nice long ride on her bike.

After she and Jordan had sex, the energy around them had shifted almost immediately. She tried to keep Jordan in the moment, safe in her arms, but felt her distance before she physically pulled away. The emotional gap they'd begun to bridge widened again. Jordan's blue eyes had turned stormy as an avalanche of emotions played across her face.

She'd tried to talk her down, emphasize the positive and reconnect, but she'd failed. Jordan had shown a glimpse of her heart, shared a fragment of intimacy, but Neela had been unable to protect it from the ghosts. She watched helplessly as Jordan walked out, as detached as she'd been the first day they met.

Neela lay there reliving the exchanges between her and Jordan since they'd met—no conversation at all, barely speaking, guarded comments, and finally sharing past hurts and disappointments. The road had been long, arduous and often frustrating, but what they'd shared today seemed like a breakthrough. So what had happened? Had Jordan suddenly realized she only wanted casual sex, that they really had no future? Or had she inadvertently offended Jordan or reminded her of the past in some unpleasant way? She had to know. Their joining had felt too right to be so easily dismissed.

Neela grabbed her cell off the nightstand and dialed Jordan's number. No answer. She tried again with the same result. On the third attempt, she left a message. "Jordan, please. Come back. We need to talk, and we can't do it on the phone. Please. Come back, or at least call."

She started to lock her phone but noticed she had several messages. Punching in her code, she waited for what could only be good news compared to what had just happened. Rosemary had left two messages, one to check on her and another to ask about her personal effects at her state office. She hadn't even thought about clearing out her belongings. The next three messages were reporters asking for interviews about her resignation.

The last voice, gruff and menacing, made her slump onto the side of the bed. "You and your girlfriend got lucky. That won't happen again. You've made a big mistake. See you soon."

Neela pushed the save button and scanned the call log. Unknown caller. Her hands shook and her head pounded again as she wiped the sheen of fear sweat from her brow. She'd thought the threats would stop once she resigned. What did this person want? If she only knew how she was exasperating him, she'd simply stop.

After a quick shower, she checked the backyard and saw Blue chase a squirrel up a tree. At least Jordan hadn't taken him and would have to come back eventually. She walked to the police car out front and handed her phone to Harry Styles. "Think you better have your tech guys listen to this message. It came from an unknown caller, and I didn't recognize the voice." Harry nodded, took her cell, and made a recording on his. "Can you get hold of Detective Bishop for me, please? I need to see her as soon as possible."

"Didn't she just leave a few minutes ago?" Phil asked. But when Harry gave him a sideways glance, he speed-dialed Jordan's number. "No answer. Goes straight to voice mail. She's on medical leave at the moment, not even light duty yet. If I was her, I'd get the hell out of town for a while."

And as far away from me as possible. Neela prayed Jordan's silence didn't have anything to do with her or their brief intimate connection, but she'd seen the turmoil on her face as she lay in her arms. While Jordan was still vulnerable from their lovemaking, some shadow from the past had reclaimed her, and Neela had been unable to protect her. Her world was spinning out of control. She'd resigned from her job with no means to support herself and Bina, and now she'd somehow pushed the woman she was falling in love with completely away.

As she walked back to the house, Neela placed a call. "Hi, Bex, sorry to bother you, but do you know where Jordan is? She left my house about half an hour ago in pretty bad shape. Any idea at all where I'd find her?"

"Stay where you are. Liz and I'll be there in about fifteen minutes."

Neela propped her leg up on the sofa while she waited for Bex and Liz, trying to ease the occasional pain shooting up her calf. For a hairline fracture, it sure was throbbing like a full-blown break. When Bex pulled into the driveway, she hobbled as quickly as possible to the car. "Let's go."

Liz's face had a fresh glow, and her lips were swollen and red. She was happy for her friend. Liz deserved someone who mattered, and from Bex's smile, the feeling was mutual. "Sorry if I disturbed something. I'm just really worried."

As they pulled out of the driveway, Neela told them she and Jordan had talked and she'd left upset. She knew Jordan well enough to know that discussing their sex life would violate their fragile trust and privacy.

Liz turned in the seat, and Neela sensed what was coming next. "What are we doing, Neela? Are you sure about this?"

"I need to talk to her."

"You know what I mean. This woman," she patted Bex's arm, "no disrespect to your friend, honey, but she's messed up. Anger is her default. I experienced that firsthand. Every time I've been around her, she's been on the edge of another explosion. You're not like that. And do I need to address the age difference? She's twenty-five going on sixteen, at least emotionally. I'm sorry, Neela, but I want more for you."

Neela stared out the window, unable to meet Liz's gaze. "I can't help it." Her voice was barely audible.

"What?"

"I said, I can't help it."

"What is it? The sex? Is it *that* good?" Liz shook her head. "I'm not buying it. If she's so closed down emotionally, the sex can't be all—"

"Stop it, Liz." Her voice filled the vehicle and Liz's face paled. They stared at each other and neither spoke for several seconds. "I'm sorry I yelled. I don't know what's going on with Jordan, but I can't just walk away from her. I…care."

Liz nodded. "So, it's your savior complex—like with your subordinates at work, Bina, our stem-cell research?"

"No. It's more than that."

Liz appealed to Bex, who'd been quiet since Neela got in the car. "Can you tell her anything that might help? What's going on with Jordan?"

Bex looked at Neela in the rearview mirror. "I can't betray her confidence. All I can say is she's changed lately. Something is really upsetting her."

"That doesn't give her the right to treat my friend like shit." Liz raked her hand through her red hair and sat back, staring out the front window. "Where are we going anyway?"

"The bar," Bex said.

"Fucking perfect. The great combination, anger and alcohol." Liz's sigh echoed in the vehicle like an exclamation point at the end of an expletive.

When they pulled in front of the Q Lounge, Neela opened the door and started to get out.

"Why don't you let me check inside? Won't take a minute," Bex said.

"What's the matter, Bex? Afraid we'll find her between some woman's legs?" Neela cringed at the thought. After what they'd shared, as casual and temporary as it was, she still had trouble imagining Jordan with anyone else. "I'm going in." Neela placed her left foot on the pavement and then lowered the cumbersome cast to the ground. "Just help me shield this thing."

Liz stepped into the bar first, with Neela behind and Bex bringing up the rear. She stopped in the doorway to let her eyes adjust and then scanned the room for Jordan's conspicuous white hair. Nothing. As they made their way to the counter, a petite woman with long brown hair and huge green eyes came alongside Bex.

"Hey, where've you been, and where's your friend, Jordan? I'm Lilly. Remember? I've been looking for her." Bex took the woman's elbow and led her toward the other end of the bar.

"*That's* Lilly?" Liz asked Bex before herding Neela in the opposite direction.

"Stop pushing, Liz. I know about Lilly."

"Seriously? You know your girlfriend fucked her, and God knows how many others, while she was putting the moves on you?"

"Please, Liz, don't start again."

"Can't you see it? Jordan gets all worked up over you and then comes here and fucks a stranger who looks like you. How juvenile is that?"

Neela's stomach churned. She looked at Lilly and wondered if Jordan had been able to relax with her. Had Lilly seen Jordan nude, sucked her breasts, touched her sex, or made her come? Was Lilly the woman Jordan had fucked until she injured her shoulder? Her stomach lurched again and she headed toward the door. The cool air helped, but it didn't stop the images rolling through her mind. She clung to the side of the building and dry-heaved until her throat was raw.

Liz spoke softly from behind her. "I've got you, hon." She placed her hand in the small of Neela's back and guided her back to the car.

Bex joined them a few minutes later. "She hasn't seen Jordan and neither have the bartender or the regulars. What now?"

"Anywhere else you can think of to look?"

Bex shook her head. "I've checked her apartment. Left a note on her bike earlier, but it's gone now. She usually rides when she's stressed. She'll turn up when she's ready."

"Then take me home. If Jordan doesn't want to talk, I can't make her."

"Sensible." Liz nodded and crossed her arms like she'd won a victory of some sort.

"Shut up, Liz," Neela said.

Bex laughed, and Neela and Liz stared at her. "She sounded just like Jordan. That's what she always says to me when I'm right."

"Shut up, Bex," she and Liz said together.

CHAPTER SIXTEEN

Jordan had hidden out in her apartment after her intimacy with Neela, pacing like a caged animal. How could she explain her desperate need for Neela followed by her abrupt, unexplained departure? She'd tried to sleep, but the nightmares returned fueled by the fresh emotional upheaval.

She'd told Neela about Amy. Those two worlds should never have intersected. And she'd been sexually vulnerable with Neela—a first with any woman. The feelings consuming her now were the exact opposite yet they were powerfully familiar—rejection, abandonment, and the sense of not belonging. Neela wouldn't be satisfied with just-so. She'd expect Jordan's heart and soul, and she'd deserve it. After they'd had sex, she'd tried to remain engaged but she'd failed.

So for two days, she'd ignored everyone, even Sergeant Milton. She'd turned off her cell and put it in a drawer in the kitchen. The only thing waiting for her was a desk. She still wanted to compare notes with Bex about the legislative initiatives they'd reviewed, but that could wait. Their efforts weren't likely to lead anywhere useful anyway. She'd never given up on a case, and since her job was the only semi-stable thing in her life, it felt odd. But right now, everything felt odd and she needed answers.

By mid-afternoon cabin fever had gotten the best of her and she crept to the garage half expecting someone to jump out of the shadows. Bex had been by the day before and knocked on the door but thankfully didn't use her key. She'd also left a note taped to the gas tank of her Ducati. *Call me. Call Neela. Just let us know you're okay.* She threw the paper on the ground, cranked the bike, and headed west.

She knew exactly where she was going but didn't have a clue why. She'd never found answers at New Beginning. Maybe it was time to stop hovering in emotional corners like a coward and face what had happened at the orphanage. Neela believed in her, gave her courage and hope, but she'd have to do it on her own. Was she strong enough? Today maybe she'd just go for a ride and think about it all, make a plan. She craved the feel of the bike between her thighs, the wind in her face, the challenge of speed, and the relief of something habitual.

When Jordan reconnected with her thoughts again, she was in front of the old orphanage. In daylight, the sprawling building lost some of its daunting character. The gate was still rusted and overgrown with weeds. Gaping holes where windows once were still looked like soulless eyes, and the crumbling façade still refused to let go completely. But the faces occupying every darkened corner at night were absent or at least obscured during the day.

Jordan inhaled through her mouth to calm the feeling of dread and apprehension seizing her insides. Her nerves fired relentlessly, fanning the anger that had been a constant here. She pulled the creaky gate open, rolled her bike through, and lowered the kickstand.

She hadn't been inside the building since leaving seven years ago, but the ghosts had followed her out into the world. The only place to confront them was where they'd been born and where they still lived in her mind. She navigated the broken steps and pushed the partially rotten front door open. Recalling Amy's face, she found the courage to enter.

The old historic building had been a showpiece for the public and the press whenever questions arose about the care of children at New Beginning. The grand staircase that led to two floors of bedrooms was always immaculately clean and the banisters polished. Certain rooms were kept presentable as examples of good housekeeping and the appropriate use of community funds. Behind the scenes, life was more dismal, but no one ever checked behind closed doors or talked to the kids. Misappropriation of funds was obviously more important than mistreatment of children.

She walked through the communal areas, recalling the few good times but mostly bad that had occurred there. Vagrants had discarded empty beer cans, trash, used condoms, and excrement throughout the building until it no longer suited their purposes. How was the place still standing? Why hadn't it been torn down years ago?

She climbed the staircase to the second floor where she and Amy had shared room number thirteen. They'd laughed about getting the cursed room initially, until their nightmares started coming true. The door hung half off its hinges and Jordan kicked it down. Dust so thick she could taste it rose in gray plumes and settled back on the surfaces, clinging as effectively as her memories. She'd met Amy for the first time in this room, and they'd become immediate friends.

For a second she remembered huddling in the middle of her single bed with Amy, whispering about their latest plan to escape. As their hopes had soared, so did their voices until they were laughing uncontrollably. She could almost hear Amy's staccato chuckles filling the room as she turned in a circle with her eyes closed. But they hadn't laughed often.

This was also the last place she'd seen Amy before she was taken to the butcher. She fell to her knees as the sadness returned and wailed until her throat was sore. Why did she have to be sick when those boys attacked and raped Amy? She wanted to believe she could've stopped them, but even now she doubted she could've fought them all.

Her tears finally stopped and she rose, walking tentatively toward the basement annex in back of the huge complex. The closer she got, the more vivid her recollections became. When she opened the huge metal door, it was like falling back in time.

"I don't need to see a shrink, but if I did, I'd want a real one. Brownworth is a quack."

"Jordan Bishop, come here this instant." Sister Mary stood before her like a stone penguin, glaring and daring Jordan to defy her again. "He's trying to help with these...feelings."

"There's nothing wrong with how I feel. It's normal for girls to—"

"Stop right there, young lady. I don't need to hear this. Get in there and listen to Doctor Brownworth." She shoved Jordan into the room and the lock clanked behind her.

She almost retched as the stench of pipe smoke wafted up her nose. The room was dark, the useless windows covered in heavy light-blocking curtains. Books stacked on the floor like Legos appeared ready to topple. She wondered if he ever read any of them but decided she didn't care. This room was full of bad memories, pain, and the constant reminder that her life meant nothing.

Benjamin Brownworth moved his pudgy hand from the lock and placed it on her shoulder. He looked like an evil version of Santa Claus—fat, wrinkled, and red-faced in a really bad way. His full white beard was stained yellow around the mouth and nose from too many hours puffing his rancid pipe, and his breath always smelled foul.

To a thirteen-year-old girl he was too big to fight and too powerful to complain about. No one would listen. She and Amy had tried to tell the sisters about the so-called therapy Brownworth conducted in his secluded basement on the metal table behind the curtain. They wrote it off as young girls rebelling against authority.

"Get off me." Jordan shook free of Brownworth's grip and ran to the tiny sliver of a window just above ground. There were bars across the opening, but she needed to be near an exit, regardless of the likelihood she could actually use it.

"Come sit down, Jordan. We need to talk."

She kept her back to him. "You never want to talk. I know what you want, and I'm not doing it again." He stabbed the needle in her arm, and a few seconds later she passed out.

When she woke up, she was completely undressed and strapped to the cold metal table. Brownworth stood beside her, his yellow teeth exposed like a carnivore about to strike. "I asked nicely, but you always want to do things the hard way, Jordan. Your lessons won't be easy."

She struggled against the leather straps, knowing from past experience they wouldn't give. "Let me up. I don't want to do this."

"It's for your own good. Now try to relax and do as I say."

"No."

"I'll help you control your unnatural urges. Little girls shouldn't enjoy things like that. You're meant for a man's touch."

"That wouldn't be you then."

He slapped her across the face but she refused to cry.

Jordan closed her eyes and tried to squeeze her legs together, but the straps were too tight. Brownworth's fat fingers poked and rubbed her, always rough and demanding, and the more he touched her, the angrier she got.

But in spite of her resistance and protests, her body eventually betrayed her. She tried to prevent the tingling when it started, tried to keep the moisture from gathering between her legs, but the harder she fought, the more he touched her. And he enjoyed it more and more, until he finally stopped with a disgusting moan, leaving her with the pain, the throbbing, aching pain, and no way to relieve it. He did it over and over until the only things she associated with sex were anger, hurt, and the inability to find release.

"You understand now, Jordan? These feelings only cause little girls pain."

"Bastard."

As the memory swept through her, Jordan's anger surged. She grabbed an old metal floor lamp and smashed it against a three-legged chair. "You son of a bitch." The wooden pieces flew through the air, and pain shot through her shoulder. She swung again and demolished a rickety bookcase. "You sick prick." She stood in the center of the room and hit anything within reach. "Fuck you, Brownworth. Damn you for killing Amy and for touching us." With each swing her anger ebbed and her shoulder ached more. She finally collapsed on the floor, panting, barely able to breathe. Her left arm and her chest were covered in blood. "Damn you to hell."

Brownworth had abused her for as long as she could remember. She'd run away so many times she'd been placed under lockdown and allowed out only under heavy supervision for her motocross activities. If the teachers asked about her bruises or defensive behavior, she'd make up a plausible excuse. The only thing that kept her going was anger and the knowledge that one day she would escape and make Benjamin Brownworth pay. Unfortunately, she'd been too late to save Amy. "Damn you."

Exhausted, she dragged herself toward the basement door. She refused to spend another second in the place that had made her life miserable and had shaped her future in such a grotesque manner. Benjamin Brownworth and New Beginning Orphanage had done terrible things to her, but what had Neela said? *"You can change how you deal with them."* Neela had touched her emotionally; that was surely a start. Maybe being here today, purging some of her rage, would be her real new beginning.

Six months ago she'd started seeing a proper, qualified therapist to help with the memories and her sexual hang-ups. But how could she tell Neela what had happened to her and what her body craved when her mind railed against her desires? How did she explain that a monster had shaped her preferences as he'd scarred her soul? It made her sick to think about it, so how could Neela not be repulsed?

She reached the top step and pushed against the heavy metal door, but it didn't budge. She couldn't stay here. She needed to get out—now. Putting her good shoulder against the door, she shoved over and over with no result. Sweat trickled into her eyes as she pressed her back into it and tried again. Pounding with both fists, she didn't stop until her arms were exhausted and the blood from her shoulder was a slow trickle. She yelled for help, but her raspy voice echoed off the empty walls. As daylight caved to darkness, she was trapped as effectively as she'd been all those years ago and was just as terrified.

❖

"What are you doing today, Beta?" Bina held her sippy cup between swollen fingers and stared at Neela.

"What do you mean?"

"You have been moping for two days, and I have not seen our Jordan, not even to check on Blue. What has happened?"

Neela had avoided bringing up the situation with Jordan or her feelings for her, but Bina was becoming suspicious. Her mother was hard to fool. "Nothing, really. Everything's fine."

"Look at me, Neela." She glanced up and quickly returned her attention to her cup of cold coffee. She couldn't lie while looking into her mother's shrewd eyes. "Tell me."

She'd searched for a delicate way to tell her mother she was a lesbian but hadn't found one. A woman of Bina's age and culture wasn't familiar with the rapidly changing world or the way it was shaped by demands for greater personal freedom and equity broadcast over social media. But she wanted to have an honest life with no secrets. "Bina, I have something to tell you…about myself."

"You are joining the circus? I have suspected it all along."

"No." Sometimes Bina's sense of humor surprised her.

"You will stop working all the time, trying to cure me? I would much rather spend the time with you. I am so proud of you, my daughter. Your father was proud as well, and you have nothing else to prove."

Neela's heart ached. She had no idea her research priority was so obvious to her mother and that their time apart affected her so deeply. And she hadn't realized until this moment how desperately she'd tried to prove herself worthy of her parents' struggles and sacrifices. She'd wanted them to be proud of her, and hearing her mother's confirmation brought tears to her eyes. "I'll never stop trying to help you or others, but I will spend more time with you."

"So, what must you tell me? Do you steal, lie, or hurt people?"

"No, but I love differently than most women." She met her mother's gaze because she wanted Bina to know she wasn't ashamed of her life.

"I know, Beta. You love more deeply than anyone, and for that I am proud. Your heart is big and open."

"Thank you, Mama, but that's not what I meant." She took Bina's misshapen hands in hers. "Bina, I'm a lesbian. I love other women the way most women love men."

Bina's stare didn't waver. "Is that all? I have known this for years. I love you still."

Neela released a sigh. Two short sentences had abridged the complicated conversation she'd imagined. Though she'd believed Bina would understand, she needed her reassurance and acceptance. And as usual, her mother came through.

"Why does this worry you now, my darling daughter?"

She never wanted to say or do anything to color Bina's opinion of the world, but she had to know the truth. "Some people probably think you shouldn't live with me because of my way of life. Some may try to use my lifestyle against me. But you need to know that I'm not ashamed of who I am."

Bina nodded slowly. "I did not raise you to be ashamed of your life. Do not worry. These people have more to fear from their own hearts. I will stand by you always, my child." She took Neela's face between her hands. "And as long as you will have me, I will be here with you...and maybe someone worthy of your love."

Neela smiled as tears trickled down her cheeks. "I love you so much, Mama. I will always want you with me." She wiped her eyes and sipped the cold coffee that tasted like the best drink ever.

"So, again, what are you doing today, Beta?" Bina waggled her index finger. "Idle hands are the devil's playgrounds."

"Liz is putting the final touches on our new lab and doesn't want me to see it yet. We'll start work soon. So, I guess I'm moping the rest of the day."

"Find Jordan and talk to her. She is the reason for this chat, no?"

"How could you possibly know that?" Her only regret was that Jordan hadn't been part of the conversation with her mother. She had a feeling Bina's acceptance of Neela's sexuality and of Jordan would mean a great deal to her. If only she'd known what to say to Jordan two days ago to make her comfortable enough to stay, Jordan might be at her side now.

"Fix things with Jordan, Beta, and live your best life."

"I can't make her talk to me."

"Just let her know you are there if she wants to."

Neela picked up her cell phone from the counter and started to dial Jordan's number again, but it rang. "Hello?"

"Neela, it's Bex. Have you heard from Jordan?" Bex's voice sounded strained. If this seasoned cop was concerned, Neela should be panicked.

"Not since she left day before yesterday. You mean you haven't heard from her either?" The line was silent. "Have you tried her friends and relatives?" No answer. "Is her bike gone? For God's sake, Bex, say something."

"She's not answering the phone and her bike isn't at the apartment. I've even been inside. She's not there. I can't imagine, unless—"

Bex's tone was like a splash of cold water, and Neela grew even more afraid. "Tell me."

"Oh, shit. I've got to go."

"Don't hang up."

"I'll call as soon as I have news," Bex said. "It's just a wild hunch."

"*Bex.* Come and get me. It's all we've got right now, and I'm desperate." The only other times she'd felt so scared were when she thought Bina was in trouble and the night Jordan was shot. She couldn't imagine waiting at home for news when she could possibly be closer to Jordan.

"I really shouldn't let you—"

"Don't even try to stop me. What if she's hurt? I'll be waiting outside."

"Be there in five minutes."

Neela told Bina what she knew, put a meal in the slow cooker for later, and hobbled to the street just as Bex pulled up. "What did you remember?"

Bex shook her head as if arguing with herself. "She'll kill me if I take you to this place and she's actually there."

"And I'll kill you if you don't. What's the big secret?"

"New Beginning."

"New beginning of what?" Neela turned in her seat and stared at Bex as she drove, eyes straight ahead. "You don't mean the old orphanage?"

"You know it?"

"It was the most notorious child-care facility in the history of the state, if you can truly call it a child-*care* facility. That case has become the benchmark throughout the country of what not to do. We require all our social workers to…" The more she talked, the more Bex paled. When it finally registered what she wasn't saying, Neela's chest tightened. "Oh, no. Please tell me Jordan wasn't in that horrifying place."

Bex nodded.

Neela was too stunned to speak. She stared, not really seeing the trees whiz by on the shoulder of the road as they sped west on the interstate. She replayed her conversations with Jordan and realized she'd never mentioned a family. When Bina had asked about relatives, she'd seemed embarrassed and evaded the question. In their conversation about Amy, Jordan had never said where or how they met. But when she'd mentioned Brownworth, Neela should've remembered the horrible story of years ago. Why hadn't she seen it? The signs were so clear: lack of trust, feelings of inadequacy, anger, and problems with relationships, sexual dysfunction, and her discomfort with touching or being touched. It was scary how many things Jordan had going against her.

"Do you have any idea what they did to the children in that place, Bex?"

"I read the reports when she told me she'd been there. How could a place like that operate for so long?"

"You know the answer—greed, corruption, and a powerful and extensive pedophile ring. How long was she there?" Neela didn't really want to hear the answer, but she had to know.

"She was dropped off when she was only a few days old and wasn't able to get out until she was eighteen."

Neela sobbed, unable to stop the tremors in her body. She ached for Jordan, suddenly understanding and sharing her intense anger. "What have they done to you, my darling?"

Bex rubbed Neela's arm. "I'm sorry you heard this from me, but she'll need both of us if she's gone back to this place. Did something happen between you to set her off?"

Neela tried to control her crying, but her heart was breaking for Jordan and all the signs she'd missed. "We...connected, and not just sexually, for the first time." Bex was quiet, her gaze fixed firmly on the road again. "What?"

"Abandonment, rejection, not being good enough—take your pick. If she opened up to you emotionally even a little, it must've been scary as hell. She's probably second-guessing herself and wondering what to do. Vulnerability and intimacy scare her more than a gunfight. She doesn't know how to handle it, never had to. I don't mean to be cruel, and I could be entirely wrong. You know this stuff better than I do."

Neela shook her head, the enormity of the situation landing squarely in her gut. "You're not wrong. That explains a lot. What have I done?" If she'd somehow pushed Jordan back to this awful place, she'd never forgive herself.

"We're getting close. Don't let her see you so upset. She'll hate that I told you any of this. She can't stand being pitied."

Neela wiped her face and tried to control her churning emotions. The worst place in hell should be reserved for people who abused children, the elderly, and animals. "I'll be okay." She wasn't sure how, but she had to hold it together for Jordan. When Bex pulled up to the old building, Neela almost broke down again when she saw Jordan's bike parked outside.

"You should probably stay here," Bex said.

"Like hell I will."

"The building is about to fall apart. It'll be rough going with your leg in a cast."

"I don't care. I'm going with you. If she's injured, it's better if I'm there."

Bex shook her head again. "You're as stubborn as Jordan."

"Thanks. I'll tell her you said so when we find her."

"Where do you think we should start?"

"The base—ment." Neela fought a wave of nausea. "That's where Brownworth…" It seemed to take forever to negotiate through the rubble and make it to the huge basement door. A large ceiling beam had fallen across the entrance, and it took both of them to push it away. Neela fought back tears as Bex pulled on the heavy door.

"Jordan? Where are you?"

Neela heard a low moan. "She's in there." She wedged her hands in the small crack Bex had created, and together they inched the door open. She stuck her head inside and yelled. "Call an ambulance. She's bleeding."

Bex dialed. "Shit, there's no service down here. I'll be right back."

Neela squeezed into the opening and fell down beside Jordan. "Can you hear me, Jordan?" When she got no response, she placed her finger over her carotid artery, relieved to feel a faint pulse. "What's happened, darling?" Neela conducted a preliminary check for injuries. "Talk to me, Jordan. Open your eyes." She was covered in blood, but it was coming from her shoulder. Neela shucked her sweatshirt, peeled her T-shirt off, and pressed it against Jordan's shoulder. "Where is the damn ambulance?"

"Should be here any minute," Bex said. She was in the doorway trying to get it open wider. "Is she…"

"She's breathing but her pulse is very shallow. She's lost a lot of blood, and I can't bring her around." As a doctor she'd seen far worse, but never on someone she cared about. She struggled to stay calm and be useful.

"Can you help me open the door so they can get the stretcher in?" Neela started toward the door but Bex pointed. "Maybe you should put something on before they get here?"

She looked down at her bra and grabbed her sweatshirt from the floor. "Sorry." They'd just managed to widen the entrance when she heard voices upstairs. "We're in the basement. Follow my voice. Hurry."

In a few seconds, the paramedics flanked Jordan, proceeding through their checks, asking questions Neela couldn't answer, and loading Jordan onto the stretcher. When they strapped the ties across Jordan's chest, she started struggling.

"Get off me, you bastard. Leave me alone."

"Jordan, it's Neela. You're all right. It's the paramedics."

"Stop. I don't want this." Jordan thrashed and strained against the straps all the way out of the building. If she saw Neela at all, she didn't seem to recognize her.

"Jordan, please. Calm down." She followed them out, refusing to leave Jordan, and when they loaded her in the ambulance, she climbed in too. "I'm going with her. I'm a doctor, and she's a police officer. Please hurry. Bex, I'll see you at the hospital."

On the interminable ride, Neela tried to calm Jordan and reassure her that she was safe, but she slipped in and out of consciousness, battling with the paramedic. She'd probably driven Jordan back to that terrible place, and what demons had been resurrected?

Chapter Seventeen

Neela rested her head on the side of Jordan's hospital bed, exhausted but unable to sleep. She'd left only briefly during the night to take care of Bina. Every time Jordan moaned or struggled against the restraints on her arms, Neela spoke quietly and soothingly to calm her. But Jordan's gaze never clearly focused on anything.

"No...don't..." Jordan mumbled and pulled against the straps. "Let go." She opened her eyes slightly and scanned the room. Staring into the corner, her eyes bulged and grew wild. Was she sensing ghosts or danger? "Don't touch me."

Neela wiped her fevered forehead with a cool cloth. "Jordan, darling, I'm here. It's Neela. You're safe."

Jordan swallowed hard and grimaced. "Neela. Wa—water."

"Jordan, can you hear me?" She pushed the call button for a nurse and reached for the pitcher of ice chips beside the bed.

"Nee—la? What—"

"Don't try to talk, darling. You're safe now."

"Get out...of these..." She nodded toward the restraints on her arms. "Why?"

"You were trying to pull the IV out of your arm."

When the nurse came in, she checked Jordan's vitals and agreed she could have small pieces of ice until the doctor made her rounds, but she wouldn't release the restraints.

"Heather?" Jordan squinted, trying to place the woman.

"Yep, it's me, sport. Didn't expect to see you again so soon. I've bandaged that wound for the third time." She gave Jordan a stern look.

"Don't make me have to do it again. Do you need anything else, Doctor Sahjani?"

"No thanks, Heather."

Neela fluffed the pillows and helped Jordan sit. "Here." She raised the plastic spoon full of ice chips to Jordan's lips. "I'm sorry about the straps, but as soon as the doctor checks you, I'm sure she'll take them off. You're much more coherent."

Jordan sucked on the ice and licked her dry lips. Her breathing leveled, but when she looked at the ties on her arms, she hyperventilated again.

"Jordan, look at me. You're okay. I'm here and I won't let anything happen to you. I swear it."

"Did you go…to…" The agony in Jordan's downcast eyes and her clenched jaw muscles made it obvious she hated the thought of Neela finding her in the orphanage.

"Bex and I found you. You'd lost a lot of blood. You were very weak." Neela grabbed her throat, almost choking on the words. She'd come so close to losing Jordan. Where they'd found her made no difference, only that they'd done so in time.

"Never wanted you to know." Jordan couldn't meet her gaze.

"I wish you could've told me. I want to know everything about you."

"You don't. Some things are…I'm ashamed…"

She cupped Jordan's hand and squeezed. "You don't need to feel ashamed. You did nothing wrong, but we can talk about that later, if you want."

"I hate that look of pity in your eyes."

Neela forced her best smile. "What pity? The only thing you see in my eyes right now is exhaustion, relief, and a healthy dose of nausea."

"Nausea?"

"I've been spending way too much time around Bex and Liz the past two days. They're in that can't-keep-my-hands-off-her stage." Jordan smiled, and some of the tension drained from her face. "Now, you rest. I want you back home soon."

"Home?"

"With me and Bina. She's worried about you as well."

"I don't belong there." Jordan looked out the window and her eyes welled.

"You absolutely do. You've been through a lot and we want to help."

"I won't be your charity case, Neela. You deserve more."

"The last thing you are is charity, my darling. Bina and I want you with us. *I want you.* I'm not trying to pressure you into something you don't want, but you have to know we care."

"Oh my God. Does Bina know? Family is so important to her. I'm just an orphan brat." Jordan's face distorted with the kind of panic Neela had seen earlier at the orphanage.

"I haven't told her. You get to decide if and when you tell either of us anything about your past. We just want you to be safe and to know we're here for you."

"I can look after myself. Really, it's probably best if I go to my apartment."

"And who will take care of us? We need you for the step-and-fetch." She patted her cast. "I'll handle the heavy lifting for a while, and Bina will, as usual, direct from the sidelines. You're a part of our family now, like it or not. Besides, Blue misses you like crazy."

Jordan laughed at Neela's animated explanation and rubbed her thumb across the back of her hand. "Thank you."

"It's the least I can do. You saved my life, after all." Jordan's smile seemed to brighten the stark room just a little.

Jordan wasn't sure how she'd ended up in the hospital, but it was nice to wake up with Neela at her side. The last thing she remembered was being trapped in the annex. She'd never wanted Neela to know she'd been abandoned like garbage, raised, and abused in an orphanage. The experience defined who she was in so many ways—none of them good. She'd hoped to straighten herself out and eventually approach Neela again. But fate had intervened and dealt her an entirely different hand. Now Neela knew about the orphanage and probably about her abuse. When the center closed, the news had made headlines for days, with some former residents telling their stories to millions on the talk-show circuit for a few dollars.

Jordan had trouble telling her story to one person, unsure if she'd ever get it out that day in Molly's office. When the time came, could she share what happened with Neela? She couldn't bear the thought of being regarded as a victim. She'd held on to her anger to remain strong and get through the ordeal, but she was tired of fighting, and the anger tainted anything good. As soon as she was out of the hospital, she'd start reclaiming her life from the memories and the pain.

A light tap on the door announced the doctor's arrival just before she stepped inside. "How are you feeling today, Jordan?" Doctor Newkirk, a petite woman with blond hair and bright-green eyes, nodded at Neela and reached for the chart at the foot of the bed. "Are you ready to go home?"

"Yes, please." Jordan tugged at the restraints on her arms. "I'm even more ready to get out of these things."

"Promise not to pull your IV out again?" Jordan nodded, and the doctor unbuckled the straps and let them fall to the side of the bed. "Better?"

Jordan stared at the red marks around her wrists and fought down a wave of queasiness. She rubbed the indentions and breathed deeply through her mouth. When she looked up, Neela was smiling at her. She was momentarily lost in the warmth and the total absence of pity in her eyes. Slowly but surely, she could learn to accept and return these kinds of feelings.

"Everything looks in order. We can take the IV out in a couple more hours. I want to make sure you're sufficiently hydrated. Your blood pressure is back up, and that nasty wound is bandaged again. Try not to put too much stress on it for the next week."

"When can I leave?"

"I'll have the release order ready by mid-afternoon. Soon enough?"

"Not really, but it'll have to do. Thank you, Doctor Newkirk."

The doctor smiled on her way out, and Bex and Liz slid in around her. "Always the impatient one. Is she still causing problems?" Bex hugged Neela and gave Jordan's leg a squeeze. "I know you're healing and still flat on your back, but we've got things to talk about."

"Like where's my bike," Jordan said. "Hi, Liz."

"Handled. It's at your apartment."

"Thanks, Bex. But in case you hadn't heard, I'm not working, not even light duty yet."

"I know, but you need something to keep your mind sharp." Bex knew if Jordan wasn't riding or screwing, she was working. And right now she needed to concentrate on something besides what had just happened to her. "And then there's the phone call Neela got."

"What phone call?" Jordan tried to push herself up on the bed and winced.

"Careful with your shoulder," Neela said. "I haven't had time to tell you about that. Somebody left a threatening message on my cell the day…the last time I saw you."

"I thought we were in the clear after you resigned."

"So did I."

Bex waved a folder in the air. "He said Neela's made a big mistake of some sort. Not sure if he's talking about her resignation or something else. The lab guys have analyzed the message for background noise but didn't find anything. They're doing a voice-print analysis for comparison with other samples. Still nothing concrete."

"And the shooter?" Jordan's head was still fuzzy from the drugs, but she wanted to stay awake and concentrate. If Neela was still in danger, she had to help find the suspect.

"I talked to the Crimes Against Persons detectives this morning. The license plate on the SUV was stolen, big surprise there, and none of the witnesses saw enough to compile a composite. They were too busy diving behind cars after the shots. So we're back to square one."

Jordan reached for the water cup and took a big gulp, letting the cold liquid soothe her sore throat and clear her head. "I've been thinking about the Guilford Citizens for Equality group. They've always conducted peaceful protests. Over nine hundred of their members have been arrested so far for trespassing and failing to disperse because of their objections to Governor Lloyd's agenda. I suppose it's possible one of them fixated on Neela, but that seems far-fetched. Besides, this group is in favor of a woman's right to choose, so it's unlikely they'd target her because of her stance on abortion. We've got to be missing something."

Neela cleared her throat. "Do you really think now is the best time for this? You've been through a pretty rough ordeal. Shouldn't you rest a bit before launching back in full tilt?"

Jordan took her hand and tried her best to be reassuring. She definitely wasn't one hundred percent, but she had to focus on something besides her ordeal, as Neela called it. "Thank you for being concerned, but I really need to do this. Can you understand?"

"Of course, but I don't have to listen to all this police talk and be bored senseless, do I?" Neela grabbed Liz's hand and pulled her toward the door. "We'll be in the gourmet hospital cafeteria. Want anything?"

She and Bex shook their heads, and when the door closed behind them, Jordan turned to her friend. She was grateful to Bex for finding her and possibly saving her life, but she was also upset she'd taken Neela with her.

"I know what you're thinking," Bex said. "But I didn't have any choice. She'd been trying to get in touch with you for two days, and she was an emotional mess. When I let it slip I might have an idea where you were, I couldn't stop her. She can be pretty stubborn too."

"I didn't want her to know about my past there. It's not pretty."

"It's also not your fault. Crappy things happen to all of us, but we don't have to let them define who we are. Who doesn't have issues? Neela and I care about you, and we're not going anywhere. Now, can we get back to business? All this touchy-feely talk is making me nostalgic for Liz."

"I guess that's going pretty well?"

"Better than. She's the absolute best thing that's ever happened to me."

"I'm glad for both of you. Seriously. I'm afraid to hope for something that good." She pointed at the folder Bex had yet to open. "Want to tell me why you're really here before the Betadine has dried on my injuries?"

She pulled up a chair next to the bed. "You're not as drugged as I thought." She opened the folder and emptied the contents onto Jordan's legs. "Remember these?"

"The most contentious legislative initiatives coming up for approval this term."

"Right. You said you might've found something."

"Nothing in the text itself, but I started wondering who was driving these proposals and what they had to gain from them," Jordan said.

"Me too, and I bet we came up with the same person."

"Elliot Ramsey?"

"Bingo," Bex said. "He's got his fingers in a lot of pies, most of them leading back to the governor's mansion."

Jordan started to say something else, but she heard laughter outside the door. Neela and Liz came in giggling like two schoolgirls who'd been trading secrets. Liz handed Bex a coffee and placed a hand on her shoulder. "Are we interrupting something?"

Jordan nodded for Neela to sit. "Does the name Elliot Ramsey mean anything to you?"

"Seriously? You'd have to live under a rock in North Carolina not to know who he is. Ramsey is the Karl Rove of the Lloyd administration, but it goes beyond that. He was not only the governor's strategist for the last election, but he was also his moneyman. Why?"

"Where does his money come from?" Bex asked.

"Officially, he made billions in tobacco and textiles when he was younger and diversified later. Unofficially, he receives generous donations from politicians and businessmen all over the country. He's established think tanks to conduct surveys and push the conservative agenda."

"Have you ever heard of him being involved in anything shady?" Jordan asked.

Neela gave her an adoring smile. "Darling, he's a politician. I'd be surprised if he wasn't. Men like Elliot Ramsey seldom make as much money as he does without being involved in something improper. Please tell me you're not about to rattle his cage."

Jordan focused her attention on the documents scattered across the foot of her bed. "Only if he's rattling yours."

"And how do we find out," Bex asked. "It's not like we can just walk up to him and ask, and we certainly can't get a tap on his phone without a warrant."

"We do it the old-fashioned way—"

"Stakeout. I hate those damn things."

"Can I come?" Liz kissed the top of Bex's head. "I'd make the time pass a lot faster."

"I'm certain of that," Bex said, "but I'm afraid not. My partner wouldn't like it if I two-timed her with another woman on a stakeout."

"First, I need to get out of here. Then we'll talk about how. We'll keep eyes on him night and day to identify his associates. Even that might not give us what we need, but we have to start somewhere. In the meantime, Bex, see if you can quietly get a list of his business interests. That could help us narrow the field of players."

"I'm on it."

Neela had remained silent for too long, and Jordan could feel her anxiety building. She reached for her hand, but Neela stood and walked toward the door. "I'll see if I can find those discharge papers."

"What?" Bex looked at Liz. "Did I say something wrong?"

"No, honey. She's worried Wonder Woman will get herself hurt again or worse. She's not used to caring about somebody who puts herself in danger on purpose. Her life was very quiet and settled until you two showed up. Give her some time. She'll be fine." Liz gathered the empty coffee cups and dropped them in the trash on her way out. "I'll see if I can help her, and then I'll bring the car around front. Text me when you're coming down."

Jordan shook her head. "Am I destined to always be in trouble with Neela?"

"Pretty much a given." Bex stuffed the papers back in the folder. "I'll let you get dressed. Your clean clothes are in that trendy paper bag over there, but I'm getting tired of being your handmaiden so stop getting hurt."

When Bex opened the door to leave, Molly came in. They exchanged a brief nod before Molly said, "Well, looks like I made it just in time. I heard you had quite an interesting visit to the old home place."

"How did you know I was here?" Molly glanced back toward the door. "Bex. She shouldn't have called you."

"She's your friend, and she wanted to make sure you were okay. Are you okay?"

"I think so. I haven't processed it yet, but I think going back might've helped. At least I was able to vent some of my anger. We'll see."

"So, not ready to talk about it?"

"Not quite yet. Is that all right?"

Molly took her hands and waited for Jordan to look at her. "Of course. Whenever you're ready, I'll be here. Just remember, you've faced it head-on. Everything else is downhill. Let your friends be there for you. It looks like you have some good ones. Take care, Jordan."

"Thanks for coming by." Molly gave her a quick hug and slipped out. A few minutes later the nurse came in to remove Jordan's IV.

Alone again, Jordan stood and gripped the chair arm until a brief wave of nausea passed. The drug fog had partially lifted, and except for the exhaustion, she felt pretty normal. She pulled the hospital gown off and quickly dressed. When Neela returned, she was sitting in a chair by the window tapping her foot anxiously.

"I would've helped you get dressed."

"I'm fine, just a little weak. Come sit with me." She waited until Neela pulled up a chair and rested a hand on Jordan's lap. "Have I done something else to upset you, beyond the normal annoying stuff I seem to do without realizing it?"

"I'm just worried about you. It's what I do. I'm worried you're leaving the hospital too soon, blocking what happened yesterday without dealing with it, going back to work too quickly, getting involved with a man who could have you killed. Is that enough, because I could go on."

She covered Neela's hand with hers. "You're a wonderful woman who worries too much about me and everyone else. Trust me, I haven't blocked what happened yesterday, and I'm not avoiding it. I just need to deal with things in my own way, and that involves work for the time being. As for the job, taking risks is what I do, and I can't change that."

Neela leaned forward and kissed Jordan lightly, then more urgently. "I don't expect you to change anything. Just please be careful."

"You have my word."

"Let's go home." Neela stood and offered her hand.

When Jordan entwined their fingers, she felt a sliver of hope. Neela had learned one of the most horrible things about Jordan's life and was still supportive and understanding. Maybe Neela could accept the rest of her story and still care about her. Only time, a huge amount of courage, and a little luck would tell.

Bina was standing in the doorway with Blue when Neela and Jordan pulled up to the house. Blue broke Bina's hold and greeted Jordan the instant she opened the car door. "Hey there, fella. How've you been?" He licked her hand and wagged his tail like a windshield wiper gone berserk. "I've missed you too." She knelt in the grass and stroked his fur for several minutes before waving to the protection officers across the street and going inside.

When she got to the threshold, Bina grabbed her around the waist, unable to reach her neck even on tiptoes. "You have been gone too long, my Jordan. How are you?"

"Better now," she said and hugged Bina again. "I've missed your gorgeous face."

"Come in. We will have tea and cake."

She nodded to Blue, who was now posted at her side. "Looks like you've been feeding him too many cakes. Huh?"

Bina's cocoa skin flushed a bit darker before she hobbled toward the kitchen, waving her hand to say, no matter.

Neela took Jordan's arm as they walked down the hall, her cast tapping a slow rhythm. "My mother is very taken with you. Please don't break her heart."

"Does she know about…what's happened between us?"

"No, but I told her about my sexuality."

Jordan stopped and stared in disbelief. "You what?"

"I don't like secrets. That's how I live my life."

Jordan tried to imagine life without her skeletons but lost track of how her revelations would change everything. Would the relief of sharing her darkest secrets be worth the possibility of rejection? She wouldn't have nearly as many people to confide in as Neela did, but the task still seemed daunting. Neela either didn't care what others thought or was so secure it didn't matter. Could she ever be so self-confident about her personal life?

"What did Bina say?"

"She already knew, and nothing has or will change between us. We've always had a wonderful relationship. Don't be self-conscious. I don't usually discuss my sexual trysts with my mother. That would be taking honesty a little too far. But she thinks you hung the moon, so just act normal."

"Whatever that is." A mixture of relief and something akin to disappointment flooded through her—relief that Bina didn't know how badly she'd treated Neela and disappointment that Neela had referred to their interactions as trysts. But she was exactly right. They hadn't been anything else, so why did it bother her to have Neela state the truth? She followed Neela into the kitchen, where Bina was waiting patiently at the table.

"So…cake?" Neela asked.

"Yes, please. And then we must rest. Afternoon naps for everyone." Bina smiled. A nap was apparently cause for celebration.

"I have to meet Liz at the lab this evening, but I do need some sleep first. And you?" She looked at Jordan.

"I'm exhausted. A little downtime sounds excellent, right after that cake."

Thirty minutes later, the dishes were in the dishwasher, Bina was in bed, and she and Neela headed down the hall to their respective rooms. Neela stopped at the guest-bedroom door. "Want to come to my room? Just to sleep."

"Better not. I'm on my best behavior with Bina. Besides, I think we both really do need to rest. Looks like you haven't slept in days."

"Thanks, darling, that's certainly what a girl wants to hear, especially after she's given up her beauty sleep to keep vigil at your bedside."

"Jeez, I didn't mean it like that. I'm really grateful."

Neela stood on her tiptoes and kissed Jordan. "Lighten up. I was kidding. Sleep well."

Jordan closed the door, deposited her weapon on the nightstand, and stretched out across the bed, too exhausted to undress. Her mind immediately went to the annex, but before she could process what happened, she fell asleep.

CHAPTER EIGHTEEN

T"*he emergency panic button has been activated. The police are responding.*"

Jordan woke to a disembodied voice and the sound of alarms throughout the house. She sat up and immediately grabbed her head, still groggy from blood loss and drugs. Reaching for the bedside table, she almost tumbled headfirst to the floor. How long had the alarms been going off? She glanced at the clock, four in the morning. As she rose, she retrieved her weapon from the nightstand and worked her way down the hall.

Neela's room was closer, so she checked and found it empty. She'd said she was meeting Liz at the lab. Closing the door, she moved to Bina's suite and found her lying on the floor. "Bina, can you hear me? Are you okay?"

"I fell down, but I pushed the button just like you told me."

"Good job, and you used the audible button instead of the silent one. Are you in pain? Does anything feel broken?"

"No, but I am afraid to move."

"Will you be okay for a minute while I check the house, turn off the alarm, and let the guys know we're all right?" She hated to leave her alone, but she had to be sure the house was secure and notify dispatch not to send patrol cars.

"Yes, dear, do what you need to. I will wait here."

In a few minutes, Jordan had searched the rest of the house, reset the alarm with the monitoring company, and waved the all-clear to the protection detail out front. She returned to Bina's room and sat down beside her. "Now, let's talk about this. Have you fallen before?"

"Sure, I am good at it. Doctor says I have inflamed connective tissue pressing on nerves in my hands and feet. I drop things, cannot raise my foot or hand sometimes. He says it may eventually lead to permanent paralysis. That is why my Neela works so hard, you know. She wants to find the magic cure for all my ailments."

"Knowing your dedicated daughter, she just might succeed." While they talked, Jordan did a quick check to make sure Bina hadn't broken anything. "Let's get you up, okay?"

"You cannot lift. Your shoulder is hurt."

"Maybe we can do it together." Jordan pulled a cushioned chair to the foot of the bed so Bina could help pull herself up. She grabbed hold with her good arm on the other side, and Bina rose easily into the chair. "Okay? Anything hurting now that you're upright?"

"No, good as new. Thank you."

"Are you sure we don't need me to take you to the hospital for a checkup? Something might be fractured that I can't see."

"Absolutely not, and if you tell Neela about this, you and I will have words."

Jordan raised her hands in surrender. "And we wouldn't want that. Where to now? Family room, back to bed, what's your pleasure?"

"Bed, I think. The sun is not even up. Would you sit with me, if you are not too tired?"

"I'd like that." She helped Bina into bed before pulling the chair around. "What would you like to talk about?"

Bina pulled at a strand of her silver hair like a child. "Tell me about the first time you met my Neela."

Jordan couldn't keep from smiling as she recalled the picture etched in her mind. "I saw Neela for the first time at her office. She was so beautiful in a pale-yellow suit with a white scarf at her neck. The sparkle in her eyes seemed to light up her entire face, just brilliant. When she smiled at me, I wanted to stare at her all day. I felt warm and safe and… important that she'd noticed me. But I was also afraid of her openness, so I acted like a complete pri—jerk. I'd decided I didn't like her before we met because of her job. When she pinned me with those eyes and didn't back down, I was a goner." She was surprised by her admission.

Jordan stopped, afraid to look at Bina. She'd basically admitted to Neela's mother that she had the hots for her daughter. "Sorry, that probably didn't sound very nice. I don't mean any disrespect."

Bina chuckled. "You liked her but you did not want to. She has that effect sometimes. People see the goodness of her heart and are drawn to her."

She'd been anything but kind and caring with Neela. She'd been disrespectful and even cruel. "Bina, I...I've done things."

Bina reached for her hand and held it until Jordan met her gaze. "We have all done things we wish we had not. We are just making our way through life the best we can. The important part is to learn from those things. From what I see in my daughter's eyes, you have done nothing to lessen her feelings for you. Quite the opposite."

Jordan blinked away her tears. "I hope you're right, but I'm not sure how she'll feel when I tell her everything about myself."

"She will feel the same, as I do about her. Love does not change because of your past, only because of what you do now. When you are ready, she will be there for you."

"I hope you're right." Jordan cleared her throat and breathed more easily. "Some things are difficult to say aloud, so thank you for listening." But this was only the beginning of Jordan's secrets, and the others filled her with the worst kind of dread. "Speaking of your daughter, where could she be at this hour? She went to meet Liz. Have you heard from her? I slept too soundly to hear anything until the alarm."

"She is probably working still in the new lab. She gets lost in her research."

A tinge of jealousy niggled in Jordan's gut, but she pushed it aside. "Do you need anything else?" Bina shook her head. "I don't like leaving you alone even for a while."

"I am fine on my own. Besides, I have a very loud panic button."

Jordan kissed her forehead and on the way to the shower dialed Neela's cell. It went straight to voice mail, and she hung up. She called Bex next. "Where's Liz?"

"It's not even morning yet. She's right here beside me. Why?"

"Ask her if she knows where Neela is. She hasn't been home all night." She heard Bex and Liz mumbling and tried to be patient. Her insides were coiled knots. When she'd been on the protection detail, at least she knew where Neela was and that she was generally safe. Not knowing was the absolute worst.

"Nope. Liz left the lab on Northwood around midnight, and Neela was still working. Have you checked with the protection detail?"

"You're right. She's probably still there. Can we get together later and make a plan for surveillance on Elliot Ramsey?"

"Sure. Shoot me a text when you're ready, and I'll swing by and pick you up."

She didn't bother with good-bye, choosing instead to ring Phil. "Where are you?"

"Across from Cone Hospital on Northwood. Why?"

"Is Doctor Sahjani there?"

"Why else would I be here? Duh. I don't see how she does it. She's got the stamina of—"

Jordan disconnected the line and dropped onto the bed. Her heart was racing and her armpits were sticky. She'd been on the verge of a panic attack. She was always calm under work-related stress and thrived on the adrenaline surge, until recently. Her emotions had been crazy wild since the day she met Neela and exacerbated by her visit to the orphanage. But this feeling was different—fear, plain and simple— fear for Neela's safety. She'd lost Amy, but she couldn't handle it if she failed again.

She paced, unable to settle or decide what to do next. Turning on the shower, she stepped under a cold stream. Icy water pounding on her back and shoulders summoned the terror of returning to the annex yesterday. The fear of not knowing if Neela was safe was almost as horrifying. The prickly spray shocked her body.

She needed to run, ride, fight, fuck, or something. Pain built and centered where it always did—between her thighs. Grabbing a towel, she clenched it in her teeth and screamed, muffling the sound. She felt helpless and out of control. She slid down the side of the shower, clutching herself and crying.

Would she always be afraid of what lurked in the darkness of her mind and of her inability to protect those close to her? She'd resurrected the ghosts with her return to the orphanage, but she needed to expose them to the light to be truly free. She screamed into the towel until her throat burned and she had no concept of how much time had passed.

"Jordan! Jordan, are you all right?"

She saw a figure through the glass door coming toward her. "Don't touch me. Go away."

"Jordan, it's Neela. I'm coming in."

"No! You can't see me like this." Was she afraid for Neela to see her crying or naked? The idea of either made her cower farther into the corner. "Go away, please."

"Jordan, listen to me. I have your robe. It's warm and soft, and I'll close my eyes while you put it on. Deal? I know you're freezing in there and you're scared. I can help."

Neela held the robe open so she couldn't see Jordan's body. Jordan breathed like she was giving birth until the pain passed and she could stand. "Okay."

"I'm right here, and I'll hug you when you're covered. Just so you know."

Jordan tucked her arms into the hefty robe and tied it around her waist. She brushed the wet hair off her forehead and turned. Neela's face was flushed and her eyes shiny with tears. "I didn't know if you were safe. I thought—"

"I'm here." Neela kissed her lightly and toweled some of the water from her hair before leading her to the bedroom. "Would you lie down with me? I really need to hold you right now."

Jordan climbed on the bed and pulled the robe tighter around her. "I'm so sorry. I'm not usually such a basket case."

"I know. You're usually tough and in control, except when you're mad at me." Neela teased and snuggled behind her, resting her arm around Jordan's waist. "I've got you."

Jordan tried to relax into Neela's embrace and accept being held. She'd always been the bodyguard, sleeping with one eye open. She couldn't remember ever feeling this protected and safe. The tension in her shoulders and back eased, and the muscles in her thighs that always seemed so firmly clenched slowly loosened.

Neela stroked her arm, and something warm and soft settled inside her. Neela touched her without expecting anything in return, gave without being asked, and didn't judge—components of intimacy Jordan imagined but had never experienced.

"Are you all right?" Neela asked.

"You make me believe that's actually possible. Thank you."

"You don't have to thank me. I'm here because I want to be, because I care about you."

Jordan took a deep breath and made the first step into her dark past with a potential partner. "How much do you know?"

"Are you sure you want to do this now? There's no rush, darling."

"Please, Neela. I'm not sure how far I'll get, but I have to try."

Neela hugged her again and lowered her voice. "I know people in positions of authority violated the trust of their offices. I know children experienced things no child should ever have to. And I know you are the bravest and most resilient person I've ever met to have fought so long, for yourself and Amy, and survived. What else do I need to know?" Her arm tightened around Jordan's waist.

"I don't have a family. My parents didn't care enough to keep me when I was born. Nobody wanted me, even when I was a baby. I've never really belonged anywhere. I think I eventually just stopped caring. Who wants to be with someone who has no past, no family, and no memories to share?"

"A blank slate."

"A what?"

"You're special. In stem-cell research the embryonic cells are master cells. They can become any other type of cell, which is great. We call them biological blank slates. You're like a blank slate. You survived a horrible childhood, took care of yourself, and now you're shaping your future. Your job puts you in all kinds of situations, and you make them better—like our master cells. Every experiment, every situation has side effects, and you've made the best of yours. You're pretty amazing."

"You have a way of making everything sound positive and fresh. And that's pretty amazing, but I want you to know everything." Jordan's chest constricted as she tried to breathe. She sat up on the side of the bed, unable to bear Neela's inevitable withdrawal when she told her the rest of her story. "You need...to know...what he...did to me." She spat the words between sobs like intermittent blasts of a machine gun.

"No, I don't. You're here. You're dealing with what happened, and I don't need to know anything more."

"But…I want…to be able…to touch you…and let you…touch me." Jordan felt her anger bubbling up. "I'm so mad." She paused. Was she doing the right thing?

"You have a right to be angry. It's how you protected yourself and got through the pain."

"He…tied me down." She rubbed the red streaks around her wrists from the hospital straps. "And touched me…all the time. He was always so rough."

Neela tried to ease her back onto the bed, but she shrugged away from her touch. Jordan wouldn't be comforted until it was all out. She had to know if Neela would turn away from her. "I felt things…it felt… good…and I *hated* that. I didn't want…to feel good with him." She grabbed a pillow, pressed it against her face, and screamed until some of the rage passed.

"Oh, Jordan, that was just your young body responding naturally to stimulus. You didn't do anything bad. Everybody likes to be touched. *He* made it bad. I'm so sorry, darling."

"When he got me…worked up…he came and then stopped. I hurt all the time. My arousal always hurt, and he wouldn't let me relieve it." Neela was quiet except for an occasional sob she tried to suppress. "You've seen…how I am…sexually. I don't want to always be… aggressive and untouchable like he taught me. I want to feel what you do. I have to know."

Neela placed her hand on Jordan's shoulder and made her look her in the eye. "Have to know what?"

"If I can ever be…like other people. If what I like makes me… abnormal?"

"What are you saying, Jordan?"

Jordan ducked her head and forced the words out. "I want to be with you…see if I can have regular sex, not like I've done before." She looked up quickly and saw Neela's surprised face. She turned back toward the wall. "You don't want me. I've spoiled it."

"Jordan, look at me. I'm just shocked at your courage and honesty. I don't think you're sick or weird or abnormal or any of those other words rolling around in your head. People who care about each other experiment with sex. Normal is relative. And just so you know, I've enjoyed everything we've done—all of it. But if you want to try something different, I'm up for that too."

Had she heard right? Neela wasn't disgusted by her. She didn't think she was fucked up beyond repair. She couldn't stop staring at Neela, searching for some sign of rejection or judgment, but finding none. Jordan felt like she'd won half the battle, but the hardest part remained. "Does that mean you'll do it?"

"Are you actually asking me to have sex with you?" Neela couldn't hide the hint of humor in her voice, and it helped Jordan relax.

"I guess I am."

"I'd be honored." She stroked the scar across Jordan's lip. "But I'm still stuck on you *asking*."

Jordan stretched out beside Neela again and took her in her arms. "Okay, now you're just messing with me, aren't you?"

Neela wrinkled her gorgeous nose and nodded.

"You're the most amazing woman I've ever met. I know you'd never do anything to hurt anyone. It's not in you. And I can't imagine trying this with anyone else. I have to get my life back, all of it. Can you understand that?"

"Of course I understand, and I'll do whatever you want."

"Really?" Jordan had been so uncertain about her request that the realization it might actually happen was temporarily overwhelming. "Really?"

"Now you're making me beg again?"

"I'm surprised you still want to be with me after how I've treated you. And I'm so sorry for everything. I have no excuse, and I don't know how I'll ever make it up to you, but I will."

"You've already saved my life. What more could I ask?"

"For me to treat you with dignity and respect, like someone I care about…because I do, you know…care about you. I want more than just an occasional fuck, Neela, much more." Her sexual hunger still hovered just beneath the surface, but a more powerful need made her cling to the comfort and safety of Neela's arms. Something was happening that she didn't understand. Perhaps Neela was easing her transition from the horrors of the past to the possibilities of the future.

"I care about you too, Jordan."

She snuggled against Neela's neck and allowed the warmth of her body to sink in and heal the rough edges of her soul. "I'm really enjoying this—a lot."

"Me too, darling, me too."

❖

Jordan shivered against her, and Neela tried to imagine a childhood so damaged by the evils in Jordan's past. She fought the urge to be sick. She'd gouged divots in her palms from clenching her fists. People in positions of authority were held to a higher standard, and the staff at New Beginning had failed miserably. No one could justify what despicable people had done to Jordan while others stood by. Neela felt so inadequate. Jordan's guilt and shame were deeply embedded, and all she could do was comfort her and be patient.

"Thank you for listening," Jordan said. "I was so afraid to tell you."

"Shush, it's all right, darling. You don't have to be afraid now."

Jordan nuzzled just below her collarbone. "You're so incredibly soft. This space right here," she kissed just above her breast, "is like heaven." Jordan looked up at her. "Can I open your shirt just a little?"

"Of course you can," Neela said. Jordan's tone was tentative, something she'd never heard before, and the vulnerability of it opened her soul.

Jordan fumbled with the tiny buttons on her blouse until the first three came loose to just below her bra. "So beautiful. You're like a lightly toasted treat." Neela felt Jordan's heat rise as she edged closer. She was like a match; once ignited she burned hard and fast.

Jordan gently traced the mounds of Neela's breasts and her breath hitched. "Jor—Jordan." If Jordan was serious about trying something different, she'd better divert her before things went much further.

Jordan pulled back. "I'm sorry. I probably shouldn't."

"Would you let me try something?"

Jordan's lust-hooded gaze shifted to one of fear and uncertainty. "I'm a little worried right now, but okay. I said I wanted to learn."

"Do you trust me, Jordan?"

"As much as I've ever trusted anyone."

"Roll over on your back." Jordan's eyes searched hers for several seconds, and then she rolled over, clutching the robe around her. "You can keep that on if you want. I'd like to touch you, slowly, softly. Do you think that would be all right?"

"Maybe."

"I'll tell you exactly what I'm doing so you won't have any surprises. Okay?" Jordan nodded. "If you'd like to tell me what you're feeling, I'd like that. If you want me to stop at any point, just say so."

The corners of Jordan's mouth inched upward but stopped short of a full smile. "I like a challenge, remember?" She was trying to be brave, and Neela admired her even more.

"I'm going to slide my hand inside the robe just enough to touch your neck and shoulders. Probably a good idea to give the left one a miss though."

Jordan chuckled. "Yeah, it's had a workout the past few days."

Neela feathered her fingers across the hollow at the base of Jordan's neck and out across her collarbone. "Your skin is beautiful. If I'm lightly toasted, you're definitely sun-bleached." The temperature of Jordan's body rose under her fingers, and Neela's pulse responded. Every time Jordan had touched her before, she'd imagined what it would feel like to reciprocate. Reality was much better than the dream. Touching Jordan was like drenching her body in sensation, involving every sense—her pale beauty, her incredible scent, the silkiness of her skin, the soft deliciousness of her mouth, and the slight hitch in her breathing as Neela caressed her.

"A nice thing about making love is there's no rush. Enjoying the slow, steady burn of buildup can be the best part." She looked at Jordan's face. Her eyes were closed, and she held her bottom lip between her teeth. The delicate features of her face twisted into an anxious façade. "Relax. Concentrate on *my* hands as I touch your body. What do you feel, Jordan?"

"Scared, but it tickles a little too, and then shivers run down my body."

"That's great. Your skin is getting warmer and flushing light pink. So beautiful." She inched lower, barely brushing the swell of Jordan's breast. "May I?"

"Uh-huh." Jordan tensed, preparing to be touched. "I'm not sure I can, Neela."

"Please. Trust me. I won't hurt you, and I'll stop whenever you say."

"Okay."

Neela dipped her hand into the robe and barely swept her fingers over Jordan's breast. The nipple puckered immediately against her palm and she almost moaned aloud. "God, Jordan, you're so responsive." She glanced up again. "Are you all right with this?"

"So far. It's nice, but when you touch my breast it's like…lightning to my crotch."

"Perfect." Moisture gathered between her legs as Jordan described her response. "I'm feeling the same thing and you haven't even touched me."

"Really?" Jordan opened her eyes for the first time and met her gaze.

"Yes, my darling. Making love is all about give and take. And the greatest gift is your trust, your willingness to share yourself with me. It's an honor I'll cherish forever. You have no idea how arousing trust and intimacy can be."

"I think I'm beginning to understand. Don't stop touching me."

She closed her hand around Jordan's breast and felt her abdomen clench when the blue of Jordan's eyes darkened and she licked her lips. "Do you like that?"

"Oh…yeah. Your hand is so soft and it fits me perfectly."

Neela didn't want to upset Jordan by asking the question, though surely someone had touched her before. But she acted like physical intimacy without sex was completely new.

"Neela, I'm starting to want…more. I'm getting really wet and hard."

Every word Jordan spoke punctuated Neela's desire. It was like making love to someone for the first time. The novelty and innocence of Jordan's responses bombarded her with so much longing she could barely remain focused. "Patience. We're trying something new, remember?" Neela opened the robe wider and cupped both Jordan's breasts, kneading the firm flesh and teasing her nipples. Jordan arched to meet her and released a long, contented groan. The tingle in Neela turned to a throb. "So nice."

"Would you…take your clothes off?" Jordan's hesitation sounded like she was ashamed to ask for what she wanted.

"Of course I will. Slowly or quickly?"

"Fast. I already miss your touch."

"So, this touching business isn't bad?"

Jordan shook her head but didn't take her eyes off Neela's hands as she undressed. Neela finished unbuttoning her blouse and shucked it off with her bra, tossing them both on the floor. As she unzipped her jeans, Jordan reached for her hand. "Can I help?"

"You can do anything you like." Jordan rose and slid the zipper down slowly from the waistband, and with each audible click, Neela's body grew hotter. "That is so sexy."

Jordan tugged her jeans off and reached for her bikinis, peeling them off in no rush. "I've never undressed anyone this slowly before. It's kind of hot."

When Jordan stared at her body, Neela felt a rush of arousal. She tried to close her legs, suddenly embarrassed by how wet she'd become.

"Don't." Jordan placed her hands on her knees and continued to stare. "You're so beautiful. I've never seen a woman so excited, so close up. Is that all for me?"

"Absolutely." She grabbed the opening of Jordan's robe, wanting desperately to strip it off her shoulders. Her hands trembled. "May I please remove this?"

Jordan clutched the robe for a few seconds as a series of emotions played across her face. When she loosened her grip, she took the robe with her and flung it across the room. "Okay?"

Neela couldn't speak. Jordan's body was more gorgeous than she'd imagined. Her ivory skin was like a protective covering of a delicate flower. Her rosy nipples and the dark dusting of hair between her legs were the only color on an otherwise flawless canvas, aside from the angry injury on her shoulder. The first time she'd seen Jordan she likened her to a chiseled alabaster goddess. The reality was breathtaking.

"Is something wrong?" Jordan's skin flushed, and she tugged a corner of the sheet to cover herself.

Neela stopped her. "Everything is absolutely perfect. You're perfect. I've never seen a body so blatantly sexual. Come here." She held out her hand, and Jordan moved cautiously down beside her. "I'm not sure if I can go slowly anymore. I'm so turned on I can hardly breathe."

"Then don't try. I need you, Neela."

"But…I thought you wanted…"

"I want you." Jordan rolled on top of her, and when they pressed together for the first time in full skin-to-skin contact, Neela fought back the initial spasms of orgasm. Jordan growled deep in her throat and shifted gently until their breasts and crotches locked intimately.

"Jordan, you feel so good. I've dreamed of this moment." She kissed Jordan's neck and sought her mouth.

As their kiss deepened, Jordan pumped and ground against her, her urgency rising. "Help me go slow, Neela."

Her pleading shocked Neela just enough to refocus on Jordan. She eased to the side, took Jordan's hand, and slowly guided it to her sex. "Inside me, Jordan. Slowly. I want to feel every inch of you."

Jordan entered her gradually, drawing a steady moan from Neela that she couldn't control. "Exquisite." When their lips met again, Jordan hesitated. She traced Neela's lips with her tongue and gently eased inside while stroking her at the same pace. Neela's body rocked instinctively against Jordan as she took her with her tongue and her hands. She'd meant to be the patient one, the teacher, but Jordan's touch unraveled her, and she surrendered as she'd always done with her.

"Oh, Jordan. I feel so much. You shatter me."

"Do you like this…agonizing pace?" Jordan's eyes were pools of conflicting emotions. The pain in her face was obvious as she tried to give Neela what she wanted while holding back her natural instinct to free her urges.

"You're doing great. I love the way you're touching me, gently but with purpose. Don't stop. Please."

Jordan bit her lip and closed her eyes, lines of concentration forming across her forehead. She moved her knee between Neela's legs, using it to control her deliberate thrusts.

"Yes, that's it. Slowly. Take me slowly. Suck my breasts." As she said the words, Neela knew she wouldn't last much longer no matter what the pace. Jordan always bypassed her normal responses and went straight to her come button.

Jordan lowered her head, and when her mouth closed over her breast, Neela felt the first pulses of orgasm spiraling up from her toes. "Yes, yes. So soft and sweet. I'm close, darling."

Jordan shielded her teeth with her lips and nibbled Neela's breasts, then scraped her bare teeth over her nipple time after time until Neela begged. But Jordan seemed in a sexual feeding haze.

"You taste so good, Neela." Suddenly she pulled out and stared into Neela's face. "Can I…" Her eyes glanced down.

"Yes, *please.*"

While gently massaging her breasts, Jordan kissed her way down Neela's torso. She lightly licked the tip of Neela's clit, then blew on it, licking and blowing until Neela felt she would explode. "Jordan. Please, make me come."

Jordan looked into her eyes and claimed her with her mouth, sucking and flicking until her climax ripped from her and detonated every nerve ending. She jerked and spasmed and continued to meet Jordan's exquisite mouth until she could barely breathe. "Oh. My. God."

She was boneless for several seconds, waiting for her pulse to slow and her breathing to calm enough to speak. When she became aware of her surroundings again, Jordan was rocking against the bed, her hand thrusting hard between her legs. "Jordan. Stop."

"Hurts." Her voice was small, her breathing erratic, and her cobalt eyes glazed with pain.

"Come here, my darling." She tried to pull Jordan up beside her, but she resisted.

"Have to do this." She coiled in on herself, clawing for satisfaction.

"No, you don't. I'm so sorry I got carried away. Let me help, like you helped me."

Jordan's forehead creased and relaxed with each breath as she pushed through the hurt and uncertainty. "Not sure I can."

"Let's try. Please. Do it for yourself…and for me." She urged Jordan up beside her, and this time she didn't resist. "Relax, and show me what to do." She skimmed her hand down the flat plane of Jordan's abdomen and stopped just above her pubic mound. "I want to touch you so badly, to help you feel what I just felt, to be connected when you do."

Jordan withdrew her hand, tentatively took Neela's, and placed it over her sex. "Are you sure you want to do this? It could take a long time. I don't come easily."

"Certain, and I don't care if it takes hours. I'll enjoy every minute. Tell me."

Burying her head in Neela's shoulder, Jordan mumbled, "Just rub my clit?"

Jordan sounded like she didn't deserve to ask for what pleased her. She had to help her understand how natural her desires were. "I would love to touch you." She dipped her fingers into the juices around Jordan's opening and scissored her stiff clit between two fingers as Jordan had demonstrated. Jordan moaned and her legs tensed. "You feel so good, Jordan. You're so wet and responsive. I love it." Jordan's muscles relaxed slightly. "Is this hard enough?"

"A little more pressure." She followed Jordan's instructions and watched the emotions warring across her face—trepidation, fear, guilt, and eventually an inkling of pleasure. "Yeah, that's good. I like that. Is it all right for you?"

"I'm in heaven. Just let it go, darling. Enjoy the feelings. You're safe with me."

Neela slid her leg across Jordan's thigh, unable to see the passion in Jordan and remain unaffected. Her slick arousal coated Jordan's leg and she groaned. "See what you're doing to me? You're so sexy and beautiful. You make me ache."

"Faster and harder."

Neela quickened her pace but felt Jordan begin to slip away—her body tensed, her eyes clenched shut, and she rocked harder against her hand as if chasing something lost. "Jordan, open your eyes." No response. "Look at me, Jordan." When Jordan's eyes locked on hers, they were distant and unresponsive. "Jordan, it's Neela. Stay with me. Feel me. I will never hurt you."

As Jordan refocused, her body relaxed and she breathed a long exhale. "I'm okay." She cupped Neela's hand, buried in her sex, and squeezed. "Your finger feels so good there. Work it faster. Help me come, Neela. I really want to with you."

Neela felt like she'd been bathed in hot coals. She shivered from a flood of emotion and rubbed her throbbing clit against Jordan's thigh. She stroked Jordan's flesh, matching the pace of her hips until she felt the first twinge of orgasm. "Can I go inside?"

"No! Just rub." Jordan's gaze focused on Neela's hand working between her legs. "Yeah. Good." Neela stroked a quick-quick, slow-slow rhythm until Jordan's legs stiffened and her heels dug into the mattress. "Hard—er."

Neela rode Jordan's thigh, feeling her own orgasm only seconds away as she watched Jordan slowly unraveling beneath her touch. "I'm with you, Jordan. Come for me."

Jordan's hands clutched the bedding on each side of her and, with a gasp that seemed to rise from her depths, finally emptied in her hand. "Oh, Neela. Don't stop yet. Pull. There's more." She milked Jordan's clit until she thought she couldn't possibly come any longer, but she kept pulsing in her fingers, so beautifully free and responsive. Eventually they both collapsed on the bed, Jordan bringing an edge of the sheet with her.

Neela tugged the cover out of her hands. "Don't try to hide this body from me again, ever. You're amazing, and I never want to stop looking at you and touching you."

"I never thought anyone would really enjoy having sex with me, not the way I am."

"Nothing is wrong with the way you want to be loved. Do you hear me, Jordan? I think you're perfect. My God, that was awesome."

"But...I didn't let you go inside or use your mouth." Her skin flushed again and she picked at a wrinkle in the covers.

Neela slid up beside her and wrapped her in a cocoon of arms and legs. "You will. Besides, we have to save some of the good stuff for later. If we did everything at once, you might get tired of me. Before long you'll beg to be finger fucked and devoured like a delicious snack."

"*Neela!*"

"What's the matter, sport? I thought you liked it primal." She smiled and kissed the corner of Jordan's swollen lips.

"Oh, you're messing with me again, aren't you?"

"Maybe just a little."

Jordan hugged her, and Neela had never felt so completely and utterly connected to another person. Sure, they had some challenges, but she was more confident that at least they were both willing to face them now—in and out of the bedroom.

CHAPTER NINETEEN

Jordan woke three hours later still wrapped in Neela's arms. She eased out of her embrace, edging far enough away to take in every inch of her—the cute painted toenails, a tiny scar beside her left kneecap, her adorable outie belly button, dark-chocolate nipples atop milk-chocolate breasts, full kissable lips so evocative they should be outlawed, long silky hair, and slender, delicate fingers that had brought Jordan's body back to life.

When Neela had touched her the first time, she'd watched her, unable to connect the visual with what she was feeling. She had been unable to imagine anyone touching her so intimately without inflicting pain. She'd temporarily frozen. But this was Neela, and she would never judge or hurt her. The moisture she used to dread now aroused promise and excitement. She wasn't naive enough to believe she'd been cured, if there was such a thing for what she'd experienced, but Molly's therapy had given her hope, and last night Neela had given her a chance.

Yet could she surrender everything, give herself completely to Neela? After all, fondling was basically just masturbation, in her opinion, whether she did it or allowed someone else to. Would she ever permit Neela to penetrate her and make love to her orally—that was the epitome of vulnerability. A shiver of anxiety swept through her.

"Why are you staring at me?"

"Because you're just too gorgeous not to stare at. I'm trying to figure out how you bewitched me so completely. From the moment I met you, I knew I was in trouble."

"I cast a spell over you." Neela's eyes raked over her naked body before she reached for Jordan's leg but then paused, waiting for permission. She wasn't taking anything for granted, and that made Jordan care for her even more.

"It's okay. I won't run."

Neela wiggled closer, threw her leg over Jordan's, and pulled her down beside her. "Good, because my legs are too weak to chase you this morning, aside from the fractured one, of course." Her expression turned serious. "Are you all right?"

"I'm better than all right. No one has ever brought me to orgasm, and it was so long and intense. Thank you for that, but mostly thanks for your patience. I never imagined finding someone who would understand what I've been through and try to help me deal with it. You're amazing."

"Trust me. It was my pleasure."

"But you understand, this doesn't mean—"

"I know." Neela kissed her so softly Jordan couldn't believe her tenderness. "It's only the beginning, but I'm in it for the long haul. Get used to it. So, what's on—"

A soft knock sounded at the bedroom door and Bina announced, "Coffee, tea, and quality time in ten minutes. I expect both of you to be presentable."

Jordan threw the blanket over her head. "Oh, my God! Your mother caught me in bed with her daughter. How will I ever face her? I'm totally freaking right now."

"Well, at least everybody knows everything, so life just got a lot simpler. Get dressed. This probably isn't a good time to keep her waiting."

Was it really so simple, Jordan wondered as she crept down the hall to her bedroom for a quick shower? Were family dynamics really that straightforward? She had no personal experience, but at work, she'd seen mostly the opposite. As she dressed, she hoped that she'd know what to say to Bina. Jordan had to relay her respect for Neela and for the sanctity of their home in spite of the indiscreet situation. Though she'd treated Neela poorly in the beginning, she wasn't and never could be simply another conquest.

Neela met her in the hallway just before they entered the kitchen and threaded their fingers together. She tried to pull away, but Neela held fast. "Trust me."

Jordan took a deep breath and tried to act casual. Neela kissed Bina's cheek and guided Jordan toward the table, where two cups of coffee waited.

"Stop right there," Bina said. Jordan felt the blood drain from her face and she froze. "Where is my good-morning greeting from my new daughter?"

"*Mama.*" Neela gave her a scathing look, but Bina ignored her.

Jordan kissed Bina's other cheek and took a seat across from her. "Bina, I'm so sorry if you think—" Jordan wanted to explain before things got any further out of hand, but she wasn't sure exactly how to do that without causing even more discomfort and confusion—at least *she* felt uncomfortable and slightly confused.

Bina waved her hand in her customary manner, warding off any attempts to sidetrack her. "We will speak frankly. Quality time demands it." Jordan and Neela nodded but remained quiet. "This is the first time my Neela has taken a woman to her bed with me in the house." Neela started to speak, but Bina stopped her. "I know you have had others here, but never while I am home. That you have chosen to do so with Jordan says you care deeply for her and wish me to accept her into our family. Is this what you are saying, Beta?"

Neela looked at Jordan and her brown eyes filled with tears. The connection between them was like a current, strong and true. If anyone had tried to pull them apart at that moment, Jordan would've fought with everything she had.

"Yes, Mama, if she'll have me."

Jordan's vision blurred and she couldn't see Neela or Bina. "I— I—" She pulled for breath and her heart felt like it would burst. "Why? I don't have anything…no real home, no relatives, no past to speak of. Why would you want me?"

Bina cupped Jordan's hand in hers. "Because my Neela loves you, and she deserves only the very best."

Jordan tried to swallow as she looked at Neela.

"It's true. I'm in love with you, Jordan. I have been for some time, as unimaginable as that seems." When Jordan opened her mouth to answer, Neela placed a finger over her lips. "Don't say anything until you're certain how you feel. I know you've got a lot going on right now. Take your time. You'll get no pressure from me...or Bina." She looked to her mother for confirmation.

"Very well, but you will make the right decision. It is the only one." Bina smiled and raised her teacup with effort. "This is truly a good morning."

Jordan took sips of her coffee so she wouldn't choke on the lump in her throat. Neela was in love with her. How was that even possible? She'd treated her horribly in the beginning, and she had nothing to offer a woman who valued family so highly. And she and Bina wanted her to share their lives. Could she take the risk—to care deeply enough to be hurt and to bond with a family that could one day discard her? But as she looked at the two women beside her, a barrier collapsed inside and some of her anger evaporated like steam off her coffee. The tears started. "If you'll excuse me, I'd like to check on Blue."

She escaped to the backyard, and Blue almost knocked her down as he greeted her. "Hi, fella. Have you been good and played nice for Bina? She's a bit frail, so you have to be careful with her. No jumping on her like you do me. Okay?" She scratched behind his ears and settled on the grass, swiping at her tears. "I think they like us. Do you like it here?" He nuzzled her neck and licked her hand. "Nice play space, huh?"

Blue looked toward the house before Jordan heard the back door open. She waited, her hand buried in Blue's fur, needing the connection to something solid, as Neela made her way to her and joined them on the grass.

She settled close enough that their legs touched the length of their thighs with her cast out to the other side. Heat instantly surged between them. "Are you all right?"

"Yeah. Just a little shell-shocked, I guess."

"I'm sorry about that. I hadn't intended for my mother to tell you I'm in love with you, but she always gets to the crux of the matter. It's a gift, or a curse."

Jordan kept petting Blue. "How do you...love me, Neela?"

"With my entire heart." Her grin was adorable, and Jordan appreciated her attempt to lighten the mood.

"I mean, really? After how I treated you? And I still don't know if I can open up totally, emotionally and sexually. The worst part is, I probably don't deserve you. And please don't say I saved your life because that's not enough."

"It might not mean much to you, but my life is pretty important to me." Neela nudged her, trying to get her to smile.

"I didn't mean that. Your life means everything to me."

Neela circled her arm around Jordan's waist and leaned into her. "Jordan, you've made a decent life for yourself in spite of what you've been through, maybe because of it. Your friends see what a wonderful person you are. Animals love you, and they can sense bad energy." She nodded at Blue. "I think you're the most interesting, exciting, kindhearted, and challenging woman I've ever met. Yes, you have issues, but who doesn't? And Bina Sahjani thinks you're pretty spectacular. I didn't even get a sermon about sneaking a woman into my bedroom. That's saying something."

Jordan laughed at that one. "Well, she is a pretty good judge of character, isn't she?"

"The best. But none of that is as important as how you feel about yourself. The rest of us can only offer encouragement until you see it. And I know you're not there yet."

"If you're so smart, what am I thinking right now?" Jordan pressed their bodies closer and stared into Neela's brown eyes. Her skin heated and tingled with arousal.

"I'd say from the flush on your cheeks and the slight hitch in your breathing you're thinking about how great my hands felt on you last night and—"

"Whoa! TMI," Bex said from behind them.

Jordan scooted away from Neela and raised her hands in frustration. "Really? How about a knock before you barge in?"

Bex waved her hand from side to side. "Hello, the great outdoors. Wide open."

Liz stood behind her smiling. "I think it's great to see supercop all mushy."

"Liz, not helping." Neela kissed Jordan's cheek and tried to get up, but her cast made rising from the ground difficult. Jordan stood and offered her hand. "Thanks, darling. Think I'll check on Bina."

Jordan leaned in and spoke softly. "I love it when you call me that." And she absolutely did. The way Neela almost whispered the word and the emotion behind it was like an aphrodisiac. She wanted to take her where she stood, but more importantly, she wanted to feel worthy to take her.

"Maybe you should wait a second, Neela," Liz said. Bex shook her head but Liz continued. "You should probably hear what Bex has to say."

Jordan could tell by the way Bex was acting that her news wasn't good, and she wanted to protect Neela as much as possible. She glared at Liz.

"I don't care how long you stare at me with those cold blues, detective. Neela has a right to know what's going on. It's her life we're talking about here."

Neela appeared torn, like a referee between opposing sides, so Jordan stepped in. "Go ahead, Bex. Liz probably has a good point. Neela shouldn't be kept in the dark."

The three of them settled on the deck as Bex paced and talked. "I've been going over Elliot Ramsey's business interests. He's got his sticky fingers in projects everywhere to promote conservative and free-market agendas. And he's the primary financier for, wait for it, the only abortion clinic in the state that will still be operational if Governor Lloyd's bill passes."

"What?" Jordan wasn't sure she'd heard correctly. "He finances an abortion clinic?"

"The only one that will still meet the state's requirements if Lloyd's anti-abortion bill passes?" Neela looked stunned. "That's not possible, is it?"

"The man can make chicken salad out of chicken shit, financially speaking," Liz said.

"Then that gives him—" Jordan stopped and tried to signal Bex with her eyes to shut up, but she didn't get the hint.

"Motive," Bex said. "Exactly. He'd want this bill to go through more than anyone. It would mean big money in his pocket. And with Neela retired and now able to throw all her clout behind stopping the bill, he'd be more inclined to try to silence her." She stopped pacing and met three sets of glaring eyes. "What?"

"Shut up, Bex," Jordan said.

But the damage had been done. Neela's face was ashen. "You mean this whole sordid mess isn't over yet? And I've just made it worse by resigning? Great. Why didn't the bastard tell me what he wanted in the first place? I might've accommodated him." She seemed to reconsider her statement. "Nah, not a chance."

Jordan moved to the arm of Neela's chair and rubbed the back of her neck. "Don't worry. We'll figure this out and put an end to it soon. I promise."

"I know you will." She kissed Jordan's hand and brought it to her cheek. Her skin had gone slightly cooler, and Jordan clenched her teeth. Nobody was going to threaten or hurt Neela again, not as long as Jordan drew breath.

"Right. Bex, let's get moving on this. I don't give a good goddamn who's working the assault or who's on protection detail. We're on Elliot Ramsey, or at least I am, until I know exactly who's behind the attempt on Neela's life. After hearing this, I have a feeling he's the key. You probably have to get back to Milton, but I'm still on medical leave, so my time is my own."

"You're not leaving me out. I'm due some off days. No reason I can't take them now." They bumped fists and smiled at Neela and Liz like teenagers who'd just scored with the prom queen.

Liz hooked her arm in Bex's. "Walk me to my car, lover. You want a lift to the lab, Neela, or are you taking your car?"

"You go. I'll be along shortly." When Bex and Liz disappeared around the corner of the house, Neela turned to Jordan. "Promise you won't do anything crazy. Ramsey is a powerful man, and he'll probably go to extremes to protect his money and his reputation."

"Crazy? Me do something crazy?" Neela wasn't smiling. "Okay. I just want to find out for sure if he's connected to all this. I can do that without raising any alarms, and I promise I'll be careful." She hugged Neela and throbbed from their proximity. Her hunger for Neela never seemed to lessen, but now warmth and a genuine desire to connect intimately mitigated the hunger. "Neela, I feel…"

"I know. I feel it too."

Neela kissed her, and the power of their connection grounded her. "Damn, Neela. You make me ache so bad—but in a good way, not like before. I need you to touch me again, soon."

"I can't wait, my darling." She nipped Jordan's bottom lip with her teeth and play-shoved her toward the steps. "Now go. Do your job so I can do mine. This cast isn't the only thing making walking a problem right now."

"Jeez, you two, give it a rest," Bex said as she reappeared from the front grinning like she'd won first prize in the matchmaking contest.

"You're one to talk," Jordan said. "See you later." She waved as Neela went back in the house, and she and Bex walked the backyard with Blue at her side. "What do you think we should do?"

"Have a double ceremony as soon as possible before one of us gets arrested for lewd and lascivious conduct. We've got a couple of super-hot women on our hands. And from what I can see, we're both goners. No?"

"Afraid so, but I'm talking about Ramsey at the moment, not our suddenly full and illustrious love lives."

"I think we should watch his house. If he's mixed up in threats and attempted murder, he won't be stupid or careless enough to handle it himself, and he won't contact his lackey at his prestigious state-capitol office."

"He'd also be crazy to make contact at his home, but people get lazy, especially rich people. So, when do we start?"

"How about tonight? Got any other plans?" She nudged Jordan's shoulder and immediately apologized when she winced. "Sorry, wrong side."

"Can you pick me up around ten?"

"Sure, but where?" She smiled one of her annoying smirks.

"Here would probably be good, and no smart-assed comments. I bet you're not sleeping alone either."

"No, but Liz's mother isn't in the house. Just saying. You've got brass ones, partner."

"It's not like that, Bex. I care about Neela, a lot, and Bina knows it."

"Good. I'll try to make sure you don't screw it up." She jumped over the back fence and headed toward her car before Jordan could smack her. "See you at ten."

❖

Neela shuffled the slides under the microscope one at a time, praying for a different outcome, but each one produced the same result. The stem cells in their most recent sample had deteriorated, and the injured cells had taken over. "Damn it." She pushed the trays across the table so hard they teetered near the edge.

"Calm down, honey." Liz rubbed her back. "We knew this was a possibility when we started. Every experiment has side effects. It's not the first time we've lost this battle, and it probably won't be the last."

"I know, Liz, but Bina's getting more fragile every day, as are all the other people suffering in the world. It's just so hard."

"You're giving us way too much credit and responsibility. Not everybody in the world knows about little ole us or the work we're doing." Liz guided her away from the worktable. "Let's go get a coffee. We've been at this since noon yesterday, and in case you haven't noticed, it's morning."

"I feel like such a failure. You don't know how hard my parents struggled to provide my education. Why isn't this working? If we do make a breakthrough, it'll probably be too late to help the most important person in my life. And I couldn't help my subordinates because I quit my job. I have no idea what's happened to most of them now. And I'm not sure if Jordan will ever—" She couldn't voice this particular fear to Liz. She'd violate Jordan's trust, and she would never purposely do that.

Neela followed Liz, shucked her gloves, and retrieved her cell phone from her coat pocket on the way to the canteen. "I'd like to check on Bina and call—"

"Supercop?" Liz batted her eyes and tried to look innocent. "Obviously you two have made progress. How did that happen? Let me guess. She tied you down, made you submit to her will, and fucked you senseless."

"Not funny, Liz." Images of Jordan's past flashed through her mind, making Neela cringe.

Liz hugged her. "Oh, honey, you know I was kidding. Whatever nerve I stepped on, I'm really sorry. I only want the best for you."

"I know. I'm sorry too. Temporarily lost my sense of humor."

"As long as Jordan makes you happy, I don't care if she runs with wolves and eats raw chicken for dinner. Seriously."

Neela laughed, and some of the tension of her work failure and the memory of Jordan's ordeal fell away. "Thanks. So what do we do now?"

"Why don't we go somewhere else, talk about work strategy, and compare girlfriend notes? I'd love to know what supercop is really like in bed, strictly academic, of course."

"Strictly prurient, you mean. Absolutely not. This is one woman I will not discuss."

"I've never heard you say that before. She must be the one." She finger-quoted the air.

"I'm certain of it."

"And what about her? Are you the one for her? Nothing's worse than having to tell someone who thinks you're the love of her life that she's not yours."

"That's not happening. Jordan just needs a bit more time to figure out some things. I'm certain she'll come around."

"Are you sure, honey?" She placed her hand over Neela's. "Are you sure she won't play this out to the end and then walk away?"

"If she does, she does, but I have to take the chance, Liz. I've never felt anything like this before. She totally unravels me and challenges me to reexamine things I always took for granted. She's like our lab experiments. I never know how it's going to turn out, but I'll always keep coming back. If she left today, I wouldn't regret a minute I've spent with her. At last I know what it feels like to be in love. Can you understand?"

Liz was gazing at her, a faraway look in her eyes. "Totally. I feel exactly the same way about Bex. Guess we've both hit the jackpot."

"Guess so." Neela nudged Liz, picked up her cell, and dialed Bina. "Hi, Mama. You all right? Did you sleep well?"

"Fine. Will you be home soon?"

"On my way. Sorry, but Liz and I have been working all night. I'll see you soon."

"*Don't* hurry. Everything is fine here, just fine," Bina said.

"You sure you're okay? Your voice sounds strange."

"Fine, Mrs. Scott."

The line went dead, and a splash of fear coursed through Neela. She stared at the phone, her hand shaking.

"What's wrong, Neela?"

"Something's happened. Bina just used a contraction and called me Mrs. Scott. Her voice sounded strained."

"What do you mean she used a contraction?"

"She never does that, thinks it's improper English." Neela was sprinting as she spoke.

"Maybe she's having another episode, light-headed, not thinking clearly."

"It's more than that. I could tell by her tone. She was trying to tell me something. I have to go. I'll call you later." She ducked into the lab and grabbed her purse, not bothering to change out of her scrubs. Fear kept her upright and moving forward. If she paused to think about what might be going on at home, she'd collapse in an immobile heap.

As she ran to her car in the parking lot, she saw a note stuck under the windshield wiper. She pulled it off and waved her protection officers over. Leaning against the side of the car, she ripped the envelope open as Phil and Harry came across the street and joined her. *What's the point of police protection if they're never around when I need them?* She kept the thought to herself as she stared at the words plastered across the page.

You didn't take the hint.
Do you know where your mother is?

CHAPTER TWENTY

I feel like Phil and Harry. Three piss breaks, four cups of coffee, a box of doughnuts, and fuzzy teeth were all we accomplished last night." Bex tried to stretch her legs, but the car seat didn't go back far enough. "The only things we learned were Elliot Ramsey has a drop-dead gorgeous wife and drinks too much Scotch. Any other observations?"

"Don't forget his propensity for watching porn on his laptop. Yuck. I'm scarred for life." Jordan cranked the car and started toward home. As she made the turn at the corner, her cell vibrated. She checked the readout. "Jesus. Bina just activated the silent alarm. She's in trouble." She floored the accelerator. "Call Neela."

Before Bex could dial the number, Jordan's phone buzzed again. "Yeah?"

"Jordan, Bina's in trouble. Something's wrong. Get home *now*." Neela was yelling.

"Neela? Slow down. Tell me what's going on."

"I just told you. Something is terribly wrong. Bina called me Mrs. Scott. She sounded rattled. She's trying to warn me. I don't know—"

"Neela, where are you?"

"Who cares where I am. Take care of Bina. Hurry!"

Jordan flipped on the blue lights and siren as Neela's voice faded. "Jordan, it's Phil. She's with us. Somebody left a threatening note on her windshield implying her mother was in danger. We're running emergency to the house. We'll meet you there. "

"She just activated her silent alarm too, but don't tell Neela."

Jordan tossed the phone to Bex. Blood pounded in her ears so loudly the siren faded into the background, and she narrowed her focus to the tapered tunnel she navigated through traffic. "Oh, hell, no. This is *not* happening." Bex was quiet beside her except for the occasional "clear on the right" to let her know she could proceed through an intersection.

She cut the siren a block from Neela's house, jumped out, and ran. As her feet pounded the pavement, she'd never moved so slowly. Her mind was twenty feet ahead, but she felt like she was running in wet cement. A strange car was in the driveway, and she pointed for Bex to cover it. She ran straight toward the door and then through it.

Feet first, she rammed the door and it came loose from the frame. At the end of the hallway near her bedroom, a man held Bina's left arm, jerking and pulling to make her walk, but she resisted. Her face telegraphed the pain every forced movement caused. When Bina saw Jordan, she dropped limply to the floor and rolled away. Jordan didn't stop running until she rammed the man in the chest with her shoulder and brought him down.

As he fell backward gasping for breath, Jordan straddled him, pounding him with both fists. His head moved from side to side with each punch like a rag doll, but she didn't stop. "You. Do. Not. Hurt. My. Family." She punctuated every word with another strike, seeing only his hands on Bina and the anguish on her face.

"Jordan! Stop!" Words from somewhere penetrated her rage. "Stop! You'll kill him." Bex was trying to pull her off the bloody man.

"I don't care. Let go of me." She jerked loose and hit him again.

"Jordan, darling, stop." Neela's voice was stressed, but still calming and very close. She sounded okay, but what about Bina? She pressed her knees into the man's shoulders to keep him pinned to the floor and turned to look for Bina. "Bina is fine. You saved her. Stop now."

Neela put her hand on Jordan's arm and urged her away. As soon as Jordan crawled off the intruder, Phil and Harry rolled the guy over, handcuffed him, and escorted him outside. She slid to where Bina sat huddled on the floor in Neela's arms. "Are you all right? Did he hurt you? At all? Anywhere? Tell me? Let's get her to the hospital and make sure." Neela was checking Bina for injuries, asking similar questions.

"Both of you stop. No hospital." She slapped at Neela's hands. "I am fine, but Jordan is hurt, once again." She pointed to her left shoulder, stained with fresh blood.

As the adrenaline drained from her, Jordan slumped against the wall. She shook all over. When she'd fought for herself as a teenager, she often felt losing the battle would've been a blessing. But seeing the terrified look on Bina's face, she knew this was a fight she could not lose. Everything important in her life now had depended on it. She smiled in spite of the pain in her shoulder because Neela and Bina were finally safe.

Neela pulled her into the huddle with Bina and wrapped an arm around both of them. "My family is okay. Thank you, my darling. Now, let's get you to the hospital again."

Jordan was coming down from her adrenaline high and things started to register. The appreciation and love in Neela's eyes was palpable. Bina rubbed her arm and constantly thanked her. Maybe she finally deserved the gratitude and caring looks these women gave her, not because she'd done something heroic, but because she would have given her life for either of them without question.

Neela helped Bina to her feet and extended her hand to Jordan. "Let's go."

"I can't go back to the hospital. Heather and Doctor Newkirk will have me committed. This will be the fourth time they've had to patch me up."

"Guess that's a chance we'll have to take," Neela said.

"Can't you just put a fresh bandage on? I'm not leaving the two of you until I'm certain you're okay, and then I'll go to the station and question this guy. He's got some explaining to do, if he's not in the hospital." She looked to Bex for reassurance.

"He'll be fine, just a few cuts, nothing serious."

"I'll be with you in a minute, Bex." Jordan returned her attention to Bina. "Are you really okay? You don't need to go to the hospital? Are you sure?"

"I am absolutely fine. Stop worrying so much."

"Do you know how he got in the house?"

"No idea. I had just gotten out of bed and was going into the kitchen. He was standing in the hallway. I heard no alarm or breaking glass." Bina shrugged. "Sorry. I am not much help."

"You did exactly the right thing by activating your silent alarm, and when I came through the door, I couldn't have asked for a more perfect response. I'm very proud of you." Jordan hugged her, and Neela helped her into the kitchen.

Neela made chai tea for Bina and settled her at the table with her morning meds before she and Jordan went into the bathroom. Neela stripped the old bandage off her shoulder. "I'm against this. What if I miss something? You should have x-rays. What if you've injured something I can't—"

Jordan kissed Neela to calm her and because her concern was so heartwarming she couldn't resist. So this was what it felt like to be part of a family, to have people care about you and your well-being. She was almost dizzy from the realization that this could be her life. "I'll be fine." She kissed her again, and Neela pressed her hard against the bathroom wall, as if she was suddenly unable to stand.

"I could've lost you and Bina today. My God." Jordan felt her lips tremble against hers. "I never want to feel that helpless again." Neela fisted Jordan's hair in both hands and held her close as her kiss deepened until Jordan felt she might collapse.

"Nee—la. Can't breathe."

Neela stepped back and rubbed her mouth with the back of her hand. "I could devour you right now. And before you say it, yes, part of what I'm feeling is the adrenaline, but I don't care. I need you so much. I'm serious." She took a few deep breaths before returning to the task of cleaning and redressing Jordan's wound. Her eyes strayed to Jordan's lips as she worked, and her concentration filled Jordan with heat.

"If you don't stop looking at me like that, I may never leave."

"That's exactly what I want—you here with me until I've had my fill. And I'm thinking that could take years."

When she pressed the bandage in place and stepped back, Jordan kissed her lightly one last time and reached for the door handle. "I'm sorry. You know I have to see this through, not just for you and Bina, but for myself as well. Rain check on the devouring?"

"So, you're leaving me hurting and horny like last time?"

"Only temporarily, and Liz better not be here when I get back."

"No problem."

Just being in the same car with the man who had broken into Bina's home and tried to kidnap her made Jordan angry all over again. She tapped her foot against the floorboard as she made a mental list of questions. When they pulled into the station, Sergeant Milton was standing outside with two detectives from the Crimes Against Persons Squad. She and Bex helped the handcuffed suspect out of the backseat and led him toward the front door.

"Bishop, the CAP guys want to interview him," Milton said. "And you're not even supposed to be working. What the hell?"

"This one goes down to your squad, boss. It's our arrest. They can talk to him as soon as we're finished. Bex and I have been on this case from the beginning. Take a number, guys." She grinned as they escorted the suspect into an interview room. Milton's chest puffed out a bit, and she could've sworn his molten face tried to form a smile. He was probably thinking about the publicity he'd garner when the story hit the papers.

"Sit." She pointed to a chair but the suspect stood. "Suit yourself. We're getting a cup of coffee. Want anything?" He shook his head. "I'd like for you to think about something while we're gone. You'll be charged with at least two counts of attempted murder, two counts of assault with a deadly weapon inflicting serious injury, and one count of breaking and entering, kidnapping, and assault. Try to imagine how many years you'll spend in prison. And then decide if you want to take all the heat or share the love with whoever's paying you. Your choice." She closed the door behind her, and she and Bex waited fifteen minutes before going back in.

She slid her chair in front of the suspect and put a clean yellow notepad on the table. After advising him of his rights, she said, "Let's start with the basics. What's your name?"

Apparently he'd thought about her earlier comments because sweat beaded his forehead. "Ralph Younts." She gathered all the pertinent information about his date of birth, address, and criminal record and compared it to the printouts Bex had already pulled from his license.

"Let's cut to the chase. Who're you working for?"

"If I tell you, can I get a deal, time off my sentence?" He rubbed his hands together and scraped his balding head.

"Depends on what you have to tell us and how convincing you are."

"I'm serious," Younts said. "This guy has clout and could have me killed."

"It's up to you," Jordan said. "His hide or yours. Either way we're getting our pound of flesh. But if I was in your shoes, I wouldn't let some rich guy go free while I did time."

"The guy's name is Elliot Ramsey."

Bingo. She tried to keep a straight face as she imagined clicking the cuffs on Ramsey's wrists. "How do you know Mr. Ramsey?"

"My brother drives for him sometimes. When he said he needed special help, my brother gave him my name."

"What kind of help?" Bex asked.

"He wanted me to scare a couple of doctors who were part of some protest group. Write a few threatening letters, that sort of thing."

"And what else?" Jordan's anger clawed just under her skin. He was too calm, too matter-of-fact about terrorizing the women she cared about. "Did you attack Doctor Branson?" He nodded. "And...?" She made a mental note to get a sample of his hair for comparison to the ones left on Branson's body the night of the assault and a voice sample to compare to Neela's threatening phone call.

"When the woman didn't take the hint, Ramsey paid me extra to take a shot at her."

"He paid you to *kill* her." Jordan's jaw hurt from clenching her teeth.

"If I wanted her dead, she'd be fucking dead. I was just trying to make a point." Jordan was on her feet and halfway across the table when Bex grabbed her by the waistband. Younts dodged her swinging fist. "You've got anger issues, detective."

"And you've got legal issues, asshole." She sat down and clasped her hands in her lap, nodding for Bex to take over.

"How did you get past the alarm system in the Sahjani house?" Bex asked.

"You haven't done your homework, detective. Ramsey owns the company."

Jordan mentally flipped through the list of Ramsey's acquisitions Bex had compiled. "That's bullshit. We would've found it."

"Only bought it a few days ago. You can guess why." His smug grin indicated he thought he'd given them a piece of worthwhile information.

"Elliot Ramsey is a very influential man. Why should we believe he'd be stupid enough to pay you to do his dirty work?" Bex tapped her pen on the table.

"Because I have proof."

Bex's pen stopped in mid-air. "What kind of proof?"

"Audio. But that's all you're getting until I have a deal." Younts scooted his chair back and folded his arms. "The only other thing I have to say is this, lawyer."

Chapter Twenty-one

Neela checked her cell for the second time in five minutes. Two days had passed since Jordan had arrested the man who tried to kidnap Bina, and the only contact they'd had was by phone. As she and Liz packed up the lab equipment for the day, she lethargically changed clothes and thought about the lonely night ahead. Bina was spending the week with her friend, Mrs. Scott, in the Caribbean on a much-needed vacation, and she was waiting to hear from Jordan.

Liz slipped her arm around her waist. "We're going out to dinner. I won't take no for an answer. We're both police widows, and I'm tired of sitting around waiting for a phone call. Are you with me?"

She nodded, not really in the mood to go out, but less willing to face the empty house alone. "Sure, why not? I just don't understand what's taking so long. Elliot Ramsey's arrest has been in the headlines since yesterday."

"Bex told me they're conducting all the interviews so it's taking awhile. Haven't you talked to Jordan at all?"

"Several times, but it's just not enough. Know what I mean?"

"Totally. Nothing takes the place of that warm body beside you, does it?" She pulled her sweatshirt on and headed for the exit. "I'll meet you at the Thai place on Westover Terrace at six thirty. And don't be late. I feel like getting my drink on. I might even pick up a woman."

Neela shook her head. "Right. You're so gone over Bex you can't see another woman, much less remember how to pick her up." The twinkle in Liz's eye made Neela smile. "See you at six thirty."

The house was so lonely without Bina and Jordan. She went into Bina's room and watched dust flurries drift in the last rays of evening sun. Her mother's housecoat hung over the back of her favorite chair, and Neela thought about her most recent stem-cell-test failure. No matter how hard she worked, her efforts wouldn't stop the progression of Bina's severe rheumatoid arthritis. She wiped tears from her cheeks and vowed to make the remainder of her mother's life special. She'd spent too much time working and not enough with Bina. Life was just too short to focus on anything but the present. She folded Bina's faded housecoat, placed it on the foot of her bed, and then went to her bedroom to change for dinner.

Blue followed alongside her, nudging her hand and looking at her with his pitiful blue eyes. "You are your mother in canine form," she said, patting his thick white fur. As they entered the bedroom, he raised his head and sniffed the air like a bloodhound. "You smell her in this room more than I do, don't you, boy?"

She looked at her purposely unmade bed, and Jordan's imprint on her side punctuated her absence. Grabbing the pillow, she inhaled Jordan's unique fragrance, and the memory of it shot through her like shrapnel, ripping her defenses and stirring her blood. Almost losing Jordan again had merely confirmed what she'd known since the beginning. She'd told Jordan she loved her, and that knowledge swelled in her like a living thing. Her nerves were raw, and her senses screamed to be saturated with her lover.

Blue nudged her hand and she patted his head again. When she looked at the clock, she saw that she had only fifteen minutes to get across town. She changed quickly, fed Blue, and arrived at the restaurant just as Liz pulled into the lot.

"Great timing." Liz pulled her into a hug. "I have a feeling this is our lucky night."

"What are you talking about?"

"Good food, a few drinks, some sexy conversation. Who could ask for anything more?"

"My lover to share it with?" Liz opened the door, and the place erupted into cheers and applause. "What the—"

"Your wish is my command." Liz pointed to Jordan and Bex across the room, leaning against the bar. "Don't be mad. They just finished work and I told them they had to be here. It was initially a gathering of your old work crowd." Standing next to Jordan, Rosemary gave her a thumbs-up.

"Did you do all this?"

"I had a lot of help from your number one, Rosemary."

Her entire gang from the Health Department surrounded her like a mob. Everyone told his or her version of the shake-up Ramsey's arrest had caused in the governor's office.

The mood was jubilant, but she kept track of Jordan, drawn by some invisible force. She looked exquisite wearing her signature black T-shirt, boots, and leather jacket. But tonight she sported a pair of skintight leather pants that Neela ached to peel off with agonizing slowness. When their eyes locked, Jordan licked her lips and raised her glass in a toast.

Every time Neela tried to work her way to the bar, another coworker stopped her to talk. Everyone wanted to thank her for her courage and leadership through the years, to update her on their new positions with the department, on their raises, or about the new jobs they'd found. They'd followed her example and fought for themselves. Her worries about leaving her group had apparently been unnecessary.

Three hours later, she'd finally spoken to everyone personally, heard the highlights of their changes, and encouraged them to keep in touch. As the waiters cleared the tables, Jordan rose from the opposite end and walked toward her. She'd been much too far away the whole evening for Neela's liking.

"Could I interest you in dessert?" Jordan asked.

"I'm pretty picky about my sweets."

"I think you'll like this one."

"Get a room," Bex said from behind them.

"That's my plan exactly," Jordan said as she took Neela's hand and led her toward the exit. "And don't expect to see me anytime soon. I'm still on light duty, and I intend to make the most of it."

Neela started to say something but Liz said, "I know. You won't be at work either. I think the lab will survive without both of us for a few days." She took Bex's hand and they followed her and Jordan out.

Jordan led Neela to her Ducati in the parking lot. "Will you do me the honor of letting me drive you home?"

"As long and as often as you want," Neela said.

Jordan's body heated as Neela's innuendo registered. "I meant on the bike."

"I meant any way you want, for as long as you like. The answer is, and always will be, yes. Drive me, darling."

She put the spare helmet on Neela and adjusted the chinstrap, stopping only twice to kiss her before completing the task. "I've missed you. Sorry I couldn't get back sooner. There were things to—"

"Don't apologize for doing your job. It's one of the things I love about you. I assume everything is settled?"

"Yep, Ramsey's out on bail and denying everything. Younts flipped big-time and had a recording of their entire arrangement. The governor's office is distancing from Ramsey but still getting a hard look from the attorney general. Not sure if anything will come of it, but that's not my job." Jordan nodded toward the soft cast below Neela's knee. "Can you manage?"

"No problem." Neela lifted her restricted leg over the back of the bike, and Jordan shifted to accommodate the tightening between her legs.

"Hang on," she said over her shoulder as she started the bike and pulled out of the lot.

Neela slid her hands around Jordan's waist and she took a mental snapshot, one of the night's first she'd file in her memory—Neela's first ride on her Ducati, the first time Neela nuzzled her neck and whispered I love you with the wind threatening to steal her words.

"This is fantastic," Neela said. "But none of those daredevil stunts tonight." She raised her hands and outlined the curves of Jordan's torso through her jacket, hesitating briefly when she cupped her breasts. Dropping her right hand to Jordan's thigh, she worked a fingernail along the inseam of her leather pants like a zipper. Jordan's clit throbbed with each stitch.

"Neela, not fair. I think what you're doing qualifies as a daredevil stunt at the moment."

"Am I distracting you, darling?" She nibbled the soft spot just below Jordan's ear and pressed a finger along the crotch of her pants where the stitching cut into Jordan's flesh.

She lost her grip on the throttle and the bike slowed. "Please."

"Please what?"

"We'll be home in just a second and I'll show you." Jordan wheeled into the driveway and pulled around to the garage. She took

Neela's hand and, without a word, led her into the house. They shucked off their helmets as they headed down the hallway toward Neela's bedroom. "Now, Miss Roaming Hands, do you have anything to say in your defense?" She kissed Neela, her immediate rush of desire followed by heat and moisture.

Neela's arms encircled her neck and they merged in a fire more melting than raging. She rubbed her breasts against Neela's and pressed their pelvises together. "I need you."

"I know, my darling. I'm crazy for you. Can we please go to bed?" Neela stepped back and unbuttoned her blouse, letting it fall to the floor along with her bra. "Please hurry, Jordan. This will be fast and furious. No time for leisure niceties this round." She shucked her jeans and bikinis in one motion and stood before Jordan nude and waiting.

"My God, you are so gorgeous." The dark triangle between Neela's legs shimmered with arousal, and Jordan almost lost her footing as she tried to undress without taking her eyes off her. "You're already wet."

"You mean you're not?" Neela's hand covered the crotch of her boy shorts, and she flinched. "Sorry. Am I being too forward? Do you need me to slow down?"

"I'm fine. You're just so fucking amazing. You make me forget I have a problem."

"Because you don't have a problem. You're absolutely perfect, and I love you just the way you are. Come here." She guided Jordan to sit on the foot of the bed. "May I please take your shorts off? I want to see you naked again. I've been thinking about this for two days."

Jordan nodded, and Neela shimmied the shorts down her legs and tossed them on top of the pile with the rest of their discards. "Neela, I want to tell you something."

"Can it wait?" She kneaded Jordan's breasts, her brown eyes hooded with desire and her breath quickening.

Jordan placed her hands on top of Neela's. "No. It can't. I need to say this before we go any further."

Neela sighed and rested her hands on Jordan's thighs, looking into her eyes. "Yes, darling?"

Jordan kissed Neela's palms and took a deep breath. Her pulse hammered in her ears and her heart pounded painfully against her chest as Neela's adoring stare freed her. "I'm in love with you, Neela. Totally, completely, absolutely, no doubt in love with you. I wanted to tell you now, not while making love to you or after an amazing orgasm. Do you understand?"

Once she'd spoken the words, she knew she'd loved Neela from the beginning. She'd hungered for her since that first day, and she'd been inexplicably jealous of Rosemary and Liz because of their connections to Neela. Her feelings all made sense now; even her bad behavior had been her subconscious way of trying to deny how much she cared. Neela was hers, and she belonged to Neela mind, body, and soul.

Neela's eyes were wide and brimming with tears, but she hadn't spoken.

"Are you all right?"

Neela nodded.

"Would you please say something? I'm feeling a little exposed, and not just because I'm naked."

"Jordan, I—I'm just so beyond happy. I love you so much, but I thought it would take months, maybe years for you to feel the same way."

"And you were willing to wait that long?" Neela's sincerity bathed Jordan in another layer of security and love.

"I would've waited forever, my darling. You're the love of my life."

"And you're mine. I've never felt this way before, Neela. You've completely changed me, in a totally good way."

Neela wiggled her eyebrows and slid her hands back to Jordan's breasts. "Does that mean we can have sex now?"

"No. It means we can make love." She ran her fingers through Neela's long hair. She couldn't wait to feel Neela on top of her with those silky tresses feathered across her body. "Come here, please. I need you."

"Not yet. I was wondering if I might possibly have dessert now." She fingered Jordan's slick folds and brought her hand to her lips. Jordan shivered from the intimacy as much as from her touch. "You did promise dessert."

Jordan's thighs tensed as she imagined Neela pleasuring her with her mouth. "I'm not sure. I've never let anyone do that before."

Neela knelt between Jordan's legs, looked into her eyes, and ran her hands up and down Jordan's thighs. "I'm not just anyone. I'm the love of your life, and I won't do anything you don't want me to."

She lowered her head and kissed the length of Jordan's thigh from her knee to the join of her torso. Her lips were hot, but she cooled her path with tongue licks across her skin. Jordan shuddered as tiny jolts of heat shot through her. She grew wetter and thought about closing her legs, but stopped as Neela moaned with pleasure.

Jordan leaned back and watched Neela kiss her way up her legs. She was so close to her clit Jordan could feel every cool inhale and every heated exhale of her breath. Neela's hair fanned across her lap, and the smooth strands stroked her like a thousand tiny fingers. "That feels so good, Neela." She shifted her hips, eager for contact, as the pressure built. "So…hot."

Neela placed her thumbs in the joins of Jordan's thighs and massaged, pulling away from her clit as she encircled her belly button with kisses. Jordan felt like Neela was worshipping her with her mouth, tasting and savoring every inch of her while honoring Jordan's boundaries. When Neela buried her tongue deep in her belly button, Jordan arched off the bed. "Jeez-us."

Neela paused only slightly and looked up at her. "Do you like that, darling?"

"I'm in love with your mouth right now. Don't stop."

Neela massaged the top of Jordan's hips and licked the tender inside of her thighs. Jordan looked down, and the bright-red tip of her engorged clit stuck out, begging for attention. She throbbed at the sight and clenched the muscles of her sex to stop the pain. Neela sucked and nipped the skin of her thighs and abdomen, licking and leaving fire with every pass. Jordan rocked forward, desperate for release.

"Nee—la."

Neela didn't look up or slow as she lapped Jordan's body and moaned like she was enjoying a delicious treat.

"*Nee—la!*" Jordan put her hand under Neela's chin and raised her head from her lap.

Neela wiped her mouth with the back of her hand, her face flushed and her brown eyes ringed with flecks of golden fire. "Yes?"

"I need…" Her thoughts bypassed the insecurity of her exposed position, the fears of her past, and went straight to the love pulsing between her and Neela like a mutual heartbeat.

"What do you need? What do you want right now, Jordan?" Her gaze flicked from Jordan's eyes to her crotch, and she captured her bottom lip between her teeth.

"I need—I want—" It was ridiculous, but she couldn't say the words. After all the years she'd spent fucking women and saying every word in the urban dictionary for every form of sex, she felt foolish that she couldn't ask for what she wanted so desperately from the woman she loved so completely.

"Show me."

"I love you, Neela." Jordan cupped Neela's face and guided her to the aching between her legs. "Please, Neela, please."

Jordan closed her eyes and tensed in preparation for her touch, but nothing happened. When she opened her eyes, Neela was staring at her clit, so close she felt her breath. "What's wrong?" She tried to pull back but Neela held her close.

"You're absolutely stunning. I'm about to come just looking at you." Jordan's clit twitched. "You liked hearing that, didn't you?" Jordan nodded, and Neela blew soft breaths across her heated folds. Jordan felt another trickle of moisture. "So beautiful." She blew again and dipped her head lower. "I'm going to lick you now, darling, and I may never stop."

When the tip of Neela's tongue lightly stroked the side of her clit, Jordan jerked away. The sensation was too intense, painful almost, like an electric shock.

"Do you want me to stop?" Neela asked. Jordan shook her head. "Jordan?"

"N—no."

Neela circled the sensitive tip with her tongue in short, infrequent passes, as if she expected Jordan to stop her. The contact wasn't enough and Jordan lifted her hips slightly. Neela's strokes increased around and around the base of her clit. She gasped for breath, feeling light-headed.

"Um-mmm." Neela's guttural moan sent another spike to Jordan's sex.

"More, Neela."

She grabbed Jordan's thighs and pulled her securely against her mouth. When Neela's lips closed around her folds and her tongue flattened against her clit, Jordan fisted Neela's hair in both hands and held her in place. "Oh. My. Yes." She fell back on her elbows and looked down, meeting Neela's lust-glazed stare. "Oh-hhhhh, yes."

Neela's tongue darted in and out, and with every stroke, Jordan rode her exquisite mouth closer and closer to orgasm. Just when she thought she couldn't handle any more stimulation, Neela slid a finger inside her, clamped her mouth closed, and sucked.

Jordan fell back on the bed, her limbs slack as the powerful climax claimed her and held her suspended in its grasp. Everything inside her gathered between her legs and burst free at once. She tried to scream but the energy was diverted. She emptied over and over as Neela devoured her. Her arms were weak and shaky, but she held Neela's head tightly against her, unwilling to lose their connection.

When the last pulse of orgasm clenched Neela's fingers and the final vibrations drained out Jordan's toes, she untangled her hands from Neela's hair and covered her eyes. Her cheeks were wet and she sobbed aloud.

Neela urged her up on the bed and joined her, bringing a sheet to cover their heated bodies. "Oh, my darling, are you all right? Please talk to me." She wiped tears from her face with the edge of the sheet, her eyes full of concern. "I didn't ask about entering you. I was just so carried away. Did I hurt you?"

"No." Her voice sounded small and uncertain.

"Are you sure? You sound like you're remembering something bad. I'm so sorry. I shouldn't have rushed you."

Jordan rolled toward her and kissed her until her lungs begged for air. "You didn't hurt me, Neela. I've never felt so free and alive and loved. I guess I'm crying from the joy of it. You've done this for me, and I love you even more."

"I didn't do it, Jordan. You took a chance. I loved every minute of it."

"You did?"

Neela snuggled into the crook of her neck. "You couldn't tell? I came twice."

"Just giving me head?"

"You're so damn sexy and responsive and just delicious. But the greatest turn-on was feeling you let go with me. I was completely swept away. Thank you."

Jordan hugged her and entangled their legs. "How could I have missed that all my life? No words can describe how I felt coming with your mouth on me."

"It's pretty spectacular. In my book the best and most intimate way to make love—the sight of you desperate for my touch, your moans, the heady taste of you, and your smell." She pulled back a bit. "Before we go any further, I have one question."

"Anything." Jordan's spirit soared with the knowledge she could answer any question Neela had without reservation. She'd finally found her place. Neela and Bina were her family, and nothing was more important.

"Your smell has always baffled me. It's the epitome of innocence, exactly the opposite of what you put out to people. What *is* that?"

Jordan ducked her head and mumbled, "Baby oil."

"Baby oil? Seriously?"

"It's a good moisturizer and I like the fragrance. Is it all right?"

"It's perfect. Just like you, my darling."

"Well…maybe not perfect. I was a little hesitant at first with the whole going-down-on-me thing."

"I know. Maybe in time, you'll become more comfortable."

She stroked Neela's long hair. "You know I've got a lot of work ahead of me. The memories won't just disappear."

"I know, darling, but I'll be with you every step. You're not alone anymore."

Neela kissed her again with the same patience and compassion she'd shown since the beginning. This was what love felt like. This was what Jordan had been searching for all her life—a feeling of connection to another human being and the certainty she'd do anything for Neela and their life together and vice versa.

She rolled Neela over and tried to top her, but Neela flipped her. "I suggest lots and lots of practice, starting right now."

"I couldn't agree more," Jordan said. Neela slid down her body and settled between her legs. This time Jordan opened to her without hesitation.

THE END

About the Author

A thirty-year veteran of a midsized police department, VK was a police officer by necessity (it paid the bills) and a writer by desire (it didn't). Her career spanned numerous positions including beat officer, homicide detective, vice/narcotics lieutenant, and assistant chief of police. Now retired, she devotes her time to writing, traveling, home decorating, and volunteer work.

Books Available from Bold Strokes Books

The Chameleon by Andrea Bramhall. Two old friends must work through a web of lies and deceit to find themselves again, but in the search they discover far more than they ever went looking for. (978-1-62639-363-9)

Side Effects by VK Powell. Detective Jordan Bishop and Dr. Neela Sahjani must decide if it's easier to trust someone with your heart or your life as they face threatening protestors, corrupt politicians, and their increasing attraction. (978-1-62639-364-6)

Autumn Spring by Shelley Thrasher. Can Bree and Linda, two women in the autumn of their lives, put their hearts first and find the love they've never dared seize? (978-1-62639-365-3)

Warm November by Kathleen Knowles. What do you do if the one woman you want is the only one you can't have? (978-1-62639-366-0)

In Every Cloud by Tina Michele. When she finally leaves her shattered life behind, is Bree strong enough to salvage the remaining pieces of her heart and find the place where it truly fits? (978-1-62639-413-1)

Rise of the Gorgon by Tanai Walker. When independent Internet journalist Elle Pharell goes to Kuwait to investigate a veteran's mysterious suicide, she hires Cassandra Hunt, an interpreter with a covert agenda. (978-1-62639-367-7)

Crossed by Meredith Doench. Agent Luce Hansen returns home to catch a killer and risks everything to revisit the unsolved murder of her first girlfriend and confront the demons of her youth. (978-1-62639-361-5)

Making a Comeback by Julie Blair. Music and love take center stage when jazz pianist Liz Randall tries to make a comeback with the help of her reclusive, blind neighbor, Jac Winters. (978-1-62639-357-8)

Soul Unique by Gun Brooke. Self-proclaimed cynic Greer Landon falls for Hayden Rowe's paintings and the young woman shortly after, but will Hayden, who lives with Asperger syndrome, trust her and reciprocate her feelings? (978-1-62639-358-5)

The Price of Honor by Radclyffe. Honor and duty are not always black and white—and when self-styled patriots take up arms against the government, the price of honor may be a life. (978-1-62639-359-2)

Mounting Evidence by Karis Walsh. Lieutenant Abigail Hargrove and her mounted police unit need to solve a murder and protect wetland biologist Kira Lovell during the Washington State Fair. (978-1-62639-343-1)

Threads of the Heart by Jeannie Levig. Maggie and Addison Rae-McInnis share a love and a life, but are the threads that bind them together strong enough to withstand Addison's restlessness and the seductive Victoria Fontaine? (978-1-62639-410-0)

Sheltered Love by MJ Williamz. Boone Fairway and Grey Dawson—two women touched by abuse—overcome their pasts to find happiness in each other. (978-1-62639-362-2)

Asher's Out by Elizabeth Wheeler. Asher Price's candid photographs capture the truth, but when his success requires exposing an enemy, Asher discovers his only shot at happiness involves revealing secrets of his own. (978-1-62639-411-7)

The Ground Beneath by Missouri Vaun. An improbable barter deal involving a hope chest and dinners for a month places lovely Jessica Walker distractingly in the way of Sam Casey's bachelor lifestyle. (978-1-62639-606-7)

Hardwired by C.P. Rowlands. Award-winning teacher Clary Stone, and Leefe Ellis, manager of the homeless shelter for small children, stand together in a part of Clary's hometown that she never knew existed. (978-1-62639-351-6)

No Good Reason by Cari Hunter. A violent kidnapping in a Peak District village pushes Detective Sanne Jensen and lifelong friend Dr. Meg Fielding closer, just as it threatens to tear everything apart. (978-1-62639-352-3)

Romance by the Book by Jo Victor. If Cam didn't keep disrupting her life, maybe Alex could uncover the secret of a century-old love story, and solve the greatest mystery of all—her own heart. (978-1-62639-353-0)

Death's Doorway by Crin Claxton. Helping the dead can be deadly: Tony may be listening to the dead, but she needs to learn to listen to the living. (978-1-62639-354-7)

Searching for Celia by Elizabeth Ridley. As American spy novelist Dayle Salvesen investigates the mysterious disappearance of her ex-lover, Celia, in London, she begins questioning how well she knew Celia—and how well she knows herself. (978-1-62639-356-1)

The 45th Parallel by Lisa Girolami. Burying her mother isn't the worst thing that can happen to Val Montague when she returns to the woodsy but peculiar town of Hemlock, Oregon. (978-1-62639-342-4)

A Royal Romance by Jenny Frame. In a country where class still divides, can love topple the last social taboo and allow Queen Georgina and Beatrice Elliot, a working class girl, their happy ever after? (978-1-62639-360-8)

Bouncing by Jaime Maddox. Basketball Coach Alex Dalton has been bouncing from woman to woman, because no one ever held her interest, until she meets her new assistant, Britain Dodge. (978-1-62639-344-8)

Same Time Next Week by Emily Smith. A chance encounter between Alex Harris and the beautiful Michelle Masters leads to a whirlwind friendship, and causes Alex to question everything she's ever known—including her own marriage. (978-1-62639-345-5)

All Things Rise by Missouri Vaun. Cole rescues a striking pilot who crash-lands near her family's farm, setting in motion a chain of events that will forever alter the course of her life. (978-1-62639-346-2)

Riding Passion by D. Jackson Leigh. Mount up for the ride through a sizzling anthology of chance encounters, buried desires, romantic surprises, and blazing passion. (978-1-62639-349-3)

Love's Bounty by Yolanda Wallace. Lobster boat captain Jake Myers stopped living the day she cheated death, but meeting greenhorn Shy Silva stirs her back to life. (978-1-62639-334-9)

Just Three Words by Melissa Brayden. Sometimes the one you want is the one you least suspect. Accountant Samantha Ennis has her ordered life disrupted when heartbreaker Hunter Blair moves into her trendy Soho loft. (978-1-62639-335-6)

Lay Down the Law by Carsen Taite. Attorney Peyton Davis returns to her Texas roots to take on big oil and the Mexican Mafia, but will her investigation thwart her chance at true love? (978-1-62639-336-3)

Playing in Shadow by Lesley Davis. Survivor's guilt threatens to keep Bryce trapped in her nightmare world unless Scarlet's love can pull her out of the darkness back into the light. (978-1-62639-337-0)

Soul Selecta by Gill McKnight. Soul mates are hell to work with. (978-1-62639-338-7)

The Revelation of Beatrice Darby by Jean Copeland. Adolescence is complicated, but Beatrice Darby is about to discover how impossible it can seem to a lesbian coming of age in conservative 1950s New England. (978-1-62639-339-4)

Twice Lucky by Mardi Alexander. For firefighter Mackenzie James and Dr. Sarah Macarthur, there's suddenly a whole lot more in life to understand, to consider, to risk…someone will need to fight for her life. (978-1-62639-325-7)

Shadow Hunt by L.L. Raand. With young to raise and her Pack under attack, Sylvan, Alpha of the wolf Weres, takes on her greatest challenge when she determines to uncover the faceless enemies known as the Shadow Lords. A Midnight Hunters novel. (978-1-62639-326-4)

Heart of the Game by Rachel Spangler. A baseball writer falls for a single mom, but can she ever love anything as much as she loves the game? (978-1-62639-327-1)

Getting Lost by Michelle Grubb. Twenty-eight days, thirteen European countries, a tour manager fighting attraction, and an accused murderer: Stella and Phoebe's journey of a lifetime begins here. (978-1-62639-328-8)

Prayer of the Handmaiden by Merry Shannon. Celibate priestess Kadrian must defend the kingdom of Ithyria from a dangerous enemy and ultimately choose between her duty to the Goddess and the love of her childhood sweetheart, Erinda. (978-1-62639-329-5)

The Witch of Stalingrad by Justine Saracen. A Soviet "night witch" pilot and American journalist meet on the Eastern Front in WW II and struggle through carnage, conflicting politics, and the deadly Russian winter. (978-1-62639-330-1)

Pedal to the Metal by Jesse J. Thoma. When unreformed thief Dubs Williams is released from prison to help Max Winters bust a car theft ring, Max learns that to catch a thief, get in bed with one. (978-1-62639-239-7)

Dragon Horse War by D. Jackson Leigh. A priestess of peace and a fiery warrior must defeat a vicious uprising that entwines their destinies and ultimately their hearts. (978-1-62639-240-3)

For the Love of Cake by Erin Dutton. When everything is on the line, and one taste can break a heart, will pastry chefs Maya and Shannon take a chance on reality? (978-1-62639-241-0)

Betting on Love by Alyssa Linn Palmer. A quiet country-girl-at-heart and a live-life-to-the-fullest biker take a risk at offering each other their hearts. (978-1-62639-242-7)

The Deadening by Yvonne Heidt. The lines between good and evil, right and wrong, have always been blurry for Shade. When Raven's actions force her to choose, which side will she come out on? (978-1-62639-243-4)

Ordinary Mayhem by Victoria A. Brownworth. Faye Blakemore has been taking photographs since she was ten, but those same photographs threaten to destroy everything she knows and everything she loves. (978-1-62639-315-8)

One Last Thing by Kim Baldwin & Xenia Alexiou. Blood is thicker than pride. The final book in the Elite Operative Series brings together foes, family, and friends to start a new order. (978-1-62639-230-4)

Songs Unfinished by Holly Stratimore. Two aspiring rock stars learn that falling in love while pursuing their dreams can be harmonious—if they can only keep their pasts from throwing them out of tune. (978-1-62639-231-1)

Beyond the Ridge by L.T. Marie. Will a contractor and a horse rancher overcome their family differences and find common ground to build a life together? (978-1-62639-232-8)

Swordfish by Andrea Bramhall. Four women battle the demons from their pasts. Will they learn to let go, or will happiness be forever beyond their grasp? (978-1-62639-233-5)

The Fiend Queen by Barbara Ann Wright. Princess Katya and her consort Starbride must turn evil against evil in order to banish Fiendish power from their kingdom, and only love will pull them back from the brink. (978-1-62639-234-2)

Up the Ante by PJ Trebelhorn. When Jordan Stryker and Ashley Noble meet again fifteen years after a short-lived affair, are either of them prepared to gamble on a chance at love? (978-1-62639-237-3)